THE
JUDAS
JUDGE

Also by Michael McGarrity

Hermit's Peak
Serpent Gate
Mexican Hat
Tularosa

THE
JUDAS
JUDGE

A Kevin Kerney Novel

MICHAEL McGARRITY

A DUTTON BOOK

DUTTON
Published by the Penguin Group
Penguin Putnam Inc., 375 Hudson Street, New York, New York 10014, U.S.A.
Penguin Books Ltd, 27 Wrights Lane, London W8 5TZ, England
Penguin Books Australia Ltd, Ringwood, Victoria, Australia
Penguin Books Canada Ltd, 10 Alcorn Avenue, Toronto, Ontario, Canada M4V 3B2
Penguin Books (N.Z.) Ltd, 182–190 Wairau Road, Auckland 10, New Zealand

Penguin Books Ltd, Registered Offices: Harmondsworth, Middlesex, England

First published by Dutton, a member of Penguin Putnam Inc.

First Printing, July, 2000
1   3   5   7   9   10   8   6   4   2

 REGISTERED TRADEMARK—MARCA REGISTRADA

LIBRARY OF CONGRESS CATALOGING-IN-PUBLICATION DATA
McGarrity, Michael.
The Judas judge : a Kevin Kerney novel / Michael McGarrity.
p.   cm.
ISBN 0-525-94547-4
1. Kerney, Kevin (Fictitious character)—Fiction.   2. Sheriffs—New Mexico—Fiction.
3. New Mexico—Fiction.   I. Title.
PS3563.C36359   J84 2000
813'.54—dc21   99-089181

Printed in the United States of America
Set in Goudy
Designed by Leonard Telesca

This book is printed on acid-free paper. ∞

For Hilary Hinzmann,
who encourages the exploration of new terrain,
and
Barney Karpfinger,
who guides the expedition.

ACKNOWLEDGMENTS

Senior Patrol Officer Fred Laird of the New Mexico State Police, now retired, provided advice, technical information, and helpful insights during my research for *The Judas Judge*. Twice decorated with the Medal of Valor, Fred represents all that is honorable in the law enforcement profession. His assistance, support, and friendship are deeply appreciated.

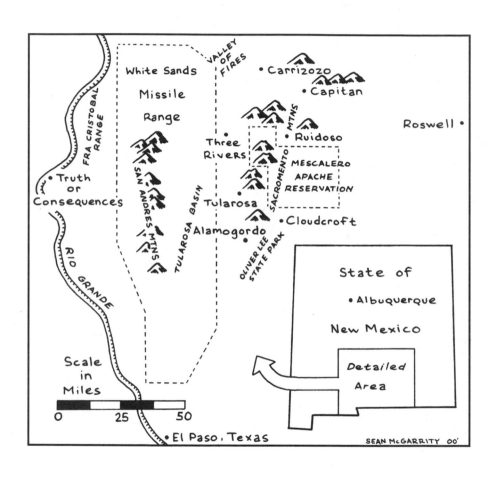

THE
JUDAS
JUDGE

1

Starting sometime after midnight, six murders had been committed along a stretch of highway in south central New Mexico. Soon after sunrise, Kevin Kerney arrived at the Oliver Lee State Park, where Sgt. Randy Shockley waited for him outside a motor home parked in an area that provided electrical and water hookups to recreational vehicles. Westward, across the Tularosa Basin, a band of low clouds mimicked the outline of the distant mountains, creating a mirage of shimmering vague foothills. The October morning was chilly, and a low sun softened the stark landscape, giving the desert a deceptively inviting impression.

Raised on the Tularosa until his parents' ranch was taken over by the army and made part of the high security White Sands Missile Range, Kerney knew the clouds would soon burn off and the day would heat up.

He eyed the motor home. It was an expensive model with a retractable awning, an air-conditioning unit on the roof, and a detachable satellite TV dish mounted on a bracket. Under the awning were a small barbecue grill, a lawn chair, and a folding metal side table. The door into the cabin of the RV was open. Painted on the side of the rig, above the manufacturer's nameplate, a bounding cartoonlike kangaroo floated in midair.

Sergeant Shockley held the crime scene log in one hand and a pen in the other. Kerney scribbled his name on the log and returned the pen. "Any witnesses?" he asked.

"No," Shockley replied. He eyed the chief's cowboy boots, jeans, and silver belt buckle, and repressed a smirk. "And nobody heard any shots. A camper discovered the body."

"Where is he?"

"Sequestered inside the visitor center with the park manager. I have an officer with them."

Across the way, a tight group of campers had gathered around a picnic table under a shelter to watch the action. Most were gray-haired, overweight, tanned, and wearing sweats and pullover tops to guard against the early morning chill.

"We're holding everybody who stayed overnight until we can take their statements," Sergeant Shockley said. "Some of them aren't happy campers."

Kerney smiled thinly at the joke. Shockley, a shift commander and the evidence officer for the Alamogordo District Office of the New Mexico State Police, smiled back. With nine years on the force, Shockley still had a cockiness about him that most cops lost after working their rookie season on the streets. He was thirty-two years old, stood five-nine in his stocking feet, and carried a hundred and forty-five pounds on a compact frame.

Shockley's record was clean. Divorced with no children, he served as an officer survival trainer at the state police academy when recruit classes were in session, and had a reputation as an instructor who enjoyed putting a hurt on cadets during hand-to-hand training.

Kerney knew about Shockley because the sergeant was the target of an internal affairs investigation. He inclined his head toward the motor home. "Who's been inside?"

"Me, a paramedic, the man who found the body, and the park

ranger. The radio message from Major Hutchinson said you were the primary investigator on this one."

"Until we get more people here," Kerney said. "Let the park manager and the witness know I'll take their statements as soon as I can."

"How many dead people do we have, Chief?"

"This one makes six."

"Looks like somebody went on a killing spree."

"So it seems. Where's the body?"

"In the back of the RV," Shockley said, "on the bed."

Kerney nodded, went to his unit, and got his gear.

At two A.M., Kerney; his second-in-command, Nate Hutchinson; and a team of agents had left Santa Fe by helicopter and flown the short hop to the Valley of Fires Recreational Area outside of Carrizozo, the scene of the first homicide. A retired couple from Iowa had been murdered in their sleep and robbed. The team had been working their way south ever since.

At the Three Rivers Petroglyph Recreation Area, a machinist from California had been killed in his travel trailer by a bullet through the heart, and at a campground near the boundary of the Mescalero Indian Reservation, a retired army master sergeant and his wife had been shot dead.

Major Hutchinson's team was stretched thin at the three crime scenes, so Kerney had taken the latest call. There was no way of knowing if it would prove to be the last.

He put on a pair of plastic gloves and went inside the motor home. The man in the sleeping nook wore only boxer shorts. Tan lines on his body stopped midway up the arms and formed a V below the neck. His torso and legs were a startling pale white in comparison.

Somewhere in his seventies, he had a full head of gray hair, good muscle tone, and two bullet holes in his chest. Above a hint of jowls, his features were angular, with thin lips and a long, narrow nose.

A large black bloodstain on a neutral gray blanket had dribbled onto the carpet. One round had caught a heart valve, and a blood spray three feet long had smeared the window and wall above the bed.

It was Friday, and Kerney had planned to fly to Kansas City to spend the weekend with his wife, Lt. Col. Sara Brannon, who was enrolled in the U.S. Army Command and General Staff College at Fort Leavenworth. But that wasn't going to happen.

Under the plastic glove on his left hand Kerney wore a gold wedding band with lapis and turquoise inlaid in a triangular pattern Sara had picked out as part of a matched pair. She had canceled her last trip to Santa Fe due to a mandatory weekend training exercise, and it had been a month since they'd been together. Aside from their honeymoon trip to Ireland in April, the most time they'd been able to spend together was four days in July. Since then, only quick weekend visits back and forth between Santa Fe and Fort Leavenworth every two weeks had been possible.

Kerney had gone into the marriage knowing it would be a part-time, long-distance relationship, and so far he hadn't voiced any complaints. But a month was a long time, and Kerney had to shut down a desire to grumble about it. He shook off his ill-humor and got busy.

He took photographs, did a crime scene sketch, and searched for evidence. He found no spent rounds or sign of forced entry, and went to take statements from the park ranger and the witness who'd discovered the body. Nate Hutchinson arrived just as Kerney finished up.

Known by his nickname Hutch, Nate ran the day-to-day operations of the criminal investigations, narcotics, intelligence, internal affairs, and alcohol and gaming enforcement bureaus. He had droopy eyelids that gave him a sleepy look often mistaken for boredom by those who didn't know him, close-cut brown hair showing a hint of gray, and the ramrod carriage of a Marine drill instructor.

"Got anything, Chief?" Hutch asked.

"The victim's name is Vernon Langsford, a retired lawyer from Ruidoso, age seventy-six. The park ranger said Langsford was a volunteer camp host. He worked three days a week and was on call at night after the park closed. When he wasn't passing out information to tourists and campers, he liked to play golf at the local courses. He was shot twice in the chest at close range."

Hutchinson cocked his head. "Twice? All the other victims were killed with one round. Why two shots for Langsford?"

"I don't know. There's no sign of a struggle. His wallet and jewelry were taken, along with a small, portable color television."

"That matches the MO at the other crime scenes. All the other victims were just tourists traveling through, Chief. Why did our killer take out a camp host?"

"I haven't a clue. From what I've been told, nobody heard shots at this location."

"Silencer?"

"Without a doubt," Kerney said, looking at the travel trailers within shouting distance of the motor home. "Why was Langsford killed quietly and not the others? Besides that, why waste time on this victim when there were more accessible targets closer to the access road? I'm almost certain the killer walked from the locked gate to Langsford's RV. It doesn't make any sense."

"Maybe Langsford's RV was the first one he could get into," Hutch said.

"Spree murderers don't operate that way," Kerney said. "They get on an emotional high, act indiscriminately, go for easy kills, and then move on."

"Are you saying Langsford was deliberately killed?"

"It's possible."

"That could mean we've got multiple murders to cover up one crime."

"That's my best guess at this point," Kerney said. "And if no more victims surface, I'll bet the farm on it. Start deep background checks on all the victims. Look for anything that could point to a motive for murder. Pay particular attention to Langsford."

"You've got it, Chief."

Kerney glanced at Randy Shockley, who was assisting an agent taking statements from impatient senior citizen campers. "Is Agent Duran at the district office?"

"He's standing by."

"We're going to get heavy media attention on this, Hutch. Get the public information officer down here from Santa Fe ASAP. Have him release a statement saying we're handling the cases as a multiple murder spree. He can fill in the blanks from there. If he has questions, I'll be around."

"You're not going to Kansas?"

"Not a chance." He lowered his voice and leaned into Hutch. "Where does Duran stand with his investigation on Shockley?"

"He's just about got it wrapped," Hutch replied. "Can you backstop him, Chief? I can't spare anybody."

"Does Shockley know the axe is about to fall?"

"He doesn't have a clue."

"Tell Duran I'm on my way."

Hutchinson left, and Kerney raised his eyes to the sweep of mountains, his gaze settling on Joplin Ridge, high above Dog Canyon. Long before the park existed, he'd come here as a boy on camping trips with his father to explore the freshwater springs and seeps that enabled lush plants and trees to thrive at the edge of a desert filled with yucca and mesquite. Spindly, eight-foot-tall ocotillo shrubs climbed the flanks of the rocky Sacramento Mountains, masking any hint of the existence of the hidden springs.

Now Dog Canyon was part of the Oliver Lee Memorial State Park. Kerney had grown up hearing stories about Oliver Lee from his grandfather, who ranched on the west side of the Tularosa Basin in the San Andres Mountains back when Lee controlled the water in Dog Canyon and a million acres of free range. To this day, people argued over whether Oliver Lee was a hero or a villain in the range wars that erupted during the late Nineteenth Century. The living descendants on both sides of the feud kept the quarrel going. It had become a peculiar form of entertainment that spilled over into local politics, bar fights, and business dealings.

Kerney nodded at Sergeant Shockley as he passed by, and thought glumly of needing to call Sara to cancel his visit.

After leaving a message for Sara and talking by phone with his boss, Andy Baca, chief of the state police, Kerney left the crime scene and drove to the district office. Alamogordo had once been a sleepy desert railroad town, but with the opening of the air base during World War II and the establishment of White Sands Missile Range after the war, all that had changed. Now the community went boom and bust and boom again on annual congressional defense appropriations.

A major four-lane highway cut through the town along the east side of the Tularosa Basin, and a commercial strip stretched beyond the city in both directions. There was the usual assortment of bars, pawnshops, cut-rate furniture stores, and used-car lots that catered to servicemen mixed in with motels, fast-food franchises, and gas stations that served the highway traffic.

Thanks to the establishment of a permanent training station for the German Air Force and the consolidation of stealth bomber and fighter squadrons at Holloman Air Force Base, the city was enjoying a comeback from the deep defense budget cuts that had occurred at the end of the Cold War. But in spite of banners on light poles proclaiming local attractions and community events, the main strip still looked seedy.

The state police district office was in a building that housed several other state agencies on a major street near the old downtown area. Kerney parked in the back lot, rang the bell, and the dispatcher buzzed him inside, where Agent Robert Duran waited for him.

A small-boned, wiry man, Duran competed in cross-country and marathon races, and had recently transferred from criminal investigations to the Internal Affairs Unit.

"What did you get from Shockley's ex-wife?" Kerney asked.

"According to the ex, he was always bringing stuff home after his shift. Booze, office supplies, a nice luggage set, a brand-new chain saw—stuff like that."

"Weapons?"

"Oh, yeah. Lots of those. He had a locked closet in the garage where he kept the goodies. When he moved out last year, he took everything with him. She saw him load up at least ten handguns, several long rifles, and a shotgun when he left."

"Did she give a statement?"

"In writing, Chief."

"Did Shockley tell her where he got the weapons?"

"He said he traded for them, or bought them used."

A handgun Shockley had reported as returned to the owner had surfaced in a recent El Paso armed robbery, and Kerney asked if Duran had talked to the owner.

"Couldn't do it, Chief," Duran said. "He died six weeks before Shockley sent the dated and signed receipt to Santa Fe. Shockley forged the owner's signature on the form."

"Did the perp who used the gun identify Shockley as his supplier?"

"He never met Shockley, but he gave me the name of the Juárez gunrunner who sold him the pistol. I had a nice long chat with the guy. Once he understood that I wasn't going to put the Juárez cops onto him, he fingered Shockley as one of his illegal weapons suppliers."

"How many weapons did Shockley sell him?"

Duran consulted his notebook. "During the last two years, Shockley sold him approximately sixty weapons: mostly handguns, all in cherry condition. The dealer paid him an average of four hundred dollars for each gun, sometimes more."

"Did you recover any of them?"

"No, but I got a partial list of makes and models from the guy—as much as he could remember. I compared it to Shockley's evidence reports. What Shockley said he'd returned to the rightful owners, he was mostly selling."

Duran closed his notebook. "The Juárez buyer isn't willing to cross the border and testify, if and when we go to trial, Chief. In fact, I had the distinct feeling he would disappear as soon as I left. I tape-recorded his statement."

"You've got enough to make your case without him."

"I've got more we may be able to use. There's been a spike in the number of stolen cars reported by the district over the last three years, beginning right about the time Shockley got his sergeant stripes. I asked the intelligence unit to do an analysis. Most of the cars were stolen on Shockley's swing and graveyard shifts. When he worked days, nighttime auto thefts dropped dramatically."

"Do you have anything connecting Shockley to the auto thefts?"

"Not yet."

"What about the money trail?"

"That, I've got. Shockley plays the market. He has four separate Internet brokerage accounts. His total investment over the past three years exceeds one hundred twenty thousand dollars. He sure hasn't been investing that kind of cash with his take-home pay."

"Inheritance?" Kerney asked, thinking of Erma Fergurson, his mother's old friend who had left him a 6,400-acre ranch, which was about to be sold to the Nature Conservancy. Even after all the taxes were paid when probate closed next month, Kerney would still have more money than he'd ever dreamed possible. Considerably more than Shockley's low six-figure market accounts.

"That's unlikely, Chief. Both parents live in Carlsbad. His father works as an auto mechanic, and his mother at a day care center. There's no family money that Shockley could tap into. Additionally, the ex-wife didn't know anything about Shockley's adventures in the stock market."

"Do you need more time?"

"I'd rather not wait, Chief. I can always bring additional charges later. I did a quick inventory of the evidence room this morning. Two handguns that should be there are missing. I think a search of his unit and his apartment will turn them up."

"Did you get a warrant for his apartment?" Kerney asked.

"Signed by a judge this morning," Duran said.

Kerney knew Duran's presence at the district office wouldn't go unnoticed for long. The back channel network could have already passed on the information. "You'd better move."

"I'll pull him in now," Duran said. "Will you do the house search for me, Chief?" He held out the warrant.

Kerney nodded and took the paperwork.

"Thanks."

"Don't talk to Shockley without backup."

"There isn't anybody I can use. Every available agent is working the homicides."

"Bring in a uniform to assist you."

Duran thought about it for a minute. "Pete Bustamante. We worked patrol together in District Seven. He's solid."

"You're sure?"

"Yeah."

"Okay. Under my orders, have dispatch instruct Shockley and Bustamante to report here immediately for a special assignment."

Randy Shockley pulled onto the state highway and checked his rearview mirror. Pete Bustamante was on his tail, following him to the district headquarters. Shockley knew Chief Kerney's orders were bogus. The dispatcher had called him by cellular phone to report that Agent Duran had been snooping around in the evidence room and looking through his paperwork. The dispatcher had no further information, but Shockley knew what was up: Internal Affairs had uncovered his weapons scam. There could be no other reason for Duran's search.

Maybe the auto theft scheme hadn't been detected. He flipped open his cell phone and called Jake's Towing Service. "Has anybody been coming around asking questions?" he asked, when Jake answered.

"Anyone like who?"

"A cop, you stupid shit."

Jake laughed. "You know I hate cops, Randy."

"Answer the fucking question."

"I haven't talked to any cops, or anybody asking a lot of questions. I would have told you if that was happening."

"When did you move the last vehicle?"

"Four days ago," Jake replied. "Delivered and paid for. We got fourteen thousand dollars for it. Do we have a problem?"

"I'll get back to you." Shockley hit the disconnect button and punched in his ex-wife's number. "Maureen."

"I told you never to call me, Randy."

"Has anyone from the department talked to you recently?"

"I have to leave for work."

"Don't fuck with me, Maureen."

"Go to hell, Randy," Maureen said with a hint of peevish satisfaction as she hung up.

Shockley checked his rearview mirror again. Bustamante was still there. He punched in the number for the district attorney's office and asked to speak to the administrator. Nicole Prince came on the line. "I hope you don't want to speak to any of the ADAs, Randy. Everybody who isn't scheduled for court is out at the crime scenes. Isn't that something?"

"It sure is," Shockley said. "I'm checking on a warrant. Did anything come in for signature this morning?"

"One of your Santa Fe agents showed up with an affidavit approved by my boss himself. He took it to Judge Witcher."

"Thanks." He waited until he got to the edge of town before dialing Bustamante's cell phone number, and watched in the rearview mirror as Pete picked up. "I've got to swing by my place for a few minutes," he said. "I'll catch up with you."

"Okay, Sarge," Pete said. "See you there."

Shockley made a quick turn off the main drag, waited for Busta-mante to pass out of sight, then floored the unit, hit the emergency lights, and cut through traffic running a silent code three. At his apartment building he did a slow drive-by, looking for cop cars or un-marked units. From the parking lot he could see no activity outside, and no sign of Duran, Kerney, or other officers.

He stopped by the manager's office and asked if anyone had been by to pick up a key. The woman said no, and Shockley gave her a bullshit line that he was expecting a friend from out of town who was going to stay with him for a few days.

As he hurried to his apartment, Shockley tried to figure out what had gone wrong. All the weapons he'd boosted had been unclaimed for at least a year, and he'd sold them in Mexico to a Juárez dealer for shipment to Central America. Everything else he'd filched during his tenure as evidence officer had been sold at El Paso flea markets, where nobody knew him.

If he could clean out the weapons stashed in his apartment before Duran could serve the warrant, he might be able to avoid prosecu-tion and hard time. Duran would have nothing more than a paper trail to go on. With a damn good lawyer the department might settle for his resignation to avoid embarrassment.

Shockley could live with that.

Inside the apartment he grabbed the .38 caliber four-inch Ruger, a sweet Colt 9 mm, and his cash box. He couldn't chance stashing the stuff in his personal vehicle, so he would have to dump it. He didn't like the idea of throwing away four thousand dollars in cash and a thousand dollars worth of weapons, but there wasn't any choice.

He checked his watch. Five minutes had passed since he'd peeled off from Bustamante. He couldn't use the apartment Dumpster—

that would be the first place Duran would look after searching the apartment. A trash bin at the supermarket a few blocks away would have to do.

He stuffed the guns and cash box into a half-full kitchen garbage bag, tied it off, and headed for the front door. Outside, he found Deputy Chief Kerney standing behind the open driver's door of a unit.

"Where are you going, Sergeant?" Kerney had his semiautomatic hidden out of sight behind his leg.

Shockley smiled. "I just stopped by to take out the trash, Chief. They pick it up on Fridays."

"Drop the bag and keep your hands where I can see them."

Shockley kept smiling. "What's this all about, Chief?"

"Drop the bag."

Kerney stood at an angle behind the open door of the unit, presenting the smallest possible target. Shockley didn't move, and Kerney studied him. The bulletproof vest under the uniform shirt bulked up Shockley's compact frame, and his eyes scanned Kerney carefully.

"Are you hiding a gun behind your leg, Chief?" Shockley asked.

"This doesn't have to get out of hand, Sergeant. Do as you're told."

"What are you talking about?" Shockley shifted his weight slightly and watched for a response. There wasn't one.

"I think you know," Kerney said.

"No, I don't." Shockley moved his right arm slightly to test Kerney's reflexes one more time. The chief didn't seem to notice.

"I have a warrant to search your apartment."

"Search my apartment?" Shockley said, feigning amazement. He dropped the garbage bag at his feet and held out his hand. "Let's see it."

"I'll show it to you later," Kerney said.

Shockley had watched Kerney hobble around on a bum leg at the crime scene. Chances were good, given Kerney's physical condition and age, that the chief didn't possess Shockley's survival skills, eye-hand coordination, and speed.

He brought his extended right arm closer to his sidearm. "I have a right to see the search warrant."

"Don't push your luck, Sergeant."

Shockley laughed. "I don't operate on luck, Chief." He heard the first faraway sound of a siren. "Backup?"

Kerney nodded. "Agent Duran."

"What am I busted for, Chief?"

"Agent Duran wants to ask you a few questions."

"Why don't I just talk to him at the office?" Shockley said, taking a side step that gave him a better angle on Kerney.

"Stay put, Sergeant. Clasp your hands together at the back of your head, and we'll stay nice and calm until Duran gets here."

"Whatever you say, Chief." Shockley said, without complying.

"Hands at the back of your head."

Shockley gauged the distance. Kerney was twelve, maybe fourteen feet away. His vest would stop Kerney's rounds, and if he moved quickly, the chief might miss him completely. He heard the sound of Duran's siren closing fast.

"Don't be stupid, Shockley. Do it now."

"I think I'll just wait for Duran," Shockley said, visualizing the moves he would make. He would have to draw and fire in one smooth motion. He practiced the sequence mentally: a quick step to the left, hand to his holster, draw, fire twice, drop, and roll.

"Hands behind your head," Kerney repeated.

"How come you don't wear a uniform, Chief?" Shockley asked, eyeing Kerney's boots, jeans, and cowboy shirt as he inched his hand closer to his weapon. "You're a deputy chief, for chrissake. You should be wearing a spit-and-polish uniform with three stars on your collar. Make the troops proud."

"Don't try to goad me."

"Hell, I thought you were some sort of cowboy wannabe when you showed up this morning. I almost laughed in your face."

Shockley locked his eyes on Kerney's face and in one fluid motion he spun sideways, drew, braced his weapon as he came up on target, and fired. He caught a fleeting image of Kerney's weapon pointed at his head before white light exploded inside his brain.

Kerney walked to Shockley's body and kicked the weapon out of his hand. The gun skidded twenty feet across the parking lot. His two rounds had torn holes in the sergeant's neck and eye, and blood was pumping out of a carotid artery, spraying over Shockley's uniform shirt.

Kerney had seen a lot of dead bodies over the years, but never one of a cop he'd shot. His gaze traveled down to the gold shield on Shockley's chest, the stripes on the sleeves, the hash marks above the cuff, the gray piping on the black trousers, the highly polished shoes, covered with a sheen of dust. The blood splatter on Shockley's face was dark brown. The sight made Kerney want to puke.

"Jesus Christ," Robert Duran said. "What happened?"

Kerney turned and found Duran at his shoulder. He held out his weapon. "Take this."

Duran obliged and Kerney walked away.

"Where are you going, Chief?"

"Give me a minute."

At the side of the apartment building, Kerney quickly lost the food in his stomach. He stood up, leaned against the wall, and didn't move until his heart stopped thudding against his chest.

The helicopter lifted off from the pavement and two Otero County deputy sheriffs moved their units to let traffic back on the side street behind the parking lot to the district office. A semi-truck pulling the mobile command center Chief Baca had ordered sent over from Las Cruces made a tight turn into the parking lot.

At least half the workers at the nearby Otero County courthouse were either hanging out windows or watching the action from the sidewalk. The crews of six television-station vans parked in a side lot were busy filming the chopper's departure, and the only thing that kept the assembled reporters from blitzing the district office were the barriers and uniformed officers the PIO lieutenant had put in place to hold the media back.

Three passengers from the helicopter—Chief Andy Baca, Deputy Chief Elias Giron, and Maj. Kurt Hagerman—converged on Nate Hutchinson. Giron ran uniform operations for the department, and Hagerman was his zone commander for the eastern sector, which included Alamogordo.

"Where is Chief Kerney now, Hutch?" Andy asked, barely glancing at the captain and lieutenant from the Alamogordo office, who waited nearby.

"Detained by the city police. The district attorney is taking his statement."

"Who let the city butt in on this?" Andy asked sharply, his normally low-key temperament worn thin from the events of the day.

"By the time we got to Shockley's apartment, the city cops had secured the area and wouldn't let us in. I couldn't even talk to Agent Duran until they'd finished with him. That took two hours."

"Has the dispatcher admitted to tipping off Shockley about the IA investigation?"

"She admits only to telling Shockley that Duran was waiting for him at the office, and that Chief Kerney had left the premises."

"Fire her ass. I want her gone within the next ten minutes."

"We can't fire her without taking progressive discipline, Chief," Capt. Willie Catanach, the district commander, said.

"I wasn't speaking to you, Captain," Andy said. "But since you've chosen to enter into this conversation, let me make a couple of things clear. I've got lawyers up in Santa Fe who will gladly defend the department against any wrongful termination suit. I'm going to let them do their jobs. Speaking of which, let me say something about your job. What Sergeant Shockley was allowed to get away with goes way beyond misplaced trust or sloppy supervision. Chief Giron and Major Hagerman are now in charge of this district. You and Lieutenant Vanhorn are relieved of duty. My office will inform you when and if you can return to work."

Catanach flinched as though he'd been slapped in the face, and Vanhorn's expression turned to stunned disbelief. Neither man moved.

"You heard the chief," said Elias Giron, who'd been chewed out privately by Andy for not having adequate evidence policies in place. "Lieutenant, give the captain a ride home. Captain, I need your car keys."

Catanach fished the keys out of his pocket and gave them over.

As the men moved away, Andy swung his attention to Hagerman. "Major, get a relief dispatcher in here now, and fire that woman."

"Yes, sir."

Andy put his hand on Nate Hutchinson's shoulder. "I want internal affairs to review all district evidence inventories. If this shit can happen in Alamogordo, it can happen anywhere."

"I'll get it started, Chief."

"Elias, I want you with the city police chief, right now. Hold his hand or sit in his lap if you have to, but don't let him out of your sight until Kerney is turned loose. If you get the slightest hint that he's planning to play political football with Kerney, call me right away. Tell the DA the minute he's finished with Kerney, I want a meeting with him before he does another damn thing. Be diplomatic."

"I'm on it," Giron said, as he walked to Catanach's unit.

Some of the tension left Andy's face. "You can brief me inside," he said to Hutch, as he glanced at the midday sun in a cloudless sky. "I keep forgetting how damn hot it gets down here in the fall. It feels like summer in Santa Fe."

He shook his head as he moved toward the door. "Six murders and a dead dirty cop, all in one day. Unbelievable. Did Agent Duran see the shooting go down?"

"He got there after the fact."

"How is Kerney handling it?"

"According to Duran, he's hammered."

"Jesus, who wouldn't be?" Andy said.

2

Kerney placed his shield and commission card on the table. His blue eyes, usually so intense, were expressionless. "I'm not doing this anymore," he said flatly.

"Did you know that you're the only deputy chief in the history of the department who wasn't appointed from within the ranks?" Andy Baca replied.

"You're not listening to me."

"I caught a lot of flak for that," Andy said.

"Am I supposed to thank you for the opportunity to be a cop again?" Kerney had been chief of detectives for the Santa Fe Police Department before a gun battle forced him into medical retirement. Andy had brought him back into harness a year ago.

His stinging tone made Andy repress a smile. "Quitting now will make a lot of people happy."

"I couldn't care less."

"It might be seen as a forced resignation."

"It's common knowledge that I'm planning to leave soon."

"Next month, under completely different circumstances," Andy said, thinking about Kerney's windfall inheritance. "Erma's estate will be settled, the land sale will be closed, and you'll be a rich man. Did you know this is the biggest murder case in the department's history? If you leave now, some people might say that you weren't up to the challenge."

"I don't give a rat's ass what people think."

"I know that," Andy said, not believing it at all, but pleased that more emotion had returned to Kerney's voice. "By the way, Major Hutchinson agrees with your theory that this wasn't a spree murder. It doesn't fit the profile. Spree murders are emotional, disorganized, unplanned, with no cooling-off period. The perp made it look good until he got to Langsford."

"I put a cop down today, Andy."

"One of the victims has to be the real target. Everyone else was murdered to cover it up."

"I know that. You're not listening to me."

"Yes, I am. You put down an armed and dangerous felon who hid behind a shield. Who refused to comply with your lawful orders, tried to kill you, and had stolen property in his possession. That's the word from the city PD and the district attorney's office. If Shockley's bullet hadn't clipped the top of the unit's door frame you'd both be dead."

"Are you saying I'm cleared?"

"For now. Because you supervise the internal affairs unit, I've asked the local DA to handle any follow-up investigation. That way we can avoid speculation about a departmental whitewash."

"Regulations require you to place me on administrative leave until the investigation is complete," Kerney said.

"Or I can relieve you from your current duties and reassign you. Give me thirty days, full time, as lead investigator on this case. Hutch will take over the division. I'm promoting him to deputy chief after you leave, anyway."

"That's not much of a reassignment," Kerney noted.

"It satisfies the regs," Andy said, as he pointed out the window at the mobile command center. "That's your office for the duration."

Kerney didn't speak for a moment.

"You still keep your rank as a deputy chief." Andy said.

"I don't give a damn about the rank. Does Hutch know about this?"

Andy nodded. "He also knows that you recommended him for your job."

"I'll do it on one condition: I leave as soon as an arrest is made within the thirty-day period. Agreed?"

"You want out that bad?"

"I'm done with it, Andy."

"Okay. You're booked into a local motel. Give me your house key and a list of what you need from your apartment, and I'll have it here from Santa Fe by morning."

"What made you so sure I'd go along with this?" Kerney asked, as he dropped his house key on the desk.

Andy smiled. "Because you're bullheaded."

"That's it? I'm bullheaded?"

"And you love a challenge. Go catch this killer, Kerney."

Kerney walked into the small office at the back end of the mobile command trailer where Nate Hutchinson was planted behind the tiny desk.

"Good deal," Hutch said, grinning at Kerney.

"Meaning exactly what?"

"Chief Baca talked you into staying on."

"Only long enough to train you for my job."

Hutch's smile spread. "Thanks for putting in a good word for me."

"You earned it on your own, Hutch."

"Thanks, anyway." Hutch hesitated before continuing. "This thing with Shockley."

"What about it?" Kerney asked.

"He didn't give you a choice, Chief."

"That doesn't give me much comfort. I could have handled it better. What have we got on the victims?"

"So far, very little, including Vernon Langsford. The state parks use a one-page application form for camp hosts that captures almost no personal data. They don't run background checks and don't gather next-of-kin information."

"How long before we get the details on Langsford and the others?"

"We found letters from family and friends in the out-of-state victims' travel trailers. I've passed the information along to agencies in Arizona, Iowa, and California. They're making contact with people now. I've asked the Ruidoso Police Department to get me what they can on Vernon Langsford."

"Why haven't we sent an agent up there?" Kerney asked.

"Everybody's still working the crime scenes, Chief."

"What's come in from the field so far?"

Hutch stood up and waved a hand at the papers on the small desk. "Here it is. I'll get out of your way. Shockley was way over the edge, Chief."

"How so?"

"During the last two years, he made at least five DWI traffic stops involving women. He coerced them into having sex and then let them go without making an arrest."

"Has a victim come forward?"

Hutch shook his head. "Shockley used his own blank tapes to record the sex acts with his unit's video camera. Duran found them in his apartment."

"Are you kidding me?"

"Some of it makes everything but hardcore porno films look pretty tame."

"I want to see those tapes."

Hutch pointed to the cassettes on the shelf next to the wall-mounted combination TV and VCR. "They're gonna turn your stomach."

"Has Andy seen them?"

"Not yet, but he knows about them."

"Has Agent Duran run down Shockley's stolen-car ring?"

"He's working on it. Chief Baca said I'm to manage the division while you take the lead on the homicides."

"That's correct."

"With Chief Baca's permission, I'm going to release what we have on Shockley to the media. I don't want anybody in or outside of the department thinking Shockley was anything but a psycho who never should have worn a shield."

"You don't have to do that for my sake, Hutch."

Hutch shook his head and stepped toward the door. "I'm not. It's for all of us, Chief. The district attorney wants to meet with you again in an hour."

"Tell him I'll be there."

After Hutch left, Kerney watched the videotapes. By the time the last one finished playing, anger flushed his face. Shockley liked to sodomize his victims. In each tape he positioned himself at the front of his unit, bent the women over the hood and held them down with a hand on their necks. Then he'd smile at the camera with a smug, satisfied look on his face. The images made Kerney almost want to shoot Shockley all over again.

He rewound the last tape, no longer feeling quite so lousy about taking Randy Shockley's life, and thought about Paul Gillespie, the small-town cop who'd been killed by a woman he'd raped. Nita Lassiter had shot Gillespie with his own handgun at the Mountainair Police Department. Kerney had solved the case with some lucky breaks and had come out of the investigation convinced that Nita Lassiter had more than an adequate reason to blow Gillespie away.

Nita's trial had concluded last month, and she'd been found guilty of manslaughter, a third-degree felony. Because of mitigating circumstances, she'd been sentenced to one year minus a day in the county jail, with work-release privileges so she could continue her practice of veterinary medicine.

A lot of cops and prosecutors around the state were upset when Kerney testified on Nita's behalf at the sentencing hearing. They didn't like the idea that a senior state-police officer could find anything redeeming about a convicted cop killer, no matter what the justification might be.

Now that he'd put Randy Shockley down, he wondered how much more character assassination he'd have to face. Maybe he'd go from being known as a turncoat who sided with a cop killer to being called a cop killer himself.

He rewound the last cassette. With Hutch making sure all of the hard facts about Shockley got out, that might not happen. For the first time in hours, Kerney smiled. It was a damn fine gesture on Hutch's part.

He checked the time, went back to the desk, and scanned through the field reports before leaving to meet with the DA.

Kerney spent several uncomfortable but necessary hours with the district attorney, who probed hard to uncover any personal relationship that might have existed between Kerney and Shockley, or any work-related antagonism that might have contributed to Kerney's willingness to use deadly force. Kerney made it clear he'd never met Shockley before the shooting and had never supervised him.

With that issue set aside, the interview shifted to Kerney's record of deadly force. The DA dug into all prior events, including a gunfight with a street drug dealer who'd blown out Kerney's knee, the shooting of a rogue army intelligence officer during a murder investigation at White Sands Missile Range, the wounding of Nita Lassiter, who had tried to commit suicide to avoid arrest, and a gun battle with assassins hired by a Mexican drug lord to kill Kerney.

The records showed Kerney had been cleared of any wrongdoing in each incident. But the DA, a burly man with a high-pitched voice who breathed heavily through his nose, quizzed Kerney carefully on each event, looking for anything that might suggest Kerney was a trigger-happy cop.

Kerney understood the DA's reasoning; compared to most officers he had an extremely high use-of-deadly-force history. At five o'clock he returned to the command center, drained but through the worst of it. The DA had let him go without scheduling another session.

Sounds of commuter traffic hummed on the street as civilian workers from the air base and White Sands Missile Range made their way up the boulevard to houses in the foothills. At the nearby media staging area, reporters washed in the glare of high-intensity lights were broadcasting live satellite feeds back to stations and networks.

To the west, diaphanous in a light haze, the far-off tips of the San Andres Mountains towered like silent sentinels over the Tularosa Basin, home of the vast White Sands Missile Range.

Kerney's personal history was tied to the Tularosa. When he was a young boy, his parents had been forced off the family ranch when the missile range expanded; and less than three years ago Kerney had met his future wife, Sara, while searching for his AWOL godson, Sammy Yazzi, a soldier stationed at the base.

Good and bad memories coursed through Kerney's mind. His early years on the ranch had been the best of his life, and meeting Sara Brannon, a strong-willed, beautiful woman, had brought him emotionally back to life in ways he'd never imagined possible. But the loss of the ranch still galled, and the murder of his godson would always remain a sore spot in his mind.

The teams of agents and uniformed personnel from the crime scenes began trickling in, and Kerney went to meet them. No new killings had been reported, and Kerney figured the chances were good that the spree was over. He listened to their debriefings, which clearly indicated that a quick break in the case was unlikely. The sum total of facts remained unchanged: six people had been robbed and killed by person or persons unknown—probably with the same handgun—within a six-hour period, in a sequence that started at Carrizozo and ended at the Oliver Lee State Park. Vernon Langsford was the only victim to be shot twice with a silenced weapon.

Why two bullets for Langsford with a silencer?

In Kerney's mind, Langsford had to be the primary target, which meant that five innocent people had been killed to cover up a pre-meditated murder.

Kerney went looking for Lt. Lee Sedillo, the assistant commander of the criminal investigation unit, who'd been gathering background information on Langsford. He found him glued to a computer screen at the front of the command trailer.

Over twenty years ago, Kerney had started his career with the Santa Fe Police Department about the same time Sedillo had joined the state police. Kerney had worked on a number of joint cases with Lee after both of them had moved into criminal investigations.

A big-boned, balding man, Sedillo had thick thighs and large but-tocks, a legacy of his years as a high-school and college football line-man. He easily carried an extra twenty pounds on an imposing frame, and had a pudgy face.

"What have we got on Vernon Langsford, Lee?" Kerney asked, as he sat in a chair next to Sedillo.

"I knew who Langsford was as soon as Hutch asked me to check him out," Sedillo replied, as he positioned the cursor under an icon on the screen and clicked the mouse. "He retired as a district court judge about six years ago, not long after his wife was killed by a letter bomb that was sent to his home. The case was never solved. Alcohol, Tobacco, and Firearms and the FBI were brought in. I'm asking for their case files right now."

"What do we have on the case?"

"A lot of digging that went nowhere." Sedillo swung his chair around and faced Kerney. "I was still in narcotics when it happened, but it created a big buzz in the department and among the politicians."

"Why?"

"Langsford had just ruled against the Mescalero Apache Tribe's casino operation, and ordered it shut down on a legal technicality. Everybody figured that Langsford was the target of the letter bomb, and the murder was tied to his ruling invalidating the gaming com-pact with the state. But nothing materialized to prove it."

"You have our case file?"

Sedillo nodded and patted a thick folder. "I almost burned up the fax machine getting it, but here it is. That's your copy."

"Have you talked to the Ruidoso PD?"

"Yeah, and they don't have much. Langsford kept a low profile. He lived alone and, except for his golf buddies, kept pretty much to himself."

"Was he under any kind of protection?"

"Not since before his retirement."

"I want a list of everyone who visited the four campgrounds during the past month," Kerney said.

"Do you think our killer reconnoitered the campgrounds?"

"We can't dismiss it as a possibility."

"Visitors pay on the honor system, Chief, if they pay at all. We'll have to gather the pay envelopes, pull the license plate information, and run motor vehicle checks. We're talking thousands of day and overnight visitors, Chief."

"I know. Get started on it tonight. Tell the team to pay particular attention to anyone who visited all of the sites on the same day, or in a very short time span."

"Will do."

"And keep working the background investigations on the other victims. We can't rule out the possibility that Langsford wasn't the only primary—or even the last—target until we're sure that we haven't missed anything. If Langsford knew any of the other victims casually as the camp host at Oliver Lee State Park, or had a prior personal or professional relationship with any of them, that could be important."

"Another long day at the office," Sedillo sighed, as he scribbled a note to himself.

"If any promising connections or motives turn up, get an agent on a plane as soon as possible to check it out."

"Are we looking at money, revenge, sex, profit, and politics as motives, Chief?" Lee asked dryly.

"All of that, plus extremists. Using a letter bomb to kill Langsford's wife goes way beyond an ordinary homicide."

"You got it." Lee paused. "Hutch told me about Shockley, Chief."

"I'm glad he did."

"You and I go back a long way. Can I speak freely?"

"I've never known you to do otherwise, Lee."

"Every member of the team knows you did what you had to do. If I hear any flak about it, I'm gonna kick some butt."

Kerney squeezed Sedillo's shoulder and picked up the letter bomb file. "Thanks, Lee, but don't waste time on adjusting attitudes. Just keep your people focused on the job."

Outside the command trailer, Kerney watched the day fade on the western horizon, tinting the San Andres with flecks of amber. The lights along Tenth Street flicked on in a hot pink that gradually turned yellow as the fluorescent filaments powered up. In the morning he would go to the mountain resort community of Ruidoso, an hour away by car, where Vernon Langsford had lived, and start digging. But tonight, he would read the file on the murder of Langsford's wife, catch a couple hours sleep, and then drive the killer's route from Carrizozo to Alamogordo, starting at the time of the first shooting.

He wanted to experience the conditions encountered by the killer: see the terrain, move through the campgrounds, drive the roads, time his movement along the route, and get a feel for the killer's efficiency.

His cell phone rang.

"I got your message that you weren't coming," Sara said lightheartedly. "Does this mean our romance has soured?"

The sound of Sara's voice made Kerney smile. "That's the last thing I need to have happen."

"Bad day?"

"Worse than bad."

"Want to tell me about it?"

"Have you got the time?"

"Now that I have all weekend to work on it, my stunning analysis of military operations in Haiti since its independence from France can wait a few more minutes."

Kerney walked away from the command trailer. "I killed a cop today, Sara."

"Was it an accident?"

"No, I had to shoot him."

"Tell me what happened."

Kerney walked to the lawn that bordered the walkway to the district office, stood under a tree that had yet to shed its leaves, and started talking to his wife.

At first light, Kerney entered the command trailer. The core of the trailer, a rectangular space with built-in workstations, communications equipment, computer terminals, and office machines, was crowded with agents who looked as sleep-deprived as Kerney felt. He found Lee Sedillo in the small office, hand on his chin, staring blankly at some papers. The FBI and ATF files had arrived, and Kerney wanted a briefing before starting out for Ruidoso.

Sedillo filled Kerney in. The letter bomb matched no signature of any other, either before or after the event. Reconstruction experts had determined the device was similar to, but not identical with, several that had been mailed to abortion clinics in the Southwest. Postal inspectors had intercepted those devices before delivery, but no suspects were ever identified. Nothing in Langsford's court docket over a ten-year period showed any rulings that could be connected to an anti-abortion issue.

"Have all the victims' next of kin been notified?" Kerney asked.

"All but Langsford's," Lee said. "His only living relatives are a daughter and son. Son's name is Eric, the daughter is Linda Langsford. Eric is single and thirty-two years old. His last known address is in Cloudcroft, twenty miles away. I sent an agent up there last night. He moved a month ago with no forwarding address. We're checking with his last employer."

"And the daughter?"

"The daughter is thirty-five, divorced, with no children. She practices law in Roswell, specializing in oil and gas leases and litigation. Her law partner said she started a vacation two days ago. He doesn't know where she is, exactly. She took off on a road trip to Colorado. I've asked all Colorado law enforcement agencies to keep an eye out for her."

"Have you found any connection between Langsford and the other victims?"

"So far, we've struck out, Chief, and it looks like we're not getting anywhere on a motive for any of the other killings."

"Have the public information officer release all the victims' names, except Langsford's," Kerney said, "and tell him to keep emphasizing the spree-killing theme."

The fairways at the Ruidoso golf course were still green, and several foursomes were out on the links in spite of the cool morning. Langsford's home, a pitched-roof, single-story ranch-style house, was on the back nine with a nice view of the tenth hole and the heavily forested peak behind the course. The house looked closed up and no one answered Kerney's knock at the front door. He walked around the exterior noting the burglary alarm system on the windows and the miniature TV security cameras above the entrances and the garage door.

A new Ford Explorer pulled into the driveway as Kerney came around the side of the house, and a leggy woman wearing jeans and a lightweight wool turtleneck got out and hurried toward him.

"Can I help you?" the woman asked.

Somewhere in her thirties, she had long brown hair and an aura of sexuality that showed in her blue green eyes and the ease of her carriage.

Kerney showed his shield and introduced himself.

"Has there been a break-in?" the woman asked.

"Nothing like that. Please tell me your name."

"Kay Murray. I work for Judge Langsford."

"Can we talk inside?"

Murray hesitated, then nodded. "Let me get my things."

Kerney watched as the woman returned to the Explorer, retrieved a large purse, an overnight bag, and a leather-covered day planner, then locked the car. Not tall, she gave the impression of height, and had a very shapely rump.

She unlocked the front door and turned to Kerney. "Give me a minute to turn off the alarm."

"Of course."

Inside, she dropped her bag and purse on the couch and placed the day planner on an end table. The living room, a deep space with a fireplace along one wall and a large picture window with a view of the tenth hole, was decorated in expensive leather furniture accented by bulky dark oak side tables, which held handsome pottery lamps. Two beautifully framed Remington prints were nicely hung on either side of the fireplace, reinforcing the strong masculine feel of the room.

Kerney looked closer at the prints and decided they were original oils, not reproductions.

"What is this all about?" Kay Murray asked.

"Judge Langsford has been murdered."

Murray pressed a hand against her mouth. "Oh, dear, that can't be."

"I take it you haven't spoken to the local police."

"No, I've been in Albuquerque for the last two days. I just got back. What happened?"

"I can't go into the specifics. I'm trying to contact either his son or his daughter."

"Vernon has very little to do with either of them. You could say he's estranged from his children. I don't think he's spoken to Eric or seen him since I've been working for him, and about the only communication he has with his daughter is an exchange of cards during the holidays."

"How long have you worked for him?"

"Five years."

"Do you know why he's estranged from his children?"

"Eric and Linda hold him responsible for the death of their mother."

"Why would they do that?"

"You know about the letter bomb?"

"I do."

"The only reason Marsha Langsford was killed instead of the judge was because Vernon was supposedly away at a legal convention, while in fact he was spending time with another woman."

"How did you come to learn this?"

Murray dropped her gaze from Kerney's face. "Vernon told me. He's never stopped feeling guilty about it."

"Did his children know about this woman?"

"Oh, yes. He'd already told Marsha he was going to leave her, and of course she told Eric and Linda."

"None of this ever came out during the investigation."

"It was hushed up by the family. But it cost the judge a good bit of money."

"He bribed Eric and Linda to keep silent?"

"I wouldn't put it that way. He gave Eric fifty thousand dollars. Linda's husband had just filed for divorce when it happened, after discovering that she'd been having an affair. I guess she didn't think she could cast the first stone."

"Who was the woman in Judge Langsford's life?"

"Is that important?"

"It could be."

"Penelope Gibben. She works for Ranchers' Exploration and Development in Roswell. Vernon broke off the relationship immediately after Marsha's death."

"Langsford confided a great deal in you."

"I'm about his only confidante. In some ways he's a very lonely man." Her face tightened. "I mean, was."

"What did Eric do with the fifty thousand?"

"He blew it. Eric has a long-standing drug and alcohol problem."

"Exactly what kind of work do you do for Judge Langsford?"

"I'm a combination housekeeper and personal assistant. I keep his books, respond to his correspondence—if he chooses not to do so himself—pay the bills, shop, and fix his meals."

"Do you write checks for the judge?"

"Only on the household account. He has his own personal checking accounts. I simply mail him the unopened bank statements if he's not here when they arrive."

"Did you work for him full-time?"

"During the spring and summer when he's in residence, I do. Then it's three days a week during the fall and winter."

"And there was enough work to keep you busy?" Kerney asked.

"Part of it was keeping him company, Mr. Kerney. Older people are sometimes willing to pay for that. It's been a perfect job for me. I'm a weaver. I design shawls, wraps, and textiles. Vernon lets me work on my craft here, when I'm not busy with any of the odds and ends that need looking after to keep things in order. I have a loom in the spare bedroom that I use as an office and studio."

"That was very generous of the judge."

"You've noticed the security system?"

"I have."

"Judge Langsford was more concerned for his safety than he was about my personal convenience. He felt my physical presence here, on a regular basis, acted as a deterrent. After all, someone once wanted to kill him."

"He felt safe in his motor home?"

"As a camp host, he did. He was always surrounded by others, all of them people who had no idea who he was or what he'd been." Murray put her hand to her mouth again. "He was murdered by that spree killer, wasn't he? I heard reports on the radio while I was driving home."

"Yes."

"How awful."

"When was the last time you spoke to Langsford?"

"Three days ago. He would always call in once a week to see if anything needed his attention."

"Such as?"

"Judge Langsford had two consuming interests, golf and investments. He'd call me weekly to get an update on his portfolio, or to ask me if some board minutes or prospectus from a company had arrived."

"Would you characterize him as well-off?"

"More than that," Murray said. "He was the only child of a man who was once the biggest natural gas producer in the state. He inherited millions of dollars before he was appointed to the bench. He owns partial or controlling interest in three companies."

She took a deep breath and let it out slowly. "I'm sorry. I just can't stop thinking about him as still alive."

"That's understandable. What will you do, now that you're out of a job?"

"I'll be fine," Murray said. "I'm showing in three galleries: one here, one in Albuquerque, and one in Santa Fe. I've been socking away the money I've made as a weaver and living off my salary. I won't be homeless, Mr. Kerney."

"How long will you be here this week?"

"I've been paid through the end of the month, so I'm at your disposal."

"Will you be in town from now until the end of the month?"

"Yes."

"Can I see your driver's license?"

"What for?"

"Information for my report."

She searched her purse, found her wallet, and extracted the license.

Kerney wrote down the information, verified Murray's home address, and got her telephone number. "I'm going to ask a judge for a search warrant, Ms. Murray. There may be information in the judge's papers that could be helpful to the investigation. It will probably be issued today. If I can use the telephone, I'd like to call and have a city police officer come and stay here until the warrant is executed."

Murray's expression turned guarded. "Why do you need to do that?"

"I don't need to do it, Ms. Murray. But it's in your best interest that I do. With an officer on site, there will be no question about the loss or removal of anything from the house while you're here."

"I wouldn't take anything."

"I don't doubt you."

Kay Murray's cautious expression cleared. "I suppose it would be a good idea. I hate to think I'd be considered a suspect."

"We can get that issue off the table very quickly, if you'll give me the names and phone numbers of the people you were with and the places you went during your two days in Albuquerque."

"You're asking for an alibi, aren't you?"

"Yes, I am."

"I'll write it all down for you," she said, reaching for her daily planner.

"And if you have it, Penelope Gibben's home and work addresses would be helpful."

Murray paused. "I'll get them for you."

"I have the feeling Judge Langsford was a very private man."

"Vernon was extremely private."

"Yet he confided a great deal in you."

"We were friends, Mr. Kerney," Murray said tightly. "Is that a crime?"

"Not at all."

The Ruidoso patrol officer, a woman in her twenties, arrived within ten minutes. Kerney briefed her on the assignment, thanked Kay Murray for her cooperation, went to his unit, called Lee Sedillo, and filled him in on what he'd learned.

"I'll run a records check on Eric Langsford," Sedillo said, "and get the search warrant paperwork started."

"Make the search warrant as inclusive as possible," Kerney said. "But have the agent who serves it concentrate on Langsford's financial and personal papers. I need to know ASAP what corporations Langsford owns or has an interest in, and the state of their financial health."

"Do you have some specific reason to follow the money, Chief?"

"There's a lot of it, Lee. That's reason enough. We'll work this angle and the theory that the prior attempt against Langsford came because of his ruling against tribal gambling."

"Two motives for murder are better than one," Lee said.

"Hang on a minute," Kerney said, as Kay Murray came out the front door of Langsford's house. She'd removed her wool sweater, and the body-hugging tee shirt she wore made her look even more lissome.

She walked to Kerney's unit and held out a key. "Am I free to go?"

"Of course."

"Then I'd rather not stay. Having that police officer inside makes me feel that I'm under arrest."

"That's not the case."

"I know, but that's the way I feel. Take the key."

"It would be better if you came back after the search is finished and locked up. That way, there will be no question that anything has been unnecessarily damaged."

"What kind of unnecessary damage?" Murray said, putting the key in her pocket.

"Opening a locked desk or a safe. Does Langsford have a safe?"

"There's a floor panel in the study closet that lifts out. Under the panel you'll find a small safe embedded in concrete. His desk key is in the pot on the fireplace mantle in the study."

"Do you have the combination to the safe?"

"No."

"Is anything else locked?"

"No. Can I leave now?"

"Yes."

"I'll get my things."

"Lee?" Kerney said, as Kay Murray moved away.

"I'm here, Chief."

Kerney read off Murray's home address, social security number, date of birth, the license plate number to the Ford Explorer, and the name of the car dealer's tag on the back of the car. "Do the usual check on Murray, and call the dealership. I want to know if it was Langsford or Murray who bought the car."

"You got a hunch, Chief?"

"I think Murray's relationship with Langsford may have been more than meets the eye. It could mean nothing, but then again . . ."

"I'll get back to you," Sedillo said.

"There's more," Kerney said. "Murray said she spent the last two days in Albuquerque. Have an agent verify that."

"You got places and names, Chief?"

"Affirmative," Kerney said. "You ready?"

"Read it off."

The morning drive into Ruidoso had been pleasant. The east-west highway through the high mountains of the Mescalero Apache Reservation provided beautiful scenery and wonderful views. But from the Ruidoso city limits on, along a long stretch of road that wound down the Hondo Valley, there was nothing but the ugly commercial strip that seemed to be so typical of every Western city.

In Spanish, Ruidoso means noisy. The name came from the fast running river that coursed through the narrow valley where the town sprang up. Once a hotbed of gambling, prostitution, and bootlegging during the Depression, Ruidoso now catered to flatlanders from Texas and Mexico who came to escape the desert heat and for the horse racing, the reservation casino gaming, high-end shopping, the trendy resorts, and the golf courses.

Kerney drove the highway trying to remain immune to all the billboards and businesses that made the mountain pass look so tacky. In his boyhood Ruidoso had been nothing more than a sleepy village.

The investigation was beginning to get complex, and Kerney

liked having his attention fully engaged. It pushed shooting Shockley out of the forefront of his mind. But the image of Shockley re-
surfaced, and with it came an automatic gag reflex that Kerney
fought down.

Kerney knew his reaction was purely tribal. The vivid memory of
Shockley's bloodstained uniform and the common bond of belonging
it represented had slammed into Kerney's psyche far more deeply
than the actual shooting itself. He wondered if he would ever shake
it from his mind.

Roswell was on the eastern plains, an hour or so down the road.
He looked forward to talking with Langsford's ex-lover, Penelope
Gibben, and started framing questions he would put to her when
they met.

3

Home of the famous UFO Incident allegedly covered up by the military shortly after the end of World War II, Roswell traded on its notoriety, spurred on by several recent television shows. The old Main Street movie house had been converted into a UFO museum and gift shop, several companies conducted tours of the UFO crash site, and retail stores sold UFO coffee mugs, hats, tee shirts, toys, and posters of aliens and spaceships.

Aside from the UFO hoopla, Roswell was an ordinary small city that touted its mild climate, small-town flavor, capable work force, and recreational opportunities as a way to draw new businesses and retirees. Laid out in a checkerboard pattern, it was indistinguishable from many other Southwestern cities. The obligatory shopping mall was near the outskirts of town and strip malls peppered the major four-lane state roads bisecting the city. Main Street had lost its draw as businesses abandoned downtown, and new housing tracts stretched over the monotonous plains.

Two blocks east of Main Street on Pennsylvania Avenue, a tree-lined street with old Victorian houses, Kerney found Penelope Gibben at home. He sat quietly in her living room and watched her cry.

Although Gibben was in her mid-sixties, in appearance she had not surrendered to senior citizen status. An attractive woman no more than five feet tall and weighing less than a hundred pounds, Gibben was stylishly dressed in a chenille V-neck sweater that displayed a single strand of expensive pearls and she wore lightweight wool slacks. She used very little makeup, but her eye shadow had smeared a bit from crying.

The living room had mahogany double doors that opened on to the entry hall, a marble fireplace, and sash windows that gave a view of the porch and front lawn. It was furnished with two armchairs in a matching floral pattern, a velvet rose-colored sofa, Colonial-style end tables, and a stout coffee table with curved legs.

"I simply can't believe it," Gibben finally said, dabbing her eyes with a handkerchief.

"I need to ask you a few questions about Judge Langsford."

Gibben's eyes blinked rapidly. "Even though our friendship ended, I've always been comforted by the thought that Vernon was nearby and not really gone. Now he is."

"I understand that you and the judge were more than friends."

Gibben's eyes widened. "Excuse me?"

"He was once your lover," Kerney said.

She folded her hands in her lap and looked at Kerney with serious eyes. "You say that with such authority."

"Do you deny it?"

"I suppose there's no need to, now. Yes, we were lovers, although I'd rather the information remained confidential."

"Tell me about your relationship with him."

"It was perfect for many years until Vernon became dissatisfied with his marriage."

"That bothered you?"

"I'm a very independent person, Mr. Kerney. I enjoy living alone. I've never wanted to marry, but I do like the company of men as long as they don't intrude on my privacy. Vernon filled my need for a lover and a friend very nicely."

There was something cold about Gibben's revelation, but Kerney didn't challenge it. "How long were you lovers?"

"Far longer than many marriages last," Penelope said. "Almost twenty years. Eighteen to be exact."

"How did you meet?"

"I met him at work, Mr. Kerney. Vernon's father started Ranchers' Exploration and Development and hired me as his secretary. I came to know Vernon through my association with the company. He owns a controlling interest in the business."

"What is your current association with Ranchers'?"

"I'm the chief financial officer."

"I understand Vernon ended his relationship with you because of the guilt he felt about Marsha's death."

"Do you know that Vernon and I were together when Marsha was killed?"

"I do."

"How could he not feel guilty? We both did. The decision to end the relationship was mutual. After what had happened, neither of us could handle it."

"Why was he considering a divorce?"

"Marsha never recovered from Arthur's death. Her depression destroyed the marriage."

"Arthur?"

"Vernon's oldest son."

"Tell me about Arthur," Kerney asked.

"It was an absolute tragedy," Penelope replied. "The children had all returned to Roswell for the holidays. Arthur was home from graduate studies in California. Linda was newly married, had her law degree, and was working for one of the large firms here in town. And Eric had just completed a drug rehabilitation program and seemed to be doing well."

"What happened?"

"Of all the children, Arthur was the best athlete. In high school he excelled at track and field. As an undergraduate he gave up competitive sports to concentrate on his studies, and became a mountain bike enthusiast. When he was home from school, he would ride up into the mountains every chance he got. A hit-and-run driver killed him on the highway to Ruidoso five days before Christmas."

"When was that?"

"Three years before Marsha died."

"Was an arrest made in the incident?"

"The driver was never found. How did you come to learn about my relationship with Vernon? Surely, Linda didn't tell you. Was it Eric?"

"Why is that important to you?"

"I know what Vernon did to keep our secret safe from the public."

"You mean the fifty thousand dollars he gave to Eric?"

Gibben smiled wanly. "Over the years before Marsha's death, Eric cost him a great deal more than that. But I don't think Vernon ever begrudged him the money. He kept hoping Eric would straighten himself out."

"I get the feeling that after the affair ended, your friendship with Judge Langsford remained intact."

"For a time. Are you going to tell me who told you about my relationship with Vernon?"

"It was his personal assistant, Kay Murray."

"I see," Penelope said flatly.

"Does that surprise you?"

"Not really. Vernon was always drawn to women who could engage him intellectually and emotionally. Marsha gave him the security he wanted in a wife, but she was not very challenging in other ways."

"You talk as if you know Ms. Murray."

"I know Vernon."

"Judge Langsford obviously looked for more than just an intellectual and emotional connection outside his marriage," Kerney said.

"Are you asking me to speculate on the nature of Vernon's relationship with Kay Murray?"

"If you wish to."

"The Vernon I knew was a vigorous man with healthy appetites who was generous with those he cared about."

"What did Eric do with the money his father gave him?"

"He bought a new van, moved to San Francisco, and became a cocaine addict. When the money ran out, he came back and has been living in Cloudcroft ever since."

"How do you know this?"

Gibben sighed. "Eric refuses to have any further contact with his father, so Vernon appointed him a corporate board member with an annual stipend of twenty thousand dollars a year, to help him out. I send him the quarterly checks."

"When did you issue the last one?"

"Two months ago. It was endorsed and cashed."

"Is Linda also a board member?"

"No. She will have nothing to do with any of the family corporate holdings. As I understand it, she makes quite a comfortable living from her law practice."

"What would you say Judge Langsford's net worth totals?"

"Sixty million dollars, easily." Tears returned to the corners of her eyes, and Gibben stood up. "I don't think I can cope with any more questions right now, Mr. Kerney. If you'll excuse me, I'd like to be alone."

"I may need to speak with you again," Kerney said. "But I'd appreciate it if you would keep our conversation private."

A tight smile crossed Penelope Gibben's face. "Surely, you must know by now that keeping secrets is one of the things I do best."

Kerney left thinking that in spite of the obvious difference in age, Penelope Gibben and Kay Murray seemed remarkably alike.

Kerney tried calling Linda Langsford's law partner at home and got no answer. The office telephone yielded a busy signal, so he decided to stop in and see if Drew Randolph was working on the weekend. He found the building on a side street across from the county courthouse. Shielded by large trees and an expanse of lawn, the courthouse had a Greek revival facade topped off by a large dome.

The law office was open, and a buzzer sounded when Kerney stepped through the door into an empty well-appointed reception area. Kerney waited until a man came out to greet him.

"Can I help you?" the man asked.

Dressed in a rib-neck jersey tucked into a pair of cotton chinos, the man stood an inch taller than Kerney's six-one frame and looked to be in his late thirties. He had an athletic build and a well-developed chest.

"I'm looking for Drew Randolph," Kerney said, displaying his shield.

"And you are?"

"Kevin Kerney."

"I'm Drew Randolph. As I told the agent who called, I have no way of contacting Ms. Langsford. She didn't leave an itinerary."

"I understand that, Mr. Randolph."

"Although I'm sure she'll call in at least once or twice next week."

"Did the agent inform you that we're investigating Judge Langsford's murder?"

"Yes." Randolph's expression turned slightly sour. "She also said, unnecessarily I might add, that I could be charged with interfering with a police investigation if I disclosed the information to the media."

"Until every attempt has been made to notify the next of kin, we want to handle the case as discreetly as possible," Kerney said.

"Surely, your people must understand that as an officer of the court I am aware of the technicalities."

Kerney smiled at the pomposity of the man. "We like to cover all the bases, Mr. Randolph. How do you think Ms. Langsford will take the news of her father's murder?"

"That's an odd question," Randolph said, leaning against the reception desk.

"I understand she has not been close to her father for some time."

"True." Randolph's eyes searched Kerney's face. "How can that possibly be relevant to Judge Langsford's murder?"

"We may need her cooperation to solve the case. If she is uninterested in lending assistance, I'd like to know it now."

"Do you know the circumstances of Linda's disenchantment with her father?"

"Somewhat."

"Then you know Linda has cut herself off from him, more or less completely."

"I understand they exchange Christmas cards."

Randolph nodded. "There is occasional, strained contact. I think a psychiatrist would say that Linda is conflicted about her father. She loves him, but she can't forgive him. She keeps him at arm's length, and at the same time can't bring herself to completely sever the tie. I'm sure she'll cooperate with you. After all, now both her parents have been murdered."

"How long have you known Ms. Langsford?"

"We were in law school together."

"Does she stay in contact with her brother?"

"Not to my knowledge. They have nothing in common. I take it you haven't located Eric."

"No, we haven't. Does Ms. Langsford frequently take vacations without an itinerary?"

"We went to law school in Boulder, and we both love the Rocky Mountains. When we started the firm, we made a pact: I'd get a week of uninterrupted skiing in the winter, and she would have her annual high-country fall color tour. Since we limit our practice to oil and gas clients, coverage isn't a problem."

"That makes sense. Did you know Linda's ex-husband?"

"Slightly. His name is Bill Kendell. He's a vice president at a bank in Albuquerque. I don't remember which one. He left here soon after the divorce." Randolph held up a hand to ward off more questions. "Please don't ask me about Linda's personal life, past or present, Mr. Kerney. I'd rather you go directly to the source for your information. I'm Linda's partner, and we have a solid, congenial work relationship, but we live totally separate lives."

"Does the firm represent any of Judge Langsford's companies?"

"We do. I should say, I do."

"Which ones?"

"I'm the corporate attorney for each company."

"Thanks for your time."

The sheriff's office was behind the county courthouse, in an old, nondescript commercial building that had been carved up into offices. The investigating officer on the Arthur Langsford bicycle fatality had retired four years ago, and with a deputy sheriff at his side, Kerney searched for the case file in boxes stacked in a back storage room. When he found it, he sat on a step stool under the glare of a bare lightbulb and read the accident report.

Just five days before Christmas nine years ago, Langsford had been hit by a car on a curve at approximately four in the afternoon, with the sun low on the horizon. Reconstruction at the scene indicated that the unknown vehicle was heading west, within the speed limit, when the driver apparently swerved to avoid a hazard in the road. Skid marks showed the driver had braked hard before hitting Arthur Langsford, who had been riding in the opposite lane. Traffic at the time had been light, and there were no witnesses. Follow-up attempts to locate either the car or the driver proved unsuccessful.

The deputy made a copy of the file for Kerney, who left thinking that a lot of very interesting information about Vernon Langsford and his family had come to light, but none of it yet seemed to have any bearing on the investigation.

He swung into the flow of traffic on the main street and called in his location and destination. Lee Sedillo came on the horn to tell him the search of Langsford's Ruidoso home was under way.

* * *

Lee Sedillo met Kerney at the door and took him to Langsford's study, where two agents were working their way through the judge's financial records and personal papers. The furnishings echoed the decor of the living room: an oversize desk stood in front of a wall of books, and a matching leather reading chair and ottoman were positioned to give a view out the window to the fairway.

"We'll toss the rest of the house after we finish here," Lee said.

"Anything yet?" Kerney asked.

"Tidbits," Lee replied. "We found a letter from Langsford's daughter telling him not to appoint her as the personal representative of his estate. Langsford did it anyhow. His will, dated two weeks after her letter, names Linda Langsford as his representative. Except for some very generous donations to charity, a million dollars to Kay Murray, and a million dollars to a woman named Penelope Gibben, the estate is to be equally divided between Eric and Linda."

"Penelope Gibben was Langsford's mistress for almost twenty years," Kerney said.

"If money is the motive, then we've gone from no suspects to at least four: Gibben, Murray, and the two children."

"The letter bomb murder of Langsford's wife still suggests the possibility the judge was killed for other reasons. What else have you got?"

"Langsford kept meticulous records, including receipts of his purchases and cash expenditures. Over the past five years, he gave Kay Murray fifty thousand dollars to help her buy a town house, and bought her a number of expensive presents—an eight-hundred-dollar lambskin jacket, diamond earrings—stuff like that."

"And the Ford Explorer?"

"Another gift from the judge," Lee said. "I spent some time at the clubhouse and talking to residents in the neighborhood. Murray's car was often here overnight when the judge was in residence."

"That's interesting. Did the judge talk about his relationship with Murray to any of his neighbors or golfing buddies?"

"Nope, and all the people I spoke with had nothing but kind words about him. He was quiet, well-liked, and had a low handicap. Most didn't even know he had been a judge. Except for Murray's overnights, there wasn't any other gossip about him."

"Has Eric Langsford been located?"

"He hasn't surfaced," Lee said. "He worked as a handyman at a Cloudcroft inn until his supervisor fired him last month for chronic absenteeism. He moved out of his apartment and hasn't been seen since."

"Check with the San Francisco PD and see if they arrested or charged Langsford with any crimes six years ago. He once had a serious cocaine problem."

"Which means he's probably still using," Lee said. "Do you want me to question Murray about the gifts she received from the judge?" Lee asked.

"Did her alibi about her Albuquerque trip check out?"

"Completely."

"Let it ride, for now. I'll follow up with her myself later on. But deepen the background check on her."

"Will do. You look beat, boss."

"I am. I'll be at my motel room in Alamogordo, if you need me."

"Get some sack time," Lee said.

"That's the plan."

The lock in the motel door turned and Sara Brannon glanced up from her laptop computer to find Kerney staring at her with a surprised expression.

She went to him and snuggled against his chest. "I've been worried about you."

Sara's body felt warm and reassuring. Kerney stroked her strawberry blond hair, lifted her face, looked into her green eyes, and kissed her softly. "Not to worry," he said. "How did you find me?"

"I called Andy, found out where you were staying, and hitched a ride out here on an Air Force cargo plane."

Kerney looked out the window of the dingy motel room onto a panoramic view of the parking lot, half-filled with rental moving vans, semi-trucks, and subcompact four-bangers.

"This wasn't the weekend together I had in mind," he said. "Nor the place."

"You don't like your accommodations?" Sara said with a laugh.

"It's the best Alamogordo has to offer, I suppose. I'm glad you came."

"I considered it my wifely duty."

"There's nothing wifely about you, Sara. That's why I married you."

Sara smiled again and kissed him quickly. "Don't sweet-talk me, Kerney. How much sleep have you had?"

"Not much in the last two days. How long can you stay?"

"I fly out from Holloman Air Force Base at six in the morning."

"Give me a few minutes to clean up and we'll go get something to eat."

"I don't want you to take me out, Kerney. Get some sleep." Sara gestured at her laptop. "I have to finish my assignment, anyway."

"You're sure?"

"Positive."

"A nap would do nicely."

Stretched out on the bed next to Kerney in the darkened room, Sara listened to his breathing deepen. Although she'd married Kerney impulsively, she had no regrets. He was, in so many ways, a perfect match for her. Aside from being sexy, he was honest and had never tried to dominate or smother her, which would have driven her away in a flash. Best of all, he fully supported her decision to continue her career as a serving army officer.

She'd never really given him a choice in the matter, and had made it clear from the start that she wasn't about to walk away from four years at West Point and ten years on active duty for the privilege of becoming his wife. But she had the growing intuition Kerney wasn't completely happy with the part-time nature of their marriage.

She stroked his hand and watched for a reaction. Kerney's breathing remained even. Quietly, she got up, found her jacket, and left the room.

Kerney woke to the smell of food. The small motel writing desk had been cleared off, moved away from the wall, and covered with a red and white checkerboard paper tablecloth. On it, Sara had arranged a picnic dinner of Mexican take-out. The centerpiece, a spray of fresh-cut flowers, was arranged in the plastic ice bucket.

"Hungry?"

"Very. How long did I sleep?"

"Six hours. According to the locals, this is the best Mexican food in town. Stay where you are. I'll serve you in bed."

Kerney sat up and propped a pillow against the headboard. "Finally, I'm getting some of the treatment I deserve."

"Careful, or you'll find this plate in your lap," Sara said. She came over with two plates, handed one to Kerney, and sat with him.

"You're a beautiful woman, Sara Brannon."

"Now, that's the kind of talk I like to hear."

They ate and talked, filling each other in on all the small events that didn't get into their letters or phone conversations. By the end of the meal, Kerney felt rested, well fed, and much more like himself.

"Have you heard from Dale?" Sara asked.

Dale Jennings, Kerney's oldest friend, ranched on the west side of the San Andres Mountains, and had been keeping his eye out for property on Kerney's behalf.

"He's been bugging me to get down there," Kerney said. "Says he knows three ranchers who might consider selling."

"Well, when are you going to take a look?" Sara asked.

"I don't know."

"Do it tomorrow."

Kerney laughed. "Yeah, right."

"Why not? You've got eight agents and a lieutenant working the murder cases. Are you feeling indispensable?"

"I didn't say that."

"Are you close to making an arrest?"

"We don't even have a viable suspect."

Sara poked him lightly in the ribs with an elbow. "Take tomorrow off."

"Can you stay over?"

"I can't," Sara said, as she cleared away the plastic plates and utensils. "But if you don't do as you're told, I'll be inclined to throw a hissy fit. You wouldn't like that."

"I don't even know if Dale can get away."

"He can. I spoke to him a couple of hours ago."

"Well, aren't you something?"

"Get used to it, Kerney."

"Used to what?"

"Having someone in your life who's concerned about you."

"Bossy is more like it."

"That, too. Are you ready for dessert?"

Kerney looked at the table, didn't see any dessert, and glanced at Sara, who slowly unbuttoned her blouse. He grinned, reached over and pulled her to him.

In a briefing room at the air force base, Sara scrolled through her paper on Haitian military incursions one last time before shutting off the laptop. She needed to add footnotes and several more references to complete it, which meant putting in a long stint at the Command and General Staff College library once she got back to Fort Leavenworth.

As a lieutenant colonel, Sara was one of the highest-ranking members of her class, and she had no intention of letting junior officers outshine her. Finishing the paper as soon as possible would give her a head start on the upcoming battle command strategy exercise that would carry significant weight in determining the honor graduate for her class. Although graduation was months away and the competition was stiff, Sara planned to win that award.

She wished there was something she could do to help Kerney. The Shockley incident had rattled him badly, and while she could give him emotional support by telephone, it hardly seemed adequate. She'd deliberately arranged Kerney's day off with Dale to explore ranching possibilities as a way to force him to take some downtime and decompress.

Sara knew from firsthand experience what it took to run a major violent crime investigation, and how wearing it could be. Serving in an army where combat assignments were closed to women, she'd carefully selected intelligence and criminal investigations as a career path that would take her as close to the action as possible. Her postings had included tours as an executive officer of a MP company in Saudi Arabia during the Persian Gulf War, temporary duty as a tactical intelligence staff officer in Bosnia, supervising a Criminal Investigation Unit at White Sands Missile Range, and commanding allied ground reconnaissance and intelligence units in South Korea.

On a professional level, she would have enjoyed the opportunity to work with Kerney on the case. Spree murders were relatively rare events, and the hands-on experience would've been invaluable. So would some more time with Kerney, she thought, especially in the sack.

She wiped away a smile when a senior airman stuck his head in the door to say the bird was ready to fly.

When he woke, Kerney found Sara gone and a love note pinned to a pillow, containing a graphic suggestion of how they could spend their next weekend together, which made Kerney smile. He cleaned up and called Lee Sedillo.

"Any progress?"

"We've finished reviewing the user-fee pay envelopes for the past thirty days. We've identified seven people who visited all four parks in a one- or two-day period. I've got agents checking every motel between Carrizozo and Alamogordo to see if any of them returned and registered as guests around the time of the murders."

"Can you link any of the seven to Langsford?"

"Negative, Chief."

"Have Langsford's children surfaced?"

"Also negative, Chief."

"Have the PIO release Langsford's name and the fact that we're seeking the whereabouts of his son and daughter to the media."

"Will do."

"Did you finish up at Langsford's house?"

"No way, Chief. There's a hell of a lot of stuff to go through. The judge was a total pack rat. I've got a man there now. Are you coming in?"

"Do you need me?"

"Nothing's breaking."

"I'll be there this afternoon."

Kerney answered the knock at the door, and Dale Jennings stepped inside.

"Where's your bride?" Dale asked, eyeing the rumpled bedcovers with a grin.

"Long gone," Kerney said. "She can only take me in small doses."

"That makes sense. She said I'm to keep you occupied all day."

"We've got the rest of the morning."

"That will do, if we get our butts in gear."

"Have you seen these ranches we're going to look at?" Kerney walked to the chair by the window to grab his jacket.

"Nope," Dale said, waiting for Kerney to turn away from the window.

"What do you think the chances are of getting four flat tires simultaneously?" Kerney asked, as he eyed his unit in the parking lot.

Dale stepped to the window. "Somebody doesn't like you, would be my bet."

"Let's take a closer look."

The tires had been punctured, but there was no other damage to the car. Kerney took a quick tour of the other parked vehicles and found no additional evidence of vandalism. He called Lee Sedillo and told him what was up.

"I'll get the tires replaced and send an agent over to ask some questions," Lee said.

"Don't waste an agent's time on this," Kerney said. "Have a patrol officer take the call."

"Who did you piss off, Chief?"

"Good question," Kerney said. "Maybe one of Shockley's buddies."

"That's a thought that worries me," Lee said.

Dale Jennings took off his feed store baseball cap, scratched his head, and hoisted a foot on the truck's front bumper. "Finding land that equals what Erma left you isn't going to be easy," he said.

Kerney nodded in agreement. The two ranches they'd toured held no appeal for him. One, situated on the back side of the Jicarilla Mountains north of Carrizozo, looked promising until Kerney spoke with the owner, who was bailing out of the cattle business because the Forest Service had fenced off the live streams and greatly reduced his grazing allotment.

The other property was west of Carrizozo, a windswept, poorly managed stretch of land within sight of Chupadera Mesa. In the best of years, four hundred acres would be needed to support one cow-calf unit.

Kerney looked at the herd of scrawny Brangus cattle moving slowly across the dusty rangeland infested with broom snakeweed. Toxic to cattle and sheep, broom snakeweed caused abortions. What grasses there were—blue grama, silver beardgrass, and sideoats grama—had been pretty much eaten down to the root.

"What?" Dale finally asked, as he studied the displeasure on Kerney's face.

"Why bother to put cattle on the land if you have to truck in feed to keep them alive?" Kerney said.

"Some ranchers don't feed much until it comes close to shipping time," Dale said.

"That's no way to treat animals," Kerney said.

"I know it. Maybe this isn't a good time for you to be looking for land."

"What's that supposed to mean?" Kerney asked.

"Maybe better land will come on the market later down the road. Want to call it a day?"

"We've got one more to go?"

"Down by Three Rivers."

"Let's check it out."

Twenty sections south of Three Rivers were up for sale, running from the arid basin to the foothills that defined the western boundary of the Mescalero Apache Indian Reservation. Once, it had been part of the Albert Bacon Fall holdings that consumed a million acres from the Sacramento Mountains to the westerly San Andres Mountains.

Fall had been a senator from New Mexico before becoming Warren Harding's Secretary of the Interior. His political career ended with the famous Teapot Dome scandal, amid charges that he had engaged in shady deals regarding national petroleum reserves set aside for the Navy.

Kerney asked Dale to take the old road to the ranch headquarters. He wanted to see the rodeo grounds that had once drawn ranching families from throughout the area for several days of friendly competition. As teenagers, he and Dale had won the team calf-roping event three years running.

All that remained under the grove of trees were some rotting boards from the judging stand and a few fence posts.

"Those were good times," Dale said, staring out the truck window as they drove slowly by.

"Yes, they were," Kerney answered.

They got permission from the ranch manager to tour the land, and took off on a dirt road that wound into the hills. Good rains over the summer had greened up the terrain, but the ground was rocky, with sparse topsoil, and only patches of bunch grass thrived.

Below them, the Tularosa Basin, once a broad savanna, spread out to the far off San Andres Mountains. Not even a half century of protection by the military had restored the fragile basin from years of drought and overgrazing. Where knee-high grasses once grew, now mesquite, saltbush, and creosote bush crowded out the more fragile native vegetation.

Inside an open gate high in the foothills, Kerney and Dale walked the land, neither of them happy with soil so poorly suited to retain moisture. In front of them, the twin peaks of Sierra Blanca on the Apache Reservation dominated the skyline.

"Not much you can do with this," Dale said with a shake of his head. "It would take a full section to run one cow."

The short wail of a siren cut off Kerney's response. A four-wheel-drive bore down upon them, emergency lights flashing, and ground to a halt next to Dale's truck. The man who got out of the truck and moved toward them wore a tribal police uniform shirt. In his mid- to late twenties, he was five-ten, with an olive brown complexion and dark hazel eyes.

"Let me see some ID," the officer said, his hand resting on the butt of his holstered weapon.

"Is there a problem, Officer?" Kerney asked, flipping open his badge case.

"You're trespassing on Apache land," the officer said, dismissing Kerney's shield with a glance. "I need a driver's license from both of you."

Dale fished out his wallet while Kerney did the same. As he watched Kerney hand the officer his license Dale thought there was something familiar about the young man, but he couldn't place it in his mind.

"We didn't see a sign." Kerney said.

The officer pointed to a placard fifty yards away and plucked the driver's license from Dale's hands. "Wait here."

"So much for professional courtesy," Kerney said, as he watched the young officer stand next to the vehicle, open a citation book, and start writing.

"We're getting tickets?"

"Looks that way."

The officer finished up and returned. "You can either pay the fine by mail or appear in tribal court," he said. The name tag over his right shirt pocket read OFFICER CLAYTON ISTEE.

"Is the ticket necessary, Officer?" Kerney asked.

"Apache land, Apache laws," Istee said, nodding at the open gate. "I'll wait here until you leave."

"Cocky young fellow," Kerney said, as Dale fired up the truck and drove through the gate.

"Apaches don't like us much," Dale said. "Actually, he reminds me of you."

"I was never that sassy."

"Oh, really? I meant his looks. He looks like you. Didn't you notice?"

"You've got to be kidding."

"Same deep-set eyes, same frame, same chin."

The memory of Isabel Istee, his girlfriend during his senior year in college, ran through Kerney's mind. The only girl he'd been serious about up to that time, she'd dumped him without warning or explanation. Whatever her reasons were, it didn't matter anymore. Or did it?

He shook his head. It wasn't possible.

"So, don't agree with me," Dale said, misreading Kerney's reaction.

"Let's call it a day, Dale," Kerney said, looking out the window, his thoughts still on Isabel.

"Whatever you say."

4

Dale dropped Kerney off at the command trailer, where Kerney's unit, sporting four brand-new tires, was parked outside. On the office desk Lee Sedillo had left a sealed envelope containing his car keys and a note. Nothing had come from the patrol officer's attempt to identify the person responsible for the vandalism. Since the investigation team was staying at Kerney's motel, Lee had queried each agent about the incident. No one had noticed the damage. Because all personnel had left the motel before Kerney, Lee speculated that the crime occurred after the agents were gone and while Kerney was still in his room. Therefore, it was not a random act.

Lee and the agents were in the field conducting interviews. Kerney spent the remainder of the day poring over the information that had been gathered in the letter-bombing homicide of Marsha Langsford. He finished up by phoning the senior ATF and FBI agents who had supervised the investigation, in the hope that some important shred of evidence had been left out of the case files.

Both agents had concentrated attention on members of the American Indian Movement, a radical Indian rights organization, most famous for the shootout with U.S. Marshals and the FBI at Oglala, South Dakota, in the summer of 1976.

The feds had identified an AIM "cell" that had remained active in the Four Corners region of the state on the Navajo Nation. It had two Mescalero members. On the telephone, the FBI agent kept circling back to the AIM group. But all the evidence showed that the group's concerns at the time were treaty rights, not reservation casino gaming.

When Kerney pointed out that no group had claimed responsibility for the letter-bomb attack, the agent dismissed his observation, arguing that the Apaches were secretive, warlike by nature, and therefore still suspect.

The ATF agent Kerney talked to grudgingly admitted that AIM had never been a suspect in any type of terrorist bombing. But that didn't hold him back from rattling on about the lack of cooperation he'd received from tribal officials during the investigation.

Kerney hung up feeling that both men wanted a quick and easy cowboy and Indian solution to the case and had conveniently blamed the tribe when their investigation stalled.

Before Kerney left to return to his motel room, Lee Sedillo arrived and informed him that the subjects known to have visited all the campgrounds on the days prior to the shootings were in the clear.

"Nothing suspicious at all, Chief," Lee said. "No connections with the victims, and no weak alibis."

"Well, that's one rabbit trail we don't have to keep following," Kerney said, as he walked to the door.

"You read my note about the tires?" Lee asked.

"We'll let the incident slide for now," Kerney said.

"Unless they know the officer, most civilians don't pay any attention to who drives cop cars. Especially unmarked units like yours."

"I've thought about that," Kerney said.

"And you're driving an undercover unit with standard issue motor vehicle license plates, not department plates."

"That, too."

"So?" Lee asked, frustration creeping into his voice.

"So, I agree," Kerney said with a smile. "Whoever doesn't like me may be one of Shockley's buddies."

"Maybe one of our own," Lee said.

"I hope not," Kerney said.

"You still want me to drop it?"

"For now. We haven't got the time."

Back in his room Kerney watched the late news, which headlined the breaking story that Vernon Langsford had been one of the spree victims. "Team coverage" spun off to review the unsolved letter-bomb murder of Langsford's wife and the search for Langsford's children.

Kerney killed the TV and the bedside light, hoping the media coverage would at least get Linda and Eric Langsford's attention. He needed to talk to them, and soon.

St. Joseph's Mission, the most imposing building in the village of Mescalero, stood on a hillside overlooking the settlement. It was built from hand-hewn stone and logs. Kerney had toured it as a child with his parents, and inside on the wall behind the altar an Apache Jesus looked down on the chapel.

Although the village served as the center of government for the tribe, there were no tidy rows of houses lined up along linear streets. Aside from the few business situated close together along the highway, the schools, government buildings, and tribal enterprises were sprinkled throughout the narrow mountain valley. Most of the homes were located off dirt roads that extended into the forest.

To Kerney's eye, Mescalero seemed deliberately turned away from the non-Indian world that passed through on the highway. As he pulled into the parking lot of the tribal headquarters building, he decided it would be a good idea to remember that observation. Inside, he found his way to Silas Kozine, a senior tribal administrator.

Kozine, a man well past middle age, had gray hair and wide, slightly downturned lips that gave his face a somber cast. He tapped his fingers together while Kerney explained the reason for his visit.

Silas Kozine's expression hardened as Kerney finished, and he said nothing for a long moment.

"I am sorry Judge Langsford has been killed, but I can't see how a murder spree that occurred off tribal land has anything to do with us. We went through this exercise six years ago, when Judge Langsford's wife was murdered in Roswell. No evidence was ever found that connected any tribal member to the crime, in spite of the FBI's attempts to prove otherwise."

"I understand the tribal police conducted an independent investigation of Mrs. Langsford's murder that concentrated on possible tribal suspects," Kerney said. "I'd like to review the file."

"Our chief of police made it clear to the FBI that there were no tribal suspects."

"It might be beneficial to take another look."

"It would have no benefit for us, Mr. Kerney. In fact, it would only give those people who think of us as uppity Indians the opportunity to point fingers and start rumors."

"I'm not looking to politicize anything, Mr. Kozine. The killer could be someone from the tribe he sent to prison, someone who felt unfairly treated in Langsford's court, someone with a personal grudge, or a casino employee who felt Langsford's ruling against gambling would destroy his livelihood. The possibilities are endless."

Silas Kozine consulted a paper on his desk. "I think your request for our cooperation comes a little too late."

"Excuse me?"

"Yesterday morning, you and a man named Dale Jennings were found trespassing on tribal land."

"That was unintentional, and had nothing to do with the investigation."

"Personally, I see it as a lack of respect. You can pay your fine at the tribal court offices, Mr. Kerney."

Kerney hesitated, decided there was no use arguing further, and stood up.

"Is there something else?" Kozine asked.

"I went to college many years ago with a girl from Mescalero, Isabel Istee. Is Officer Istee her son?"

"Yes, he is."

"How can I locate his mother?"

"Isabel is director of nursing at the Indian Health Service Hospital. You'll find her there."

Before driving to the hospital, Kerney went to the tribal court and paid both his and Dale's trespassing fines. The small, two-story hospital had a rock exterior offset by stark white window frames and an orange metal roof. Kerney announced himself at the reception desk, asked to see Isabel Istee, and nervously waited, not sure if he wanted to voice the question that had to be asked.

He recognized Isabel as soon as she stepped through the door to the administrative wing. Her small body had filled out a bit, giving her an attractive subtle roundness, and her jet-black hair showed hints of gray. Her face still held an aristocratic, almost haughty appeal, and her eyes, dark as obsidian, were still intriguing.

She walked to him with measured steps and stopped a few feet away. "I have often wondered if I would see you again, Kevin," she said.

"It's been a long time, Isabel."

She nodded and gestured toward the door. "Why don't we talk in my office."

Once inside, Kerney sat in a chair and watched Isabel arrange herself at the desk. On the bookcase behind her was a framed photograph of Clayton Istee in uniform. Two framed university degrees were displayed on the same shelf.

"What brings you to see me?" Isabel asked.

"I met your son yesterday."

"Yes."

"You and his father must be very proud of him."

"Every member of the family is."

"How long have you been married?"

"You have something to ask me, Kevin?"

"Only if you have something to tell me."

"I'm not married, and never have been."

Kerney let out a sigh. "You're not making this easy, Isabel."

"Did you come here to intrude into my life?"

"Intrude in what way?"

"We knew each other when we were very young. I have no idea what kind of man you are."

"I'm a policeman, like your son." He placed his open badge case on the desk in front of Isabel.

Isabel picked it up and studied it. "I've read about you occasionally in the newspapers. Weren't you going on to graduate school after the army?"

"I did. I dropped out."

"To become a policeman?"

"Yes."

Isabel handed back the badge case. "What you do for a living doesn't tell me who you are as a person now."

"Can words answer that question?"

"Probably not," Isabel answered, looking at the wedding band on Kerney's finger. "You're married?"

"Yes."

"Any children?"

"None that I know of. Is Clayton my son?"

Isabel studied Kerney for a long, hard minute before answering. "Why would that be important to you?"

"If I have a child I want to know it."

"I suppose you have a right to know. Yes, Clayton is your son."

"Does he know who I am?"

"No."

"Why not?"

"I've never told him. He only knows that his father was an Anglo boy I met at school. I wanted two things when I went to college, a nursing degree and a baby. I came back to Mescalero with both."

"Why didn't you tell me you were pregnant?"

"You had no desire to be a father, and I wasn't interested in marriage. You gave me what I wanted, Kevin, and I gave you what you wanted."

"That's cold, Isabel. I liked you a lot."

"I don't mean it that way. We both enjoyed each other, and I have always remembered you fondly. Every time I look at Clayton he reminds me of you."

"That's kind of you to say."

"Now that you know, what will you do?"

"That question is yours to answer."

Isabel nodded solemnly. "I appreciate that. I will tell Clayton about you. The rest is up to him. He doesn't need a father, Kevin. He's a grown man."

"I understand."

"My son is Apache, Kevin."

"I understand that, also."

"I always knew this day would come."

"I will cause you and your son no trouble."

"I'd like to believe you." Isabel stood, extended her hand, and Kerney shook it. "Thank you, Kevin."

"No thanks are necessary."

Isabel smiled. "I mean, for giving me Clayton. I made a good choice when I picked you."

"Were you that deliberate?" Kerney asked, somewhat taken aback.

Isabel laughed. "Oh, yes."

* * *

Kay Murray's town house was the last unit at the end of a long dead-end lane in the community of Alto, just outside of Ruidoso. The development, nestled in a grove of pine trees, looked to be a combination of second homes and long-term vacation rentals. Two-story mountain chalets, all with steep pitched shingled roofs, second-story decks, attached garages, and wood exteriors, were grouped in a semicircle around a common park area that contained several permanently installed barbecue grills and picnic tables, two tennis courts, and a small playground. Each house was marked with a rustic wooden street-number sign planted in the lawn next to the pathway that curved to the front door.

Kerney parked and tried to pull himself together. The thirty-minute drive from Mescalero hadn't done much to settle his mind. He'd always hoped someday to be a father. But to become one suddenly, retroactively, over the course of nearly thirty years, left him flabbergasted.

Would he have married Isabel if he'd known she was pregnant? Probably, assuming she would've agreed, which, based on their conversation, seemed completely unlikely.

He didn't know if he felt misused by Isabel or simply superfluous in her scheme of things. He decided both feelings were valid, and left it there until he could sort it out.

Kay Murray answered the doorbell wearing an angora camisole, shorts, and not much else. Kerney caught an unpleasant glint in her eyes.

"Your agents made a mess of Judge Langsford's house," she said. "I was up most of the night putting things back together."

"May I come in?" Kerney asked.

"I'm just about to do my yoga," Murray answered.

"I won't take much of your time."

"I suppose it's all right," Murray said, stepping aside.

A half-round soapstone woodstove in the center of the L-shaped room served as the focal point. Except for the couch in front of a wall of books, the furniture was sleek and very European looking. A multicolored weaving in the shape of a long, unfurled streamer dominated one wall. On the wood floor was a padded exercise mat.

Murray folded her arms and didn't offer Kerney a seat.

"Are you aware that Judge Langsford named you in his will?"

"Of course," Murray said. "He also bought me my car, gave me a sizable down payment for my house, and paid me an ample salary. What's your point?"

"It would seem that the judge was quite generous with you."

"Yes, he was."

"I'd like to know why."

"Judge Langsford appreciated my services," Murray said with a cold smile. "Haven't we already talked about this?"

"Sometimes elderly people can be taken advantage of."

"I resent that remark. Judge Langsford was sound in mind and body. I doubt anyone could have taken advantage of him."

"Do you have a boyfriend, Ms. Murray?"

"I see someone."

"Here in town?"

"Yes."

"Tell me who he is."

Murray shook her head. "That's none of your business. I refuse to let you treat me as a suspect. You already know that I had nothing to do with Judge Langsford's murder."

"I still need to speak with your boyfriend."

"So, I am a suspect after all."

"Not necessarily."

"I don't like having my privacy invaded."

Kerney shrugged. "If you don't cooperate now, I'll just keep coming back until you tell me, or find a more public way to identify him. Would you like that?"

"That's harassment."

"Why are you hiding his identity?"

Hostility seeped from Murray's eyes. "Because he's married."

"I'm sure you'd like to have me go away and never come back, Ms. Murray. Talking to your boyfriend just may make that happen."

"The man I'm seeing isn't a murderer."

"I'm sure you're right. But, one way or the other, I need to confirm that."

"His name is Joel Cushman. He's a psychologist in private practice."

"Thank you for cooperating."

"This is utterly insane."

Joel Cushman had his practice in a small office complex on Mechem Road. When Kerney arrived, Cushman had just finished a session with a client. Kerney showed his credentials to the receptionist, who quickly buzzed Cushman and directed Kerney through the appropriate door.

Cushman was standing when Kerney entered. Of average height, he had a bit of a potbelly, a soft handshake, and an inquisitive look on his face. On his desk was a photograph of a kneeling woman with her arms wrapped around the waist of a young boy.

Cushman's look turned worried when Kerney started talking about Kay Murray.

"Why on earth would you be investigating Kay?" Cushman asked.

"I understand you're her lover," Kerney said.

"Who told you that?"

"Ms. Murray."

Cushman slumped into his chair. "Yes, we're lovers."

"For how long?"

"Three, almost four years."

"How did you meet?"

"Socially, at a party," Cushman said, looking away.

"And she was never one of your patients?"

"For a time she was. But our personal relationship started after she left therapy."

"Does your wife know about Ms. Murray?"

"Listen, I don't want any trouble."

"What brought Kay to see you?"

"You know I can't be compelled to reveal that information."

"What can you tell me?"

"She's a remarkable, talented, intelligent woman. I care for her very much."

"Is your practice successful, Dr. Cushman?"

The question startled Cushman. "Yes, it's well established, and my wife is an OB/GYN."

"No money problems?"

"We live comfortably and within our means."

"Has Ms. Murray ever asked you for money or a loan?"

"Never."

"Has she ever mentioned having money problems?"

"Kay also lives within her means."

"Are you her only lover?"

"Only Kay can answer that question."

"Does that mean you don't know?"

Cushman pulled himself erect in his chair. "That's the best answer I can give you."

Kerney gazed at the framed certificates and diplomas on the office wall. "Aren't there ethical rules against sleeping with clients?"

Cushman squirmed in his chair. "I've already explained that I was not involved with Kay while she was my patient."

"If you answer my question I might be willing to forget we had this conversation," Kerney said.

"Yes, she has had another lover."

"Who?"

"Vernon Langsford."

"You've been sharing Ms. Murray with Langsford?"

Color rose on Cushman's cheeks and he said nothing.

"It must have made you jealous."

"No, it did not."

"It doesn't bother you that Langsford was elderly, rich, and sleeping with your lover?" Kerney asked.

"I have no control over Kay's decisions."

"Where were you last Friday night?" Kerney asked.

Cushman's face lost color. "Attending a Christian men's fellowship convention in Albuquerque."

"Did you travel alone?"

"Yes."

"You saw Kay there, didn't you?"

"For a while," Cushman said.

"Where did you stay?"

"We stayed at the same hotel, in separate rooms."

"How long were you with Kay?"

"From about eleven-thirty Friday night until the next morning. I had to wait for her to arrive. She'd gone out with friends for a late dinner and drinks."

"Did anyone see you together?"

"We ordered breakfast in the room."

"At what time was it delivered?"

"Seven-thirty."

"I'll need the names of the people you were with at the convention."

Cushman started scribbling down names, the pen shaking in his hand. "This in unbelievable."

"I also need addresses and phone numbers, if you have them," Kerney added.

Cushman reached for his address book.

After leaving Cushman's office, Kerney got on the horn to Lee Sedillo. "Where are you?"

"Heading your way, Chief. ETA ten minutes."

"Let's meet for coffee."

"Roger."

* * *

The café on Sudderth Avenue had horse-racing posters tacked on the walls and cheap cafeteria-style tables and chairs scattered throughout the room. Aside from Kerney and Lee Sedillo, the only other customers were two city cops on a break and a table of four men, all dressed in jeans and work boots, who were busy discussing a set of construction plans. A slow-moving waitress worked her way across the room, wiping down and setting up tables.

"San Francisco PD reports Eric Langsford was busted twice on two misdemeanor cocaine possession charges while he was living in the Bay Area," Lee said. "No other arrests in California. He's had one drunk and disorderly charge and a DWI since moving back."

"Nothing more serious?" Kerney asked.

"Nope. Langsford plays the guitar. When he's not high, he's supposedly a real good musician. He was a member of a country and western band that had a steady weekend gig at a Cloudcroft bar. When the summer tourist season ended the band got booked to do a west Texas tour. That's when Langsford left his day job. Or was fired, I should say."

"Where's the band now?" Kerney asked.

"In Van Horn, Texas, playing a small club and working their way back to El Paso. But Langsford dumped the group in a town named Marfa. He got drunk and started a fight with the band's drummer two days before his father was murdered."

"Do you have a line on him?"

Lee shook his head. "He could be crawling through every border town booze joint. I've got an all points bulletin out on his camper van."

"And his sister?" Kerney asked.

"No sightings, no contact, no nothing. A neighbor said he ran into Linda Langsford at a Roswell supermarket the day before she started her vacation. Langsford told the neighbor she was planning to camp out and do some high-country backpacking in the Rockies. I've asked Colorado and Federal park rangers to canvas campsites and check all their backcountry hiking permits."

"Have you finished the background investigation on Kay Murray?"

"Murray was born in Carlsbad, the daughter of Jean and Richard Murray. The father abandoned the family, and she was raised by the mother, who died of cancer when Murray was twenty-one years old. She moved to Roswell, took art courses at the junior college, and then went to the university in Albuquerque, where she finished a degree in fine arts.

"Starting out, she couldn't make a living as a weaver, so she got into the housekeeping business, working for yuppies and well-to-do retired couples. She's been doing it now for about ten years."

"How did she hook up with Langsford?"

"I don't know."

"Murray was Langsford's lover. She's also having an affair with her former therapist, Joel Cushman. Cushman's married. He said he was with Murray in an Albuquerque hotel the night Langsford was shot."

"Do you think Cushman and Murray may have come up with the spree killing scheme so that Murray could inherit the million dollars?"

"Maybe. But it appears that Cushman is well-off, and we know Murray hasn't been hurting for money. Cushman swears Murray was with him in his room from eleven-thirty at night until the next morning. He says they ordered room service and had breakfast together. Have the agent who backtracked on Murray talk to housekeeping, room service, and the hotel auditor. And let's take a close look at Cushman."

"Roger that."

"Have you got any documentation on Murray?"

"The usual," Sedillo said, as he pulled a file from his briefcase and passed it over. "Copies of her birth certificate, public school and college transcripts, motor vehicle records, the criminal records check, and the agent's field notes."

Kerney opened the file. "Did you hit any pay dirt with the Langsford search warrant?"

"Nothing more than what I already told you about, Chief."

Kerney scanned Murray's junior college transcript, closed the file, and stood up. "I'm going to Roswell."

"What's up?"

"Murray's home address on her junior college transcript is the same as Penelope Gibben's."

Penelope Gibben's office in the Ranchers' Exploration and Development suite on the eighth floor of the tallest building in town afforded her a view of a slice of Main Street and the old warehouse district next to the railroad tracks.

She sat behind a polished walnut desk and looked at Kerney with a wrinkled brow.

"I saw no reason to tell you Kay was my niece," Gibben said. "She came to live with me after her mother—my sister—died. It was my idea to take her in."

"Did you pay her tuition and expenses while she was in school?"

"Of course. She wanted to be more than a coffee shop waitress or a barmaid. She would have gone to college right after high school if her mother hadn't been so sick with cancer."

"So Vernon Langsford must have known Kay while she was living with you."

"Yes. He grew very fond of her."

"How fond?" Kerney asked.

"In a fatherly way."

"How did Langsford come to seek Kay out and offer her a job?"

"They kept in touch after she moved to Albuquerque. He knew she was working as a housekeeper and trying to get her career in fiber art under way. Soon after he moved to Ruidoso, he made her an offer that gave her the opportunity to earn a decent living and still have time for her art."

"Did you know Langsford left the same amount to both of you in his will? A million dollars each. He must have held you both in high regard."

"What an interesting thing to say."

"Did you know that Kay was his lover?" Kerney asked.

"I had my suspicions."

"That didn't trouble you?"

"I've already told you my sexual relationship with Vernon ended with the death of his wife."

"When did Langsford start sleeping with your niece?"

"I assume it was after she went to work for him."

"Not before? Not when Kay was living with you?"

Gibben looked at Kerney frostily.

"You and your niece are very much alike, in personality and looks. She was young, pretty, creative, and intelligent. Surely, Langsford had to be drawn to her, just as he'd been drawn to you."

"I think we've talked enough."

"Did you send her to college in Albuquerque to get rid of her?"

Penelope stood up and pointed to her office door. "Good day, Mr. Kerney."

"To have your niece—a young woman you so graciously took in—compete for your lover's attention and affection must have made you jealous and angry."

Frozen in place, Penelope Gibben didn't answer, but Kerney could see fury building in her eyes. He smiled and let himself out of her office.

Kerney caught up with Kay Murray outside her town house.

"Go away," she said, striding past him.

"Would you be more comfortable talking to me at the city police headquarters?" he asked.

She stopped and wheeled. "You're such a bully. Are you the morals police, Mr. Kerney? Is that what this is all about? Do you have some lowbrow, pernicious interest in other people's personal lives?"

"You've talked to Joel Cushman."

"You bet I have."

"I have only one question: When you were living with your Aunt Penelope did Langsford seduce you or did you seduce him?"

"Jesus, you just don't quit."

"Well?"

"It was mutual, okay?"

"That must have been hard on your aunt."

"She threw me out because of it. Vernon forced her to take me back."

"How did he do that?"

"Penelope was so entwined in Vernon's life on every basic level, that she had no choice. She needed him."

"For what?"

"All the creature comforts."

"Or did she use him?" Kerney countered.

"No, Mr. Kerney, she needed him. That's why Vernon turned to me. I used him. He never had to question the nature of our relationship. It was always clearly understood."

"Neat and tidy."

"Exactly."

"Do you think Penelope is capable of murder?"

"Murdering Vernon?"

"And his wife," Kerney added.

"No more so than I am. Neither of us are violent people, capable of murder."

"Is that a fact?" Kerney said, turning away.

"You don't believe me?"

"Why should I?"

Kay tapped her forefinger against her temple. "I get rid of people in my mind, Mr. Kerney. It's a lot cleaner and neater. Just like locking a door and walking away."

"What are you going to do with the million-dollar inheritance?"

"Use it to stay far away from people like you."

Kerney left Kay Murray standing on the walkway and started the drive back to Alamogordo. Just about every possible motive for murder—sex, jealousy, money, revenge, politics, adultery, and deceit—was bouncing around the Langsford killing, and Kerney didn't have one hard target in sight.

He ran over some suppositions in his mind. Did Murray kill Langsford for her inheritance? And if so, was Joel Cushman her accomplice? Money problems would have to surface for that notion to stand up. Or was the killer Penelope Gibben, who might be holding a grudge about being dumped for a younger woman by her ex-lover? That idea had some possibilities.

But in spite of an initial unwillingness to cooperate, all of them had folded easily under questioning, and none of them appeared to have the stealth or cunning needed to pull off a copycat spree killing to get to Langsford.

One question rang true: Why did every one of them still seem to be hiding something?

He made radio contact with Lee Sedillo and asked about Linda and Eric Langsford.

"Still nada, Chief."

"I'll be at my motel room."

"Ten-four."

Clayton Istee took a deep breath, made a fist, and knocked on the motel room door. He heard some movement inside and then the door opened to reveal a shirtless Kevin Kerney. Low on his bare stomach was an ugly surgical scar.

"We might as well get this over with," Clayton said, raising his eyes to Kerney's face.

"Come in," Kerney said.

Clayton stepped inside and watched Kerney pull on a sweatshirt. "So you're my father," he said.

"That's what I've been told."

Clayton scanned Kerney's face. "I've always wondered what you looked like."

"I hope it's not too much of a disappointment." Kerney sat on the edge of the bed and gestured at the chair. "Have a seat."

Clayton swung the chair around from the desk and sat. His body felt tight and his stomach churned. "I don't know if I'm ready for this."

"I don't know if I am, either," Kerney replied.

"You're willing to take my mother's word that you're my father?"

Kerney nodded. "Why should she lie to me?"

"Maybe you think she's just some Indian slut who's telling you a story."

"I don't think either of those things about your mother."

"Maybe you want a DNA comparison, to make sure I'm really your biological son."

"Is that what you want?"

"I asked you."

"I have no reason not to trust Isabel."

"She says you were in the army before you became a cop."

"That's right. Two years active duty," Kerney said.

"When?"

"Vietnam."

"Did you see any action?"

"Enough."

"Is that where you got that scar on your belly?"

"No, that came later. It goes with my limp."

"What happened?"

"A gunfight with a drug dealer."

"Did you put him down?"

"Yeah. How long have you been with the tribal police?"

"Five years. I joined right after I got my degree from Western New Mexico State."

"You like the work?" Kerney asked.

"I like it fine. It's funny, both of us being cops."

"It is an interesting coincidence."

"You're married, my mom says. Who's your wife?"

"Her name is Sara Brannon. She's a career army officer."

"But no kids, right?"

"No kids, at least until recently."

"You ever been married before?"

"Once, when I was about your age. It didn't work out."

"I don't want you trying to act like my father or anything like that."

"I wouldn't know where to begin," Kerney said.

"I just want to learn something about you."

"That's fair enough."

"Mom says you were raised on a ranch."

"In the San Andres, fifty miles from here, as the crow flies."

"Do your parents still live there?"

"No, the ranch was swallowed up by the missile range. My parents were killed in an automobile accident when I was coming home from Vietnam."

"Where did your family come from, originally?"

"My grandfather came here from west Texas over a hundred years ago."

"Do I have any uncles, aunts, or cousins?"

"Not on my side of the family."

"Do my questions bother you?"

"You have a right to ask them. How do you feel about having me as a father?"

"It doesn't make me any less Apache."

"I wasn't thinking along those lines," Kerney said.

"I just want to make sure you know where I'm coming from. Do you like being a cop?"

"Most of the time I do, but not right now."

"Shooting a fellow officer for stealing evidence is pretty harsh," Clayton said.

The comment caught Kerney unprepared. "Is that what you think I did?"

"Based on what your department released to the media, Shockley was unfit to wear the badge. But the state police officers I know are saying that you overreacted and blew the arrest."

"Shockley gave me no choice. Let's leave it at that."

"Okay, I understand. It's an open internal affairs investigation, and you can't talk about it." Clayton smiled. "So, the first time I ever meet my old man I bust him for trespassing. That's pretty weird, don't you think?"

"It has a certain irony. You could have let us off with a warning."

"I spend most of my time working as a tribal ranger and I've learned the hard way if you just slap wrists, people think it's an invitation to come back and trespass again. What were you doing out there?"

"Looking at some land for sale. I'm retiring soon and thinking about starting up a ranch."

"You gonna buy it?"

"No, it's pretty much worn-out, unproductive land."

Clayton nodded in agreement. "You're working that spree murder case. Langsford and all those other people."

"That's right."

"And you think an Apache did it."

"I don't know who did it."

Clayton blew right through Kerney's words. "Some sneaky Apache who's going around ambushing people."

"Are you trying to push my buttons?"

"I've known a lot of Anglos who talk liberal and think racist."

"Do you want to talk about racism or the killings?"

"Tell me about the murders."

"I think they were premeditated, designed to look like a killing spree, with Langsford the real target. Somebody who doesn't want to get caught put a lot of thought into it."

"Have you got physical evidence or witnesses to back that up?"

"Some evidence points in that direction."

"Like what?"

Kerney laid out the facts of how Langsford's killing differed from the others.

Clayton relaxed a bit and listened. Hearing about cop stuff eased some of his tension.

"Maybe you're right," he said, when Kerney finished. "Are you working a suspect list?"

"That, and we're trying to nail down the motive."

"Silas Kozine blew you off, didn't he?"

"Without blinking an eye."

"That's his job. What were you hoping he'd let you do?"

"Review your department's files. Cross-check people who were employed at the tribal casino and resort at the time of Marsha Langsford's murder, to see if anyone can be associated with the judge."

"Are you asking me for help?"

"No."

"That's good," Clayton said. "You seem to be pretty calm about finding out that you're my father."

"I'm still digesting the information."

"What my mother did wasn't wrong."

"Judging from what I've seen of you and her, I'd say she's done just about everything right."

Clayton stood up and walked to the door. "Okay, now we've talked. What happens next?"

"That's up to you."

"You haven't asked me much about myself."

"Your mother gave me the impression that it would be best not to pry."

"I'm married. My wife's name is Grace. We've got two kids, a boy and a girl, ages three and eighteen months. That makes you a grand-father. I'll see you around."

Clayton left, and Kerney stared at the closed door in stunned si-lence. He'd discovered he was a father and now a grandfather in the space of one day. It was much too surreal.

He went to the mirror and studied his face. Was he really that old? He didn't feel it inside. He could only wonder what Sara would say when he told her about the instantaneous family ties that had materialized in his life.

5

Dressed in sweats, Agent Robert Duran left his motel room for an early morning run, thinking that if everything fell into place, the Shockley investigation would be wrapped up and he could go home to Santa Fe in a day or two.

He settled into a five-minute-per-mile pace, turned off the main drag, and started a long gradual climb that would take him into the foothills of the Sacramento Mountains. The predawn streets were empty of all but an occasional car.

A mile into his run he spotted a slow-moving jogger with an awkward gait ahead of him. It was Chief Kerney. He drew even and slowed down.

"Morning, Chief."

"Morning, Robert," Kerney said. "Don't let me hold you up."

"I'm in no hurry. How's the case shaping up?"

"We're still digging into the minutiae. Lieutenant Sedillo is sending the team out to canvas gas stations, motels, restaurants, and convenience stores from here to Carrizozo."

"Have any credit card charges surfaced on the victims' accounts?" Duran asked.

"Not a one, and none of the stolen items has been pawned or sold on the streets, as far as we know. How are you doing?"

"Getting close, Chief. Instead of using the rotating list of towing services like he was supposed to, Shockley favored a local company called Jake's. El Paso PD has been running undercover surveillance on an auto chop shop. Jake made a delivery last week—a top-of-the-line Chevy four-by-four, late model, extended cab pickup truck. The theft occurred at an Alamogordo motel parking lot during Shockley's shift."

"Did our department take the call?" Kerney asked, trying to stay even with Duran, who had picked up his pace a bit.

"The city police handled it."

"Can you tie Shockley to Jake?"

"Jake has an employee, a guy by the name of Martinez, who covers the late-night runs. About five or six times during the last year Jake unexpectedly gave Martinez the night off."

"Let me guess," Kerney said, slowing down, forcing Duran to do the same. "The last time that happened was the night the Chevy was stolen."

"After Jake took a call from Shockley."

"Make the collar, and thanks," Kerney said, dropping his pace to a walk.

"For what, Chief?"

"Giving me an idea. A couple of nights ago, I drove the route the killer used. There's hardly any late-night traffic once you get out of Alamogordo. I checked all the patrol logs—city, county, and our district office. There were no traffic stops or accidents on the night of the murders. But I didn't think to survey the tow truck operators."

"I'll let you know if Jake had a service call that night," Duran said. "Are you heading back?"

"Yeah," Kerney said, trying hard to keep his breathing slow and even.

"You run pretty good on that bad knee," Duran said.

"I do a great ten-minute mile," Kerney said.

"At least you're still running. Look, Chief, if you want me to, I can ask around about the vandalism to your unit. I know some of the officers with the city, and Shockley had a couple of drinking buddies in our department."

"If the problem persists, I might do that."

"Just let me know."

Kerney nodded and watched Duran take off in smooth, even strides before turning around and forcing his bum leg to move along in his customary choppy, sloppy gait.

In the motel parking lot Kerney saw Lee Sedillo with a flashlight in hand moving from unit to unit.

"Your vehicle got trashed," Lee said, when Kerney joined up with him. "None of the others were touched."

"What did they do this time?"

"The headlights, taillights, and side view mirrors are smashed. I heard the noise about five minutes ago."

Kerney circled his unit, inspecting the damage. "Have Agent Duran look into it, Lee."

"About time," Lee grumbled. "This could turn into some spooky shit, Chief."

"Can you get me a replacement vehicle for the day?"

"Take mine. I'll put an agent on duty at the command trailer for a few hours until we can get your unit repaired."

After showering and dressing, Kerney went to the command center. The agent Lee had pulled off the street because of the vehicle shuffle was busy at a computer. He nodded at the woman, went to the tiny office, called Andy Baca in Santa Fe, and updated him on the status of the investigation. Then he started calling every towing service in the area—except Jake's. Halfway through the list, Kerney scored. A trucker had broken down on the highway in front of the Three Rivers turn-off.

"You know where the old bar is?" the towing operator asked. "It's a curio shop now."

"I do," Kerney said.

"The trucker was stalled there with a busted water pump. We had to unhitch the trailer and tow the semi into Alamogordo."

"What time?"

"I got the call about two, but it took me a while to get there. I had to go to the yard and get my big rig. I arrived at about three, three-fifteen."

"Do you have information on the driver?"

"Yeah. He's an owner-operator out of Little Rock. Hold on, I'll get it for you."

Kerney waited, listening to the man's breathing and the shuffling of papers.

"His name is Clark Beck." The towing operator read off Beck's address and telephone number.

"Did you see anything unusual while you were on the call?"

"Like what?"

"Speeders, a vehicle turning into or coming out of Three Rivers Road."

The man laughed. "Everybody speeds at that time of night. There was no traffic on the Three Rivers Road while I was there, leastways not that I can remember."

"Thanks," Kerney said.

Kerney dialed Clark Beck's number in Little Rock, spoke to his wife, and explained the reason for his call. The woman told him Beck was on a run to New Orleans, then to Atlanta, and wouldn't be back for four days.

"Does he call home from the road?"

"Sometimes," Mrs. Beck said. "Not always on his shorter trips. Is this on the up-and-up?"

"Your husband isn't in any trouble, Mrs. Beck. I just need to ask him a few questions."

"You're sure?"

"Positive."

"He follows all the regulations and weight restrictions."

"I'm certain that he does. Could you have him call me?"

"I'll give him the message."

On the off chance there had been more than one disabled vehicle along the highway, Kerney continued working the list, but nothing more developed. He hung up to find Clayton Istee standing stiffly in the doorway.

"Officer," Kerney said.

"I brought you something," Clayton said, sliding a manila folder quickly across the desk. He stepped back to the door as if to avoid any closer contact.

"What is this?"

"A list of the employees who worked at the tribal casino and resort at the time Langsford's wife was killed. My cousin is the personnel director. He got it for me."

"This won't get you in trouble, will it?" Kerney asked, as he opened the envelope.

"No."

"Thanks for doing this."

"I'm not doing it for you," Clayton said. He rubbed his palms together and stopped when Kerney looked at him. "My wife thinks I should at least let you meet your grandchildren."

"How do you feel about it?" Kerney asked, eyeing Clayton's closed expression.

"I don't know." Clayton shifted his weight. "Would you like to meet them?"

"Only if you want me to."

"I'll have to think about it some more."

"This isn't easy on either of us, is it?" Kerney said, trying to melt Clayton's icy tone.

"Have you told your wife about me?" Clayton asked.

"Not yet," Kerney said.

"Maybe it's something you'd rather not tell her."

"That's not true."

"So you say," Clayton replied, as he swung around to leave.

"Thanks again," Kerney said.

"I already told you, I'm not doing it for you," Clayton answered over his shoulder.

"Still, I appreciate it."

"Just don't read anything personal into it, okay?"

"Whatever you say," Kerney replied. He watched Clayton leave, wondering exactly what it was Clayton had tried to tell him. If it wasn't personal, where was the help coming from?

The employee list came with social security numbers and birth dates. Eric Langsford's name was on the books as a groundskeeper. Kerney made a copy and waited for Agent Mary Margaret Lovato to get off the phone. Mary Margaret had inherited her given names from an Irish grandmother. She was an exceptionally attractive young woman with long jet-black hair, a creamy complexion, and soft brown eyes that hid her toughness.

She hung up and started talking before Kerney had a chance to speak. "That was Drew Randolph, Chief. He just got off the phone with Linda Langsford. He told her about her father's murder. She's cutting short her vacation and coming home right away. He said she was totally stunned by the news."

"Where is she now?"

"Randolph doesn't know. She said she'd get back to Roswell as fast as she can. She should be there this evening."

"Good deal," Kerney said, handing Mary Margaret the employee list. "Get me wants and warrants, plus state arrest and conviction records for all the people on this list. Highlight everybody from Langsford's judicial district."

"This is going to take some time, Chief."

"I know."

Mary Margaret stood up, paused, and bit her lower lip.

"Do you have a question?"

"I just wanted to say that Randy Shockley was an asshole, sir. I attended a training course with him in Albuquerque last year. The man didn't understand the meaning of the word 'no.' "

"He came on to you?"

"Big time."

"Did you report it?"

"No, but it was pretty intense."

"The next time you get hit on or harassed by a fellow officer, report it, Agent Lovato."

Mary Margaret laughed. "Would you like a daily or weekly report, Chief?"

"It's that bad?"

Mary Margaret shook her head. "It's mostly harmless stuff. I can handle it."

Kerney studied the young woman. Quiet by nature, Mary Margaret had a self-assurance and no-nonsense style that Kerney liked. "I bet you can. But if it gets out of hand, write it up."

"In a heartbeat." She paused, looked down at her shoes and then back up. "I hope you don't mind my asking, but is somebody stalking you, Chief? This thing with your unit is getting serious."

"Either that or they're making a statement. I've put Duran on it. Work that list hard for me."

Mary Margaret smiled. "Yes, sir."

Owned and operated by the Mescalero Tribe, the resort and its adjoining casino offered luxury amenities in a lush, tranquil setting. Guest accommodations radiated out from the sides of the main lodge, providing rooms with views of landscaped lawns that ran down to the lakeshore with forested mountains in the background. Vacationers could boat, fish, golf, play tennis, and, of course, drink, dine, and gamble.

At the main lodge, Kerney found the personnel office and met with Wheeler Balatche, Clayton's cousin and the human resources director. Built low to the ground, Balatche was thick through the chest. A droopy eyelid made his face look asymmetrical.

"I remember Eric Langsford," Balatche said, in answer to Kerney's question. "He would be a hard one to forget."

"Why do you say that?"

"He worked here right at the time his father ruled against our casino operation. Nobody knew he was even related to the judge until then. But when Langsford issued his order to close down the casino, Eric went ballistic."

"What happened?"

"Well, first you gotta know Eric. He was one of those Anglos who shows up here and falls in love with Indians. He did everything he could to look like an Apache: grew his hair long, went cowboy, tried to hang out with the tribal members he worked with—that kind of stuff."

"Was he successful?"

"As long as he bought the drinks."

"How did Eric go ballistic?" Kerney asked.

"When the judge issued his ruling, I called a series of staff meetings to reassure everybody that the tribe had filed an immediate appeal that would allow us to stay open, and that nobody was going to lose their jobs. Eric got up at the meeting he attended and went into this long harangue about how his father was a racist, and that the workers should take action against him."

"What kind of action?"

"Letters of protest, picketing, a sit-in at the courthouse."

"Did he suggest anything stronger than that?"

"He ranted about how white people practice economic and legal genocide against native people, and how they should be held accountable for their crimes. He wasn't wrong, but it wasn't like we weren't aware of his brilliant political insight. We've lived with it all our lives."

"What did you do?"

"I cut him off, and after the meeting, I fired him. We didn't need a gringo agitator in our midst."

"How did he take getting canned?"

"He got upset. Not with me, but with his father. Went on about how Langsford ruined people's lives and shouldn't be allowed to remain a judge."

"Did he make any specific threats against his father?"

"Not that I can recall."

"At the meetings, did any other employees show an interest in taking political action against the judge?"

"Nope."

"You seem to remember these events with great clarity."

"It was an intense time," Balatche said, "and seeing Eric yesterday jogged my memory. He came in, stoned out of his mind, looking for a job."

Kerney stifled his surprise. "Eric Langsford was here?"

"Yeah."

"Stoned on what?"

"At least booze, and maybe pills."

"I take it you didn't hire him back."

Balatche shook his head. "And not just for being a lush, either. Eric worked here at a time when we employed a lot of Anglos. Now, we don't hire outside the tribe unless we have a shortage or a candidate possesses special skills we need. To be courteous, I let him fill out an application, but I'd never hire him again."

"Did he leave an address?"

"I'm sure he did. My secretary has the paperwork."

"Mind if I take a look?"

"Go ahead."

Eighty road miles south of Ruidoso was the tiny settlement of Pinon. It boasted a senior center, post office, general store, church, and a few dwellings scattered along a two-lane highway that looped out of the Sacramento Mountains through dry, tree-dotted foothills. To the southeast, a chain of hills sliced down to flats that wandered off in the direction of the Guadalupe Mountains. Windblown dust turned the morning sky a mixture of ivory and aquamarine, and the faraway peaks had a ghostly presence.

Never much of a settlement to begin with, Pinon stayed barely alive because of the dryland area ranchers who controlled the grazing rights on vast tracts of state and federal acreage.

On his job application Langsford had given a Pinon rural route address. Kerney stopped at the general store, asked for directions, and was sent down a paved county road that turned to dirt as it wandered through a draw. He spotted Langsford's van just off the road, parked beside a small house.

Beyond the clapboard hideaway, the weather-beaten remains of a much larger house leaned precariously on its foundation. A skeletal windmill missing blades and a drive shaft stood nearby. An old post-and-wire fence enclosed about ten hard rock acres sprinkled with juniper trees and scrub oak.

The door opened as Kerney approached the house, and Langsford stepped out. A skinny five-nine, he had a receding hairline that formed a widow's peak on his forehead, the doughy complexion of a drinker, sleepy bloodshot eyes, and a face old beyond his thirty-two years.

"What do you want?" Langsford asked, words tumbling out in a rush.

Kerney showed his credentials. "I need to speak to you about your father."

Langsford's head twitched up and down. "I knew you were a cop. Is the Judas Judge dead?"

"Do you mean your father?"

"Are we talking about somebody else?"

"No. Why do you call him that?"

"It's just a nickname."

"Not a very endearing one."

"Is he dead?"

"Yes," Kerney replied.

"Good. Let Linda bury him." Langsford swayed and planted his feet to steady himself.

"Don't you want to know what happened?"

Langsford shrugged and almost lost his balance. Kerney couldn't tell if he was drunk, wired on uppers, or both.

"He's dead. That's all that matters. It's a great fucking day."

"I need you to answer some questions."

"Sure. Come on in."

The bare walls of the front room had old newspapers stuffed in the cracks of the uninsulated clapboard siding. The door to a pot-belly stove hung open, showing a firebox filled to the brim with dead ash. In the center of the room was a daybed with a metal frame, covered by a soiled sleeping bag. An expensive acoustic guitar rested against the bed frame.

Dirty clothes, beer cans, and wadded-up paper bags littered the floor. An old phonograph turntable and two battered speakers with disconnected wires stood on a low plank shelf. Under the shelf was a clutter of cassette tapes and compact discs, but the machines to play them were missing.

"Is this your place?" Kerney asked.

"Yeah, I bought it four years ago with Daddy's money," Langsford said, as he sat on the daybed. "It gives me a place to chill when I'm not working. Got it for a song." Langsford chuckled at his joke.

"I understand you're a musician."

"And a pretty good one, too, when I'm not drinking or getting high. I'm gonna be a rock and roll star. Not quite there yet. So, the Judas Judge is really dead. What happened?"

"He was murdered."

"Cool."

"You mean that?"

Langsford snorted disparagingly and opened a pack of cigarettes. "Vernon Langsford. The great man, the pillar of the community. He was nothing but a two-faced, mean, racist pig."

"Tell me about him," Kerney said.

"That says it all."

"Give me an example."

"Okay. Let me think." Langsford raised his eyes to the ceiling. "You know what his favorite game was when I was a little kid?"

"What was that?"

"He'd chase me around the house pretending to be a vampire, or Dracula, or some weird Frankenstein, until I totally lost it and freaked." Eric smiled dolefully. "He'd always do it when we were alone in the house. Doesn't that suck?"

"Some game," Kerney replied. "Did he play it with all his children?"

"Just me. Arthur was macho, could do no wrong. Sports and all that shit. Linda was his angel, the apple of his eye. I was the oddball who liked to draw pictures, play records, watch television, and get high."

"Did he abuse you in other ways?"

"When he wasn't terrorizing me, he ignored me. I was invisible to him. If it hadn't been for music, smoking pot, and my mother, I never would have survived past the age of twelve. She saved my fucking life, man. She was the only one who cared about me in that whole fucking family. I guess she wanted to save one of us kids, at least."

"Save you from what?" Kerney asked.

"Whatever."

"That's not an answer."

"It's the best one you're going to get."

"It must have been hard on you when she died."

"She's dead because of him." Langsford reached for an empty beer can and flicked a cigarette ash into it with a shaky hand.

"You were about twenty-six when your mother died. Still living at home?"

"No, I had my own place. I was playing in a shitkicker band and snorting a lot of coke."

"Were you spending much time with your mother before the letter-bomb incident?"

"Nah, I was too stoned to go anywhere, do anything, or see anyone. I stayed away from everybody except the guys in the band and
my dealer."

"You never got busted?"

Langsford shook his head. "Not in Roswell. The only good things
my old man ever did for me was give me money to feed my habit and
keep me out of jail. He did it for himself, to keep his reputation from
being sullied by his fucked-up kid."

"He also paid for your rehab treatment."

Langsford laughed, dropped his cigarette butt in the direction of
the beer can, missed, and ground it out with the toe of his shoe. "Oh,
yeah, more than once. Top-of-the-line detox centers, man, far away
from home where nobody knew me or the family."

"He gave you money after your mother was killed."

"He didn't want me hanging around."

"He offered you the money?"

"No, I asked for it. I had to get away from there. I went to San
Francisco and stayed loaded until the cash ran out. I haven't been
back to Roswell since."

"But he kept sending you money."

"Sure. It was the only thing he had to give."

"I need to know where you were from the time you quit the band
until the time you got back to New Mexico."

"I sobered up in a whorehouse in Juárez on Sunday. That's all I
can remember. I black out when I binge drink."

"Have you been drinking since then?"

"Just some beers to keep me steady."

"Are you using anything else besides booze?"

"Downers when I need to mellow out. Uppers when I need a rush.
I try to stay high one way or the other as much as I can."

"What drugs have you taken today?" Kerney asked.

"A couple amphetamines."

"How many?"

"Four. Six. Eight. I forget."

"Come with me," Kerney said.

"Why?"

"I'm placing you in protective custody."

"Jail?"

"Yep. I'll have a doctor check you out when we get there."

"That's raw, man. I don't need that shit."

"I want you safe."

"You think I killed my old man?"

"Did you?"

Langsford looked puzzled, then shook his head. "For as long as I could remember, I've wanted that son of a bitch dead. But I usually wind up thinking of killing myself instead." Langsford closed his eyes and rocked his head back and forth. "Just nod off on a nice overdose and never wake up."

"Let's go," Kerney said, reaching for his handcuffs.

"Are those things necessary?"

"Stand up, turn around, and place your hands at the small of your back."

A pat-down search yielded enough prescription tranquilizers for Langsford to use to overdose several times over. Kerney booked him into the Otero County Jail on a protective custody hold. If he needed to, he'd use the possession charge later as leverage.

He walked into the command trailer office where Lee Sedillo was parked behind the desk. Lee looked up and started to scramble to his feet.

"Stay put, Lieutenant. Are you making any progress?"

"We still have a shitload of motels to check, Chief," Lee said, as he settled back in the chair. "Not to mention more gas stations and convenience stores. I've got people reviewing store surveillance tapes."

"Good idea. How long before they finish up?"

"Late tomorrow, maybe."

At the jail, Eric Langsford had given Kerney his written, voluntary permission to search his house and van. He laid it on the desk.

Lee read it quickly. "You found him."

"He was too stoned to hide. I've booked him into the county lockup."

"I'll pull two agents off the canvas to do the search. What are we looking for, Chief?"

"The murder weapon with Langsford's prints on it would be nice."

"Is he our killer?"

"Possibly. He's got a major booze and pill buzz going and isn't thinking too clearly right now, and he doesn't have one kind word for his father. He kept calling him the Judas Judge, whatever that means. I'll question him after he comes down from his high and see where it goes."

"Agent Duran busted that towing service operator. He said Jake implicated Shockley to the max in the auto thefts."

"Is there anything that connects Jake to the damage to my unit?"

"For that, Jake has alibis. He was on confirmed service calls both mornings. Duran has already started talking to Shockley's other buddies."

"I'll handle the Linda Langsford interview after she gets home."

"Give her another four hours. She just called from Taos a little while ago."

"You talked to her?"

"Yeah. She was upset, angry, crying, and demanding a lot of answers. I didn't give her much."

"There's not much to give right now. Keep the troops humping."

Lee nodded. "Jesus, I hope we catch a break soon." He held out Kerney's car keys. "Can I have my unit back? Yours is parked behind the trailer, all fixed and ready to go."

With the high school principal at his side, Kerney watched the school marching band go through their paces on the practice field.

As they wheeled and turned, light from the late afternoon sun flashed off the polished brass horns.

"I knew all the Langsford kids," Colby Trumble said. "I was a guidance counselor back then." He turned, looked at Kerney, and pulled at the lapel of his suit jacket as the sun glittered on his bald head. "Now I get to wear a suit and listen to everybody's gripes and complaints. Sometimes I don't know who is harder to deal with, the parents, the teachers, or the students."

"Tell me about the Langsford kids," Kerney said.

"Arthur and Linda were honor society members in the top five percent of their graduating classes. Linda was a cheerleader, and Arthur played two or three varsity sports. Exceptional kids. Well-rounded, smart, never in trouble—every parent's dream."

"And Eric?"

"Troubled, brilliant, bored, and volatile. He got in lots of fights and usually took a beating. He was an incredibly gifted musician. String instruments. Violin and guitar especially."

"Any drug problems?"

"I think he was stoned in class most of the time."

"How did his parents handle it?"

"Mostly, I dealt with his mother. She was always trying to get him straightened out."

"Was Eric ever dangerous to others?"

"No, but he constantly made threats to his classmates if he perceived a slight. Most of the time it went no further than minor altercations. Shouting matches, usually."

"Just threats?"

Trumble nodded. "It was pure bravado. He got his butt whipped when things escalated beyond the pushing and shoving point."

"How did the judge react to Eric's troubles?"

"By the time Eric reached us, we didn't see much of Judge Langsford. That's not unusual. The youngest child typically gets the least amount of parental attention, and the judge was a busy man."

"Can you get me a list of their high school friends?"

"Why are you investigating the Langsford kids? I thought it was the judge's murderer you were after."

"We still don't have a motive for the slaying."

"Do spree killers need motives?" Trumble asked.

"There's always the grudge factor to consider."

"Judge Langsford was a well-respected man."

"The defendants in his court may not have thought so."

Trumble looked at Kerney sharply. "Good point. But I can't think of any classmates of the Langsford children the judge sent to jail."

"We have to look into every possible lead," Kerney said.

"I suppose you do. Stop by my office during school hours. I'll get out the yearbooks and give you names."

"That would be very helpful."

"A lot of those students have scattered, you know."

"Their names will be helpful, nonetheless."

Linda Langsford lived outside of Roswell near an old farming area known as East Grand Plains. Set apart from neighboring dwellings, her house was sheltered in a grove of trees and cushioned by an expanse of lawn that ran down to the private road.

The house, modern and expensive-looking, had a long screened porch under a gently sloping metal roof that gave an inviting feeling of openness. The core had a barnlike high-pitched roof flattened on the top. Where the rooflines joined, a massive chimney protruded, stepped down a bit from the higher elevation, creating a spare sculptured effect.

Three vehicles were parked outside. Kerney knocked on the screen door, called out, and a gangly older man with a blocky chin and a sharp nose came to greet him. He introduced himself as the Reverend Matthew Blakemore.

Kerney showed his shield and asked for Linda Langsford.

"She's indisposed," Blakemore said solemnly, barring Kerney's entry. "Can't you come back at a later time?"

Kerney adopted a formal tone. "There are certain matters Ms.

Langsford needs to attend to, not the least of which is the release of her father's body for burial."

"I see. Come in."

A breezeway connected the porch to the interior great room of the house, where three pairs of doors led off to more private living areas. The fireplace, designed to warm both the great room and the porch, dominated the room. Drew Randolph, Langsford's law partner, stood in front of the fireplace mantel, hands behind his back.

He interrupted Blakemore's attempt at an introduction. "I've met Mr. Kerney."

Blakemore reacted with a step back. "I'll see if Linda can speak to you." He turned and left the room.

"How is she?" Kerney asked Randolph.

"Wavering between grief and shock. Exhausted. She drove like a maniac to get home."

"Is she coherent?"

"Yes."

"Has Eric tried to contact her?"

"No, but she did say there were three hang-up phone calls on her answering machine when she got home."

Footsteps on the Saltillo tile floor stopped further conversation. Linda Langsford entered the room with Blakemore behind her. Dressed in jeans and an bulky sweatshirt, she wore round glasses that seemed deliberately intended to hide her attractiveness. Long light-brown hair covered her neck. Her eyes blinked and she raised a hand to shield them from the glare of the brightly lit room.

"Mr. Kerney," she said.

"Thank you for seeing me."

"I understand I need to make arrangements to have my father's body released," she said wearily, dropping her hand.

"Yes."

"Can I do it by telephone?"

"Of course, once you've decided on a funeral home."

"Where is his body?"

"In Albuquerque, at the office of the medical examiner. I'll leave a phone number with you."

"Have you caught his killer?"

"Not yet."

"You must."

"We hope to. You and I need to talk."

Linda nodded. "I want to know everything you're doing. Can it wait until tomorrow?"

"After the funeral might be better, Linda," Reverend Blakemore interjected.

"No, Chief Kerney will need to see me before then," Linda said, placing a hand on Blakemore's arm to quiet him. "Tomorrow, Mr. Kerney?"

"That will be fine. Late morning?"

"Yes."

"I understand you had three hang-up messages on your answering machine. Did you save them?"

"No."

"Do you have caller ID?"

"I didn't recognize any of the numbers, so I deleted them. They were from unnamed callers. Why do you ask?"

"Did you receive any anonymous calls at work before you started your vacation?"

"No."

"Didn't you tell me you recently had two anonymous calls on your direct office line?" Randolph asked.

"Oh, I'm sure they were just wrong numbers."

"The callers said nothing?" Kerney asked.

"No, I just heard them disconnect."

"I think that's enough for tonight, Officer," Blakemore said.

"Of course."

Kerney walked into the night and a series of pathway lights flicked on to guide his way. By the time he got back to the motel in

Alamogordo it would be too late to call Sara. He mulled over Clayton Istee's criticism of his failure to inform her of his newfound status as a father.

He didn't think he was trying to hide anything from Sara. Or was he?

Kerney shook off Clayton's implied accusation of racism. That wasn't it at all. He was a good deal older than Sara, but that had never been an issue for him up until now. Discovering a fully grown son, and two grandchildren to boot, forced Kerney to consider a completely new mind-set. He'd never thought of himself as old before. Worn down and beat up a bit, for sure, but not old.

At his unit Kerney got in touch with Lee Sedillo and asked for a priority telephone check of recent calls made to Linda Langsford's home and office numbers.

The command trailer was empty when Kerney arrived, and a stack of field reports awaited his attention. He ran through them quickly, pausing to concentrate on the follow-up report regarding Kay Murray's alibi.

The room service waiter had positively identified Murray as the woman in Joel Cushman's room early Friday morning. The front desk attendant verified that Murray had returned to the hotel at eleven o'clock the night before. Housekeeping noted Cushman's bed had been used for more than just sleeping, and hotel security confirmed that Cushman's and Murray's cars had remained in the parking lot all night.

Cushman and Murray had used no taxicabs or shuttle vans to get to the airport, and had not booked any commercial or private flights that could have taken them within striking distance of the crime scenes.

Cushman's alibi about his time apart from Murray in Albuquerque also held up. His attendance and participation at the Christian conference was confirmed by a number of sources. Following the dinner banquet and prayer fellowship, Cushman had met with a man in

his room who'd sought him out for some informal Christian counseling, and didn't finish the session until ten o'clock.

Penelope Gibben also looked to be in the clear. On the night of
the murders, she'd attended a museum foundation function to honor
the outgoing board of directors, traveling to and from the event with
a companion. Dropped off at home after ten-thirty, she would not
have been able to make the long drive to Carrizozo and start killing
people in a timely fashion.

Kerney pushed the reports away. He had paperwork but no
progress, motive but no clear suspects, an old crime and a new crime
that might or might not be linked, and six dead people who deserved
justice.

It was time to see Eric Langsford and have a long talk.

6

Eric Langsford lolled in the straight-back metal chair, head back, staring at the fluorescent lights in the interrogation room ceiling. He unzipped the top of his orange jail jumpsuit and scratched his skinny chest.

"Man, I barely remember talking to you," he said. "You busted me, right?"

"More or less," Kerney said.

"For possession, right?"

"You're in protective custody, for now. If you cooperate, I might forget about the possession charges."

Langsford sat up straight. "I can get out?"

"We'll see. You left the band in Marfa, Texas."

"Yeah. I'm gonna kill that fucking drummer, if I ever see him again."

"What for?" Kerney asked.

"I don't take shit from anyone. He got on my case about my drinking and then dumped out all my booze. He was an AA freak who wanted to save me. I hate that kind of crap."

"I can see how that would make you angry."

Eric nodded. "I've got a short fuse."

"What did you do?"

"I threw an empty whiskey bottle that hit him in the head, and told him to get the fuck out of my room." Langsford touched a small bruise on his chin. "He busted me in the chops, so I quit the band. I couldn't stand playing with those assholes, anyway. They sucked."

"What day was that?"

"Last Wednesday, I think."

"Where did you go after you quit the band?"

"I drove to Del Rio and crossed the border. Got there late."

"How long did you stay?"

"Overnight."

"Remember where?"

"Some cheap hotel. I don't know the name."

"You left the next day?"

"Yeah."

"Where to?"

"I hit a bunch of Mexican border towns."

"Which ones?"

Langsford rattled off the town names.

"What about on the Texas side of the border?" Kerney asked.

"I stopped in Redford and McNary."

"Did you rent rooms?"

"Not after Del Rio. I slept in the van so I could save my money for booze and pills."

"What bars did you drink at?"

"Hell, I don't know. Sometimes I'd hit the bars, other times I just drank in the van. The desert is beautiful at night, man. All those stars."

"When did you get to Juárez?"

"Friday, Saturday—I don't remember."

"You stayed at a whorehouse."

"That's where I woke up."

"Where was it?"

"About six blocks in from the bridge. I thought my van had been ripped off. I found it on our side of the border in a parking lot."

"Did you get a parking receipt?"

"I don't keep stuff like that."

"What was the whorehouse called?"

"It's more like a hotel where whores take their tricks."

"The name?"

"I don't know. Why are you asking me all this crap?"

"When did you leave Juárez?"

"Sunday afternoon. I drove straight to my place."

"Have you gone anywhere, seen anybody, since you arrived home?"

"Just you, and look where that got me."

"You didn't go to the tribal resort earlier this week, looking for work?"

"Oh yeah, I forgot about that."

"I understand you got a check recently from one of your father's companies."

"Party time," Eric said smiling. "I go through Daddy's money fast. When it runs out, I find work. Like playing in a piece-of-shit band that doesn't pay squat."

"Where were you Thursday night?"

"Beats me."

"Did you meet up with anyone you knew in Del Rio?"

"No."

"How about the other places you stayed?"

"I didn't see anybody I knew."

"I understand you're a gifted musician," Kerney said.

"Once I was. After high school I was accepted at every top-flight music school in the country that I applied to. But I didn't go."

"Your father is dead, murdered."

"I remember that," Eric replied.

"What do you remember?"

"That you told me he was dead."

"Did you see your father much?"

"I haven't seen him since I left Roswell six years ago."

"You never visited him in Ruidoso?"

"What for?"

"Is that a no?"

"No. I don't go near the man."

Kerney rose. "We'll talk again."

Eric scrambled to his feet. "Do I get out of jail?"

"Not yet. I'm booking you on the drug possession charge."

Langsford screwed up his face in disgust. "I want to make a phone call."

"I'll tell the guard."

"You think I killed my old man, don't you?"

"And if you did?"

"It would make me happy," Eric said, sounding like a mischievous kid admitting to a prank.

"Because of the way he treated you as a child?" Kerney asked.

"That's not even the half of it."

"I'd like to hear the rest."

"That's my business."

"You're really not sure if you killed your father or not, are you?"

Eric smirked. "I don't think I did, but you never know. Sometimes dreams come true."

Outside, Kerney took a deep breath of the cool night air. Eric Langsford had the maturity of an adolescent, a drug-addled mind, and was clearly pleased about his father's death. Kerney couldn't dismiss the possibility that Eric had iced his old man along with five other victims. Killers came in all flavors and varieties, including the hopped-up, emotionally arrested kind.

He decided to come back early in the morning and take another crack at Eric.

* * *

Kerney knocked at Sedillo's motel room door, and the lieutenant opened up. He reported that nothing of consequence had been uncovered during the search of Eric Langsford's house and van, except for a receipt from a package goods store in Marfa, Texas, dated the same day Langsford had left the band.

Kerney summarized his interview with Langsford, placed the cassette of the taped conversation in Lee's hand, and asked Sedillo to put an agent on it right away.

"Have him backtrack on Langsford," Kerney said.

"That's a three-day swing."

"So far, he's our only suspect without an alibi."

"Did his sister have one?" Lee asked.

"I haven't gotten that far with her yet."

"I could use more people, Chief."

"Not possible. The way it stands now, if we don't get serious movement by the end of the week, we'll be down to just you and me. Did Mary Margaret run those employee names?"

"Yep, and you can forget about it. At the time of Mrs. Langsford's death there were no political activists, hardcore felons, convicts, or fugitives working at the resort or casino who we can connect to Langsford. There were two cases against employees that resulted in bench warrants for failure to pay child support. Both fathers made their back payments and got a stay out of jail card. One other employee did time for aggravated battery against a police officer, stemming from a DWI stop. But he got drunk two years ago, passed out on the railroad tracks, and was run over by a train."

"Eric says he hasn't seen his father in years—never once visited him. Get an agent up to Ruidoso in the morning, showing Eric's picture around the judge's neighborhood. That beat-up van he drives would be pretty hard to miss."

"Will do. Is that it, Chief?"

"Why is Langsford so damn happy his father is dead?"

"Maybe he just didn't like him."

"I think it goes deeper than that."

"You may be right," Lee said. "We just got the information you requested from the phone company on those hang-up phone calls made to Linda Langsford's residence. All of them were made the night of the murders from pay phones along the killer's route."

"What about the anonymous calls to her office?"

"Two one-minute calls were made one right after the other from an Albuquerque number. I've got an agent making contact now."

"Let me know as soon as you hear anything. We may have caught a break."

The phone rang. Lee walked to the bedside table, picked up, listened for a minute, and then dropped the handset in the cradle with a shake of his head. "It doesn't look promising, Chief. The Albuquerque calls came from an elderly man who misdialed a granddaughter's Roswell number. He reversed two digits."

"I want confirmation on who he is, who the granddaughter is, and whether or not anyone else has access to his telephone."

"We have an agent from the Albuquerque district office rolling on it now."

In the morning, Kerney checked his unit for damage, found none, did a short run, and called Sara at Fort Leavenworth, half-hoping she'd already left her quarters for class. She answered on the first ring.

"How are you?" he asked.

"Pumped," Sara answered. "We start the advanced military studies sequence today. The Civil War. Grant's Vicksburg campaign. I've been reading all about it. Very exciting stuff. You never call me in the morning. What's up, sweetie pie?"

Kerney told her about Isabel Istee, Clayton, and the two grandchildren.

"My, my," Sara said.

Kerney waited for more, but Sara remained silent.

"That's it?" he finally asked.

"I'm thinking."

"I swear, I knew nothing about this."

"You lead a shockingly interesting life, Kerney."

Kerney caught a hint of amusement in Sara's voice. "The Irish are cursed that way," he said.

"I'm not sure I like the idea of being married to a man who's a grandfather."

"Don't say that."

"This has thrown you, hasn't it?"

"It's a little unsettling."

"I'm a bit stunned by the news myself," Sara said. "You're absolutely sure about this?"

"I have no reason to doubt it."

"Then we'll just have to accept it."

"It's not a problem for you?"

"Well, the upside is that now I know you can father children."

"Is that supposed to be funny?"

"But I don't like the idea of an old love suddenly reappearing in your life."

"You're still kidding, right?"

"Of course I am. Don't go getting insecure on me, Kerney. This wasn't a situation of your making. When do I get to meet your new family?"

"I'm not sure that will happen. I'm not perceived as a welcome addition to the clan."

"It sounds complex. I'll try not to add to the confusion."

"Meaning?"

"Having a husband who's a grandfather isn't something I've had to consider before. But it doesn't make me love you any less."

"That's what I wanted to hear. I need to get going."

"Be careful out there, grandpa."

"Give me a break," Kerney groaned.

"You're tough, you can take it."

Agent Robert Duran checked out of the motel, threw his luggage filled with dirty laundry into the unit's trunk, and slammed the lid. Getting pulled off the vandalism case by Lieutenant Sedillo to be sent on a three-day road trip to backtrack on Eric Langsford was irritating.

Because Duran was part of the Internal Affairs Unit, Sedillo had asked—not ordered—Robert to take the assignment, knowing full well that turning down the request could sully Robert's reputation as a gung-ho officer. With his eye on an upcoming sergeant's vacancy in criminal investigations, Robert couldn't afford any bad raps about his dedication to the job.

He sat in his unit and studied a map, mentally tracing the route Eric Langsford said he'd taken after quitting the band in Marfa, Texas. The pivotal issue hinged on where Langsford had been last Thursday night. Robert decided to work Langsford's drunken travels home in reverse order, starting with his last stop in Juárez, an easy eighty-mile drive from the Oliver Lee State Park.

If he could confirm that Langsford had been within striking distance on the night of the murders and didn't have an alibi, it would make him a prime suspect.

Robert tossed the map on the seat and thought about the vandalism case he'd been forced to put on the back burner. Chasing down the person who'd disabled and damaged Chief Kerney's unit was no small matter, especially given the strong likelihood that a cop could have done it in retaliation for the Shockley shooting.

Duran couldn't see a civilian sneaking around a motel where a bunch of cops were staying, or even knowing which car Kerney drove. And some of the smug reactions from Shockley's buddies at the city PD about the vandalism made it clear that there were those who believed Kerney deserved a payback. It wasn't a stretch to believe that the situation could easily escalate into a physical attack against the chief.

With no hard target outside the department on the horizon, Duran had asked all district personnel and the agents working the spree killings to account for their time during the two incidents. It hadn't gained him any new friends or valuable information, so he'd been about to start working the bars where Shockley had hung out when Sedillo dropped the Langsford assignment on him.

So be it, he thought glumly, switching his attention to the field notes on Eric Langsford. If nothing panned out in Juárez, he would be spending his time in shitkicking bars and backwater border towns for the next three days.

Across the parking lot, he watched Chief Kerney limp to his unit, inspect it carefully, and drive away.

Last spring, Robert had worked a murder case in northern New Mexico on ranchland the chief had inherited. According to the scuttlebutt, Kerney was about to cash out the land, pay the taxes, and still have a hefty seven-figure bankroll. With that kind of money Kerney could've walked away from it all and never looked back.

That wasn't the chief's style, Robert decided, as he pulled into traffic, heading south.

After discovering that Eric had been bailed out of jail on the misdemeanor drug possession charge by Drew Randolph, who'd left with Langsford in tow, Kerney drove to Roswell.

Randolph greeted Kerney at Linda Langsford's door with a haughty expression. "Don't you think it was bad form not to tell Linda you had her brother locked up in jail?" he asked.

"I saw no reason to add to her worries," Kerney answered. "Where is Eric now?"

"In the guest bedroom, sleeping off the bottle of whiskey he drank after I brought him here last night."

"And Ms. Langsford?"

"I'll get her for you."

Linda Langsford entered the screened porch with Randolph close behind. She pressed her hand into his and kissed him on the cheek. "I'll be fine, Drew. You go along."

"You're sure?" Randolph asked, shooting Kerney a hard look.

Linda nodded, and her long hair swept across her face, hiding it.

Randolph breezed by Kerney and out the front door without a word.

"Do I need to hire an attorney for Eric?" Linda asked, pushing her hair away with a shaky hand. Dark circles under her eyes clashed with the gold frames of her glasses.

"He's only facing a misdemeanor possession charge right now," Kerney said.

"Aren't you here to arrest him for murder?"

"Do you think he killed your father?"

She shook her head to ward off the question. "And five other innocent people? I can't comprehend how anybody can do that, Mr. Kerney. Eric, especially."

"You don't think he's capable of murder?"

"Don't ask me to incriminate my brother."

"I was asking for your opinion."

"Eric told me that you suspect him."

"He has a weak alibi and admits to wanting your father dead. Why is that?"

"He told you how my father tormented him. Can't you understand his anger over that kind of treatment?"

"Anger can turn into rage and murder."

"Save the pop psychology for somebody else, Mr. Kerney. You've seen him, you've talked to him. He can barely cope. He's almost always stoned, high, or drunk. He's been this way since high school."

"I understand both you and Eric held your father accountable for the death of your mother."

"Given the circumstances, surely you can understand why."

"And now your father is dead."

"Murdered by a nameless spree killer, unless you have evidence to the contrary. Do you?"

"Was your father abusive to you?"

"My God, you don't quit, do you? My father was a stern man who expected his children to be perfect. Eric failed him because he chose to live in a drug-induced dreamworld."

"Didn't his problems with his father start long before he began using drugs?"

"That's the way Eric sees it."

"But you disagree?"

"Eric is a troubled person. He can be charming, intelligent, overly dramatic, and totally unpredictable. He also lies a great deal."

"You both stand to inherit considerable wealth from your father's estate."

The morning sun washed into the porch and accentuated Linda's angry eyes. "Look around, Mr. Kerney. Does it seem that I am in dire need of my father's money?"

"Eric's circumstances are quite different from yours."

"Did you come here to tell me about the investigation or to conduct an inquisition?"

"I need a copy of your vacation itinerary," Kerney said.

"Am I now a suspect?"

"It's merely a process of verification, Ms. Langsford. Nothing more."

"I have nothing to hide from you."

"Then it shouldn't be an imposition," Kerney said.

"Wait here."

She left, returned with her purse, emptied it on a table, and began picking through the contents. Finished, she held out a batch of credit card receipts and hotel bills. "I'd like these back," she said.

Kerney quickly fanned through the receipts. "Do these cover your entire trip?"

"Yes."

"Have you had any more hang-up telephone calls?"

"No. Why do you ask?"

"I'm worried about the anonymous calls to your house. They were made from pay phones along the killer's route on the night of the murders."

Linda's eyes widened.

"Three members of your family are dead, Ms. Langsford. I can't dismiss the possibility that you might also be a target."

"Do you actually believe someone has been killing off my family, one by one?"

"It's within the realm of possibility."

"Do you have any substantiation for your theory?"

"My assumption is that the murderer knows you. Otherwise, why would he take time from all the bloodletting to call?"

"It could be a coincidence. And my brother wasn't murdered; he was killed by a hit-and-run driver."

"Still, it's troubling. Will Eric be staying with you?"

She nodded. "Until after the funeral."

"Are you sure that's wise?"

"My brother isn't a killer, Mr. Kerney. I have nothing to fear from him."

"Do you want police protection?"

"That's totally unnecessary." She took off her glasses and rubbed her eyes, "Please go, Mr. Kerney. I'll be fine."

Kerney stopped at the Roswell district headquarters, arranged to put Eric Langsford under surveillance, and faxed Lee Sedillo copies of Linda Langsford's credit card receipts along with instructions to start the verification process. From the looks of what Linda had given him, she'd spent the night of the murders in a small Colorado town six hundred miles away.

At the high school, Colby Trumble sat with Kerney and went through the yearbooks, pointing out former students who'd been friends with the Langsford children. As expected, Arthur and Linda had been quite popular, while Eric's buddies—kids Trumble characterized as marginally socialized—had been few and far between.

Kerney asked for the guidance and counseling records on the Langsford children, and after checking with his superiors, Trumble complied, although it took a while to dig the paperwork out of storage. As Arthur and Linda's counselor, Trumble's efforts had been focused on college placement, but with Eric the issues had been mainly disciplinary in nature. Trumble had referred Eric to a private psychotherapist who still maintained a practice in town.

The referral notation in Eric's counseling file cited family problems, and Kerney asked Trumble to elaborate.

"I could never get him to talk to me about it, specifically," Trumble replied. "It came out as generalized anger toward his father, sister, and brother."

"Eric gave you no hints?" Kerney asked.

"No. But he was spiteful about his siblings in a way that went beyond feeling merely alienated or envious, and his reaction to his father bordered on hatred. Only his mother escaped his vindictiveness."

"How did Eric display his anger about his family?"

"With snide remarks, cutting comments, and sarcasm. He called his father the Judas Judge."

"He used the same expression with me," Kerney said. "Do you have any idea what it means?"

"He felt bitterly betrayed by his father, but I never learned why."

It took a while for Kerney to get in to see Dr. Lillian Joyce, the psychiatrist who'd treated Eric Langsford. A tall woman in late middle age, Joyce had a calm, receptive manner and serious, thoughtful eyes. Her office seemed more like a comfortable sitting room, and Kerney guessed that the expensive armoire against a wall concealed a writing desk and a computer.

Kerney made his pitch for information about Eric Langsford, which Dr. Joyce greeted with a shake of her head.

"You can't possibly expect me to release privileged information to you," she said.

"What can you tell me?"

"Eric was the disruptive member of a dysfunctional family."

"Meaning?"

"Meaning, Chief Kerney, that individual work with Eric wasn't the treatment of choice. The entire family needed to be in psycho-therapy. That's why my time with Eric was unproductive."

"It sounds like serious stuff," Kerney said.

Dr. Joyce smiled. "Many families need therapy. It's not that unusual."

"What was the degree of family dysfunction?"

"At the time I felt it was severe and persistent."

"Severe enough to lead to violence?"

"Eric didn't stay in therapy long enough for me to find that out."

"Take a guess," Kerney said.

"Determining family psychodynamics isn't guesswork, Chief Kerney."

"Let's step away from the family for a moment. Generally speaking, would current research and case studies lead to you believe an individual with personality traits similar to Eric's might be prone to act violently?"

"The potential for violence would most likely be present. But I couldn't speculate on the degree of it or the direction it might take."

"But it could run the gamut from thoughts of violence all the way up to and including lethal acts."

"Yes, of course. But isn't that true of all of us, given the right set of circumstances?"

Kerney left Joyce's office chewing on her words, and the fact that she hadn't shut him down completely. She'd stayed within ethical boundaries during the conversation, but she was clearly troubled by what she knew about the Langsford family.

He needed to put together Joyce's strong hint that what he knew about Eric should be tied to the entire Langsford family.

A few miles past the Mescalero boundary, flashing red lights of a tribal police unit appeared in Kerney's rearview mirror. He pulled onto the shoulder of the highway and watched Clayton Istee dismount and walk toward him.

"Was I speeding, Officer?" Kerney asked, when Clayton arrived, knowing full well he'd been traveling a good ten miles an hour over the limit.

"Yeah, but that's not why I stopped you."

"What can I do for you?" Kerney asked.

"It's more like what I can do for you," Clayton said. "I know somebody you might want to talk to."

"And who might that be?"

"Are you interested or not?"

"I'm interested," Kerney answered.

"Follow me," Clayton said. "But when we get there, let me do the talking at first."

"Does this person have a name?"

"If he wants to tell you, he will."

Clayton swung his unit around in the direction of Ruidoso, and Kerney followed. They turned off on a graded tribal dirt road that wound through narrow mountain canyons and descended into a large meadow ringed by old-growth pine trees.

A modern wood-frame cabin with smoke drifting from a chimney sat in a clearing at the edge of the meadow. A young man about Clayton's age, wearing jeans and a denim jacket, stepped out on the porch and watched the vehicles approach. Shoulder-length hair fell loose behind his ears. High cheekbones and a small chin gave him a gaunt appearance.

Kerney stayed at his vehicle and let Clayton take the lead. The man raised his chin in a greeting to Clayton, and they talked briefly before approaching Kerney's unit. He got out to meet them.

"Clayton says you're okay," the man said, looking Kerney up and down. "Is this off the record?"

"Is that the way you want it?"

The man searched Kerney's face before nodding.

"Then it's off the record."

"Clayton said you want to know about Eric Langsford."

"Whatever you can tell me," Kerney said.

"I worked with Eric at the resort, before his mother got killed. We used to drink and gamble together after hours. When he'd get a check from his father's company we'd go on a spree with the money."

"Go on."

"I got fired from the job but kept hanging with Eric at the casino and the racetrack in Ruidoso for a couple of years, until I joined AA and got into recovery."

"And?"

"If he had money and I was tapped, he'd always give me some. I owed him maybe two thousand dollars."

A long stretch of silence prompted Kerney to ask, "Is that it?"

The young man glanced at Clayton for reassurance and got a nod. "Once, he asked me to pay him back what I owed, but I didn't have that kind of cash. So he asked me to rob his father's house in Ruidoso."

"When was this?" Kerney asked.

"A little over four years ago, in late summer—August, I think. Eric had me drive him around his father's neighborhood so he could point out the place to me. He said he'd get me a list of things to steal and where I could find them."

"Did he?"

"Yeah, about a week later. He wanted me to do it, like, right away, but I chickened out."

"How did Eric find out what was inside his father's house?"

"He didn't say."

"What did he want you to steal?"

"Jewelry, a coin collection, handguns—stuff like that."

"Handguns?" Kerney asked. Not one weapon had been found in the search of Judge Langsford's house.

"Yeah, I guess the judge had quite a collection."

"And Eric knew exactly where to look for everything?"

"I guess so."

"What did he say when you backed out of the plan?"

"That he'd do it himself. That he'd ripped off things from his father when he was a kid."

"Did he do the job?"

"I guess so. About a week later, I saw him at the casino betting heavy, and asked if he'd ripped off his old man. He smiled and nodded like it was a big joke."

"Did he say anything?"

"Something about how he could never steal enough from his asshole father to make up for his shitty childhood."

"I appreciate your taking the time to talk to me," Kerney said.

"No problem," the man said, as he walked away.

"How did you connect this guy with Eric?" Kerney asked Clayton.

"He told me the story a couple of years ago, after he stopped drinking and got into treatment. I thought it might interest you."

"Eric told me he'd never been near his father or the house in the last six years. Not once."

"So you caught him in a lie," Clayton said.

"Either that, or his brain is just fried from staying stoned and loaded for years."

The half-friendly expression on Clayton's face vanished. "I'm sorry if I wasted your time."

"You didn't. This case is a tough nut to crack. I've got enough motives for a dozen murders, a screwed-up family a shrink described as needing treatment, a suspect who wants to believe he killed his father but can't remember doing it, and no hard evidence that points to anyone else."

"So, you've got no Apache suspects," Clayton said somewhat smugly. "I told you there weren't any."

"So far, you've been right."

"But that won't stop you looking."

"Give it a break. I don't give a damn what the killer's ethnicity is, as long as I catch him." Kerney paused. "I told my wife about you this morning."

"Yeah? How did she take it?"

"She teased me about being an old man with grandchildren."

"That's it?"

"I'd like her to meet you and your family."

"Why?"

"Because she's part of my life."

"Or is she just curious about your bastard Apache son?"

"Believe it or not, that subject wasn't broached. You don't let up on this race thing, do you?"

"Why should I?"

"Maybe you just don't like the idea that your father is a gringo."

"Maybe I don't." Clayton switched his gaze to his unit. "You can follow me out."

"Whatever you say."

Kerney clamped down on his anger as he drove behind the tribal unit. Butting heads with Clayton was no fun, and yet twice the kid had voluntarily helped the investigation, which meant something. He needed to see beyond Clayton's fierce Apache pride and his leeriness about Anglos.

He smiled and waved at Clayton as he pulled onto the highway, and got a curt nod of acknowledgment in return.

Kay Murray wasn't at her town house, so Kerney drove to the Langsford residence, where he spotted her Explorer parked in the drive. He rang the doorbell incessantly for a few minutes before Murray opened up. Her face was clear of emotion, but anger rose in her voice when she spoke.

"The voyeur cop returns for more fun and games. I have nothing to say to you."

"This isn't a game, Ms. Murray. I understand Judge Langsford's house was burglarized some time back. Were you working for him then?"

Murray's expression turned to puzzlement. "A burglary?"

"A little over four years ago."

"Nothing like that ever happened here."

"Supposedly, Eric broke in and took some of his father's possessions."

Murray laughed sharply. "Did Eric tell you that?"

"Do you have a different version?" Kerney asked.

"Only if you're interested in the truth. Eric didn't break in. He came here demanding that his father give him what he wanted. He even brought a list with him."

"And Judge Langsford complied?"

"Only after Eric refused to take money instead."

"He turned down money?"

"That's right."

"Why?"

"He wanted things the judge prized. He said that writing a check would be too easy."

"He wanted to hurt his father," Kerney suggested.

"I suppose."

"Do you have any ideas on the subject?"

Murray raised her hands in a theatrical gesture. "For past sins. For the death of his mother. For a shitty childhood. How should I know?"

"Or some family secret?" Kerney proposed.

"Every family has them."

"But you don't know what they are?"

"Why should I?"

"How did Eric get Judge Langsford to give him what he wanted?"

"He was half-loaded and waving a gun around."

"So, it was robbery."

"No, and it was never reported to the police. Vernon talked Eric into putting the gun away."

"What kind of gun was it?"

"I don't know. A revolver of some sort."

"What did Eric leave with?"

"Everything on his list. Some of his mother's jewelry, his father's handguns, Arthur's coin collection, and Eric's stamp album. All of it quite valuable."

"How valuable?"

"Eighty, a hundred fifty thousand dollars. In that range, at least."

"That's quite a haul. And the judge just handed everything over?"

"Yes."

"Why would he do that?"

"To get him out of the house, I would imagine."

"Did Eric want anything that had belonged to his sister?"

"I don't think so."

"Did the judge discuss Eric's visit with you afterwards?"

"No."

"Did Eric ever come back here after that visit?"

"No."

Kerney took his hand off the front door. "I need a list of the handguns the judge gave Eric."

"I wouldn't know where to look," Kay Murray said. "Go find the killer, Mr. Kerney, and stop wasting your time butting into other people's personal lives." She slammed the door shut in Kerney's face.

Driven by southerly winds, a brown haze of dust and pollution settled over Roswell. The sky was low and dreary, and the mountains to the west were a trivial outline against the horizon. The exquisite, radiant light and the vast conjunction of earth and sky, once so familiar and appealing, were fast becoming a rarity as industry along the Mexican border belched smog that drifted onto the high plains. Middle-class retirees seeking the warmth of the Sun Belt added to the problem, as did the traditional dryness of a New Mexico desert autumn.

As Kerney wheeled into Linda Langsford's driveway, the sour feeling in his gut intensified. Not because the sky was less beautiful. Other things were piling up on him. Sara was hundreds of miles away, and he didn't get to see her enough. Clayton viewed him with hostility. And to top it off, he worried that his dream of ranching was nothing more than an overblown, forty-year-old fantasy.

Modern ranching was far more complex than Kerney's childhood experiences on the Tularosa. Could he do it? Did he even know how to do it? Was he too old to try? Even the thought of the heap of money he stood to get from the sale of the land Erma Fergurson had left him didn't soothe his unsettled feelings.

His parents had raised him to work hard, enjoy what life brings, and never waste anything. What would they have said about his good fortune? Certainly they would have expected him to put the money to good use and to spend it wisely. They would have wanted him to build something of enduring value. But figuring out how to do that was starting to get harder than Kerney had ever imagined possible.

He shut the car door and stared at the stark architectural lines of Linda Langsford's house, which now seemed incongruous in comparison to the nearby farms, pastures, and fields. The house said something about Langsford, but Kerney wasn't sure what it might be.

He tried to get his head straight, but the lousy mood persisted. The most important case of his career was filled with contradictions and going nowhere. As he walked up the pathway, the appearance of the house ate at him along with everything else bouncing around in his head.

7

Under the close watch of a surveillance officer, Linda Langsford was at a funeral parlor making arrangements for her father's services. Eric answered Kerney's knock, looking scrawny and undernourished in what appeared to be some of Drew Randolph's clothes. His eyebrows twitched as he stared at Kerney.

"I'm not talking to you," he said from behind the screen door.

"You'd rather go back to jail," Kerney countered.

"For what?"

"I'll think of something."

"I didn't murder my father or any of those other people."

"That should make talking to me a whole lot easier."

"Okay, come in."

Kerney stepped through the door. "Now, you're absolutely sure you didn't kill your father?"

Eric nodded as he padded barefoot into the living room and sat on the couch. "That's right. Do you know my bitch sister doesn't have any uppers or downers in the house? Not even a Valium prescription. There's not a damn thing to get high on except booze."

"You don't seem to like your sister very much."

"We're not that close. Never have been."

"She had Randolph bail you out."

"That was for appearances, man. We've got to grieve together publicly now that the old man's been iced. Linda's big on shit like that."

"Four years ago, you ripped your father off."

Eric smiled gleefully. "You heard about that? I held him up at gunpoint, man. It gave me a big charge. What a rush."

"Why didn't you just take his money?"

"I wanted things that mattered to him. Stuff he wouldn't want to give me. Money would've been too easy. That's all he ever offered."

"You took Arthur's coin collection, your mother's jewelry, and your own stamp album."

"That's right."

"Things with a sentimental value."

"Bullshit, sentimental," Eric snorted. "He was a control freak. Nothing ever really belonged to us. He picked out every coin, stamp, and piece of expensive jewelry and kept it all locked in his safe. My mother had to ask him when she wanted to wear any of the good jewelry he bought for her. Can you believe that crap?"

"What did he buy for Linda?"

"Daddy's darling girl got money."

"What for?"

"Anything she wanted. Clothes, shoes, trips to Europe, dancing lessons, shopping sprees, cars—whatever."

"When I talked to Dr. Joyce she said the whole family needed therapy."

"Family therapy was her thing, man. To hear her talk, everybody needed it. Seeing her was a total waste of time."

"She must have had her reasons."

"I don't want to talk about it."

"What did you do with the guns you took from your father?"

"I sold them, along with everything else."

"You didn't keep any?"

"Nope."

"What kind of gun did you take to your father's house?"

"It was a Saturday night special." Eric spread his thumb and fore-finger. "A .25 caliber semiautomatic."

"Kay Murray said it was a revolver."

"She's wrong."

"Where is the gun now?"

"I traded it to get high. Is that the kind of gun that was used to kill my father?"

"No."

"Have you checked out my alibi yet?"

"You lied to me, Eric."

"About what?"

"You said you hadn't seen or visited your father in six years."

"I forget a lot of things when I'm stoned."

"You weren't high when you said it."

"So I lied."

"Did you use pay phones to telephone Linda last week?"

"What for?"

"You tell me."

"No, I didn't call her."

"Did you see your father last week?"

"No."

"Talk to him on the phone?"

"No."

"Hire someone to kill him?"

Eric grinned. "That's always been my favorite fantasy."

"Did you?"

Eric shook his head.

"Why did you hate him so?"

There were footsteps on the porch, and a voice snapped out. "That's enough!"

Linda Langsford stormed up to Kerney, her face crimson red. "Why are you here again?" she demanded.

"To return your receipts," Kerney answered calmly, holding out the credit card slips. "I made copies."

She disregarded the papers and gave her brother a scathing look. "What has he been asking you?"

"If I robbed the Judas Judge," Eric said.

Kerney dropped the credit card slips on the coffee table.

"Don't call him that," Linda snapped.

"Fuck you. I can say what I want."

Linda's body tensed. "You're a mess, Eric." She swung to face Kerney. "Don't come back here without calling in advance, and don't talk to Eric again until he has legal counsel."

"As you wish," Kerney said.

"Go," she said flatly.

"We'll need to talk again, Ms. Langsford."

Linda smiled belligerently. "I'll be the judge of that."

Crammed into the command trailer with Lee Sedillo and the agents working the case, Kerney listened to progress reports. Days of intense legwork without any headway had dampened everyone's spirits. Kerney masked his own disappointment by focusing on the details of each agent's assignment.

After the last agent's briefing, Kerney met with Lee in the small office. "What's pending?" he asked.

Sedillo sat at the desk and rubbed the back of his neck. "Two things: Eric Langsford's whereabouts at the time of the murders, and the verification of his sister's vacation itinerary. I had to pull Duran off the vandalism investigation to do the legwork on Eric."

"Where is he?" Kerney asked.

"El Paso. He hasn't checked in yet, so I'm assuming he hasn't got anything, and the bed and breakfast where Linda Langsford spent the first two nights of her vacation has shut down for the season."

"Where's that?" Kerney asked.

"Creede, Colorado, in Mineral County—wherever that is. I've

got a call in to the sheriff, asking him to locate the owners and have them contact us. A husband and wife run the place."

"I've been there," Kerney said. "It's a small old mining town in the Rockies, northeast of Alamosa. There are a lot of summer vacation homes but not too many year-round residents. It shouldn't be hard to run down the B and B owners."

Lee nodded. "I hope so. About the only thing we've done so far is wipe out the overtime budget for the year."

"I want the team to go back over everything again one more time. All of it—the parks, motels, eateries, gas stations, convenience stores—the works. This time, have them concentrate on Penelope Gibben, Kay Murray, Eric Langsford, and his sister. They are the only ones who stand to profit from Langsford's murder."

"Gibben and Murray have solid alibis, Chief," Lee said.

"*Seemingly* solid alibis," Kerney replied.

"We'll work it again," Lee said without much enthusiasm.

"Let's take a closer look at the Langsford family." Kerney handed Lee a copy of the names Colby Trumble, the high school principal, had provided. "Friends, neighbors, school chums, relatives, teachers, business associates—whoever knew them. Let's see if we can turn up any more private family scandals. You know the routine."

"You still think this wasn't a spree killing?" Lee asked.

"Give me the killer's motive that triggered the event," Kerney said. "Was it simple robbery? If we had one confirmed report that a victim's credit card had been used, any stolen items had been pawned or sold, or a check had been forged, maybe I'd buy it. But even that wouldn't explain why the perp used two bullets on Langsford and one with everybody else.

"Aside from all of that," Kerney continued, "we may have a murderer who is systematically wiping out the Langsford family. Changing his MO with each crime. Up to now, the killings have been widely spaced apart. But that could change."

"You think he's going after Linda Langsford?"

"The phone calls made to her residence on the night of the murders bother me. Spree killers get off on bloodletting, so why stop to
make the phone calls unless there's a reason? With this type of killer,
you'd expect him to be spraying bullets around, pumping round after
round into his victims. That didn't happen."

"Good points," Lee said.

"Let's assume the killer had some firearms training. Contact every
gun dealer, weapons instructor, and shooting range in the state. Find
out if any of our possible suspects have experience with handguns."

"Including Linda Langsford?" Lee asked.

Kerney shrugged. "Why not?"

"You want gun sales records searched also?"

"You bet. Start with Brady Bill felony checks."

The phone rang and Lee grabbed the receiver. He listened, gave a
terse thanks, and hung up.

"That was the Roswell district commander. Eric Langsford took
five hundred dollars out of his sister's purse and split. Surveillance
didn't even know he was gone. He left out the back door."

"When?" Kerney asked.

"No more than an hour ago. Linda Langsford just called it in."

"Find him."

The message light on the motel telephone blinked at Kerney. He
called the front desk, and the clerk told him Kay Murray was in the
lobby waiting to speak to him.

She rose quickly from the chair when Kerney entered the lobby.
Her long brown hair fell in soft curls around her face, and she wore
tight-fitting, faded blue jeans and expensive high-heeled boots that
made her look alluring and provocative.

With apprehensive eyes, she smiled shyly as Kerney approached.
"I've treated you badly and I've come to apologize," she said.

"There's no need for that."

"At least let me buy you a drink to make amends."

Kerney nodded in the direction of the motel restaurant, and her expression lightened.

They settled at a table in the almost empty lounge, where the smell of alcohol and cigarettes blended with the aroma of greasy restaurant food. With cheap paneling, mass-produced seafaring prints on the walls, a fishing net hung from the ceiling, and low-end captain's chairs and tables, the decor matched the menu.

"I know you have a job to do," Kay said, after the bartender brought the drinks. "But I'm very protective of my personal life."

Kerney said nothing.

"Does that make any sense?"

"Of course it does."

"I'm a private person. It's the way I survive."

"You don't have to explain yourself to me, Ms. Murray," Kerney said, hoping she would.

"Please, call me Kay. I know I've been impossible with you, and I want you to understand why. I'm not conventional in the way I live, and I stay away from those who are quick to judge."

She reached out and touched Kerney's hand. "I know you weren't doing that. But your questions made me feel that way. I had to settle myself down and get it clear in my mind that you were just doing your job. Will you forgive me?"

Kerney felt an unexpected arousal at her touch. He pulled his hand back and picked up his drink. "Of course."

"So now what?"

"Excuse me?"

"Now that you know all my secrets, are they safe with you?"

"I doubt I know all of your secrets," Kerney said.

Murray laughed. "No, you don't."

Kerney switched the wineglass to his left hand so she could clearly see his wedding band. She didn't seem to notice. "Would you mind a few questions?" he asked.

"About?"

"Judge Langsford."

"Go ahead."

"Eric characterized his father as cruel, heartless, and controlling."

"That's unfair. Eric and his father were as different as night and day. Vernon was vigorous and virile—very charming with women. Eric has almost no sexuality at all. There's no spark to him. He's virtually a eunuch. At the most, sexually amorphous."

"Did Vernon favor Linda?"

"He doted on her. She was his only daughter."

"Why did you become Vernon's lover?" Kerney asked.

The question brought an amused smile to Kay's face. "You change subjects neatly. He always interested me sexually. I particularly liked the way he treated Penelope. I got to see them together a lot when I lived with her."

"What drew him to you?"

"I was his type."

"What type is that?"

"You could say a younger version of Penelope." Kay smiled as she leaned forward. "See? Now you know another secret about me. I like men. Do you know what a single woman really needs?"

"What's that?"

"A good mechanic and a great lover."

Kerney smiled. "I hope you've found both."

"I keep my antennae up for likely prospects," she said with a lilt.

"Did you get to know the judge's family while you lived with Penelope?"

"Only through her. Vernon was very good at compartmentalizing his life, if you know what I mean. And Penelope was, in some ways, a throwback."

"How so?"

"She was more a courtesan than a mistress, and very honest about her needs. She had all the freedom she wanted, none of the burdens of a wife, and a reliable lover who wasn't overly intrusive. I came to appreciate her view of life."

"So did Vernon, apparently."

Kay leaned back and searched Kerney's face with her eyes. "You mean the money he left us in his will. You make it sound almost immoral. Would you be more approving of us if Vernon hadn't been a rich, generous man?"

"I only note it."

"Why bring it up at all? You know I am clearly not a suspect."

"You do have a good alibi. I wasn't accusing you."

"There isn't one person you're investigating who had a dire need for Vernon's money."

"Except Eric."

"Vernon would have provided for him even more than he did. All Eric needed to do was get off drugs and clean himself up."

"Which, if my reading of Eric is correct, would have meant caving in to his father's wishes. That's something I don't think he was willing to do."

Kay gave Kerney a weighty look. "That's an interesting concept."

"Maybe the family liked having Eric be the oddball, to keep things in a crazy kind of balance."

"What benefit would Eric possibly get out of that?"

"Attention."

"Did you come up with this theory all by yourself?" Her tone was playfully mocking, as though she was talking to a misinformed child.

"No. Eric's former therapist reminded me of the concept." Kerney switched gears. "No one seems to want to talk about Arthur. Penelope told me his death devastated Marsha Langsford, and that Vernon was about to leave her when she was killed."

"Arthur was her firstborn."

"A hard loss, certainly. New Mexico is a community property state. Would Vernon have been willing to give her half of his considerable assets in a divorce settlement?"

"Are you suggesting Vernon may have killed his wife?"

"The thought crossed my mind."

"Do you think everyone is capable of such evil?" Censure crept into her voice.

"I think under certain circumstances people can and will do anything imaginable. Did you know Arthur at all?"

"No. That's not to say I didn't know who he was. Why is he important to you?"

"Three members of one family are dead. That raises my interest."

"All died years apart under different circumstances. You won't let this drop, will you?"

"Did you come here to probe my intentions?" Kerney asked.

"You think I have a conniving purpose," she said slowly, watching for a reaction.

Kerney smiled broadly. "Do you?"

The softness on Kay's face vanished, replaced by a icy, shut-down stare. She opened her purse and dropped some bills on the table. "I've made a serious mistake. I thought you were someone who could understand."

"I'd like to."

"You play word games, Mr. Kerney," she said, as she stood up. "I think you're a cold man."

Kerney couldn't resist. "Not at all what a single woman needs."

Her eyes ate into him, venomous. "Screw you."

Kerney stayed at the table after Kay Murray left and ordered a chicken salad sandwich from the bar menu. Only the mayonnaise made it palatable, but he ate it anyway.

What had brought Kay Murray down to Alamogordo to see him? He didn't think for a minute her motives were spurred by genuine attraction, although she tried to play it that way until the tactic broke down. Did she just need to confirm that she wasn't under suspicion?

Kerney doubted it.

He was no moralist when it came to other people's lives. Experience had taught him never to trust the shibboleths of conventional morals and ethics. They often sugar-coated unpleasant truths.

He could buy the idea that Murray was a lusty woman, but why was it important for her to make him aware of that fact? It went way beyond a causal come-on, Kerney decided, or a simple need to be understood. Which meant she was either protecting herself or hiding something she didn't want uncovered.

The more he learned about the people in the judge's life, the more it seemed that Langsford's personal relationships went way beyond unconventional. Where that might take him, Kerney couldn't begin to guess.

He put some bills on the table to cover the tip, and a hand touched him on the shoulder. He looked up as Barbara Jennings leaned down and kissed him on the cheek.

"I hope that isn't your supper, Kerney," Barbara said.

Dale, Kerney, and Barbara had been best friends in high school, and Dale like to tell the story of how he fell in love with her the first time he saw her barrel racing at a county fair rodeo.

No more than five foot three, Barbara's light brown hair framed her widely spaced eyes and full mouth. Her face, now creased with the fine lines of middle age, held a perpetual look of curiosity about life, which she matched with a wide range of personal interests.

Years of ranching hadn't erased her sweet features, and in some ways she was prettier than ever.

Kerney smiled broadly and stood up to hug her. "It's good to see a friendly face for a change. How are you?"

"Just fine," Barbara said, as she motioned Kerney back to his chair and joined him at the table. "I'm in town for a daylong seminar on bull fertility tomorrow. Dale has me doing all the breeding stock buying. He says I'm better at it than he is, and he's right."

"Where is Dale?"

"Tending to the ranch."

"And the girls?"

"They're staying at our apartment in Truth or Consequences, and going to school."

"Are you still living in town with them during the school year?"

Barbara nodded. "I'm there most weeknights. But we're all at the ranch on the weekends. I was hoping to buy you dinner, Kerney, but not here. Can you stand to pick your way through another meal while you keep a woman company?"

"It would be my pleasure," Kerney said, gesturing for the bartender. "But first let me buy you a drink."

Barbara told him a glass of wine would do nicely, and Kerney placed their order.

"Are you really going back to ranching?" Barbara asked, after toasting Kerney with her glass.

"That's the current plan."

"Dale would like that."

"And what do you think?" Kerney asked.

"I love the ranching life, but I could do with a little more security. It's an iffy business at best, especially for us small producers. But you'll have a fair chance at success since you'll own your land outright."

"What would you do in my shoes?"

"Ten years ago, I would have said get into breeding stock. But now even that niche is crowded. Some ranchers have switched to elk ranching."

"I've heard about that."

"They harvest bull antler velvet, sell private hunting permits, slaughter for the market, or breed for other producers."

"Is it profitable?" Kerney asked.

"It can be. One bull elk hunting permit costs on average nine thousand dollars, and on the private game parks there's no state restriction on the number of permits."

"It sure can't be the same as raising cows," Kerney said.

"It's not. A few other ranchers have switched to buffalo. The Livestock Board treats them as domestic animals, if they're not from a wild herd," Barbara said. "Several large outfits here and in Montana are trying to develop a national market for buffalo meat."

"Sounds like folks are looking for a way to get by."

"As long as beef consumption and slaughter prices stay down, they've got to do something."

"Not a rosy picture."

Barbara laughed. "And you want to put yourself into it. I swear, Kerney, you haven't changed: still bullheaded stubborn."

"Maybe not so much anymore."

"That would be different." Barbara scooted her chair closer. "Now, enough of this ranch talk. How is Sara?"

"Stunned by the recent revelation that I'm a grandfather."

"Say that again," Barbara said, lowering the glass from her lips.

"It's true," Kerney said, launching into the story of Isabel and Clayton.

About the only thing Robert Duran felt good about after a day of pounding the Juárez streets was the overtime pay he was earning. Night along the Juárez tourist strip made the city look even more dirty and vulgar. After hoofing around the city from one sleazy hotel to the other, Robert crossed the Rio Grande into El Paso. Technically back in the States, he saw little difference between Juárez and the dilapidated neighborhood that bordered the river. Like Juárez, the area smelled of stale booze, urine, automobile fumes, and garbage. All the retail businesses sold the same cut-rate crap featured in the Juárez tourist traps.

He walked toward the old downtown El Paso plaza, noting an absence of whores on the street, fewer gaudy neon signs, almost no street vendors, more vacant commercial buildings, and a number of cheap hotels.

Canvassing the Juárez strip hotels had yielded no confirmation of Eric Langsford's supposed stay in the city. But that didn't mean anything; most of the hotel clerks had been totally disinterested in assisting a *norteamericano* cop, even if he looked like one of *la gente* and spoke good Spanish—of the northern New Mexico variety.

To reduce the possibility of vandalism to his unmarked unit, Robert had parked in the underground lot of the one decent hotel near the El Paso plaza. He was halfway there when he stopped and looked up at a flickering, humming neon hotel sign. Maybe Langsford had stayed on the Texas side of the border, and not in Juárez at all.

He looked back down the dingy street. There were at least six more hotels within sight and another half dozen up ahead. He ducked into the nearest one, flashed his ID and a photo of Langsford, asked his question, and checked the guest register. Nada, but at least he got cooperation from the clerk. He worked each hotel down the block, changed direction, and finished up at the new high-rise hotel near the plaza where his unit was parked.

He stood in front of the lit-up building with its Spanish accent decor and glass front lobby and decided to make one more inquiry before calling it a night.

Robert showed the woman at the registration desk Langsford's photograph and she recognized him immediately.

"When did he check in?" Robert asked.

The woman clicked away at her computer keyboard. "Last Wednesday."

"When did he check out?"

"Late Saturday morning."

"Method of payment?" Robert asked.

"Cash."

"Did he make any phone calls?"

"Only one, on Wednesday night, to an escort service called California Coeds."

"Let me have the phone number," Robert said, "and a copy of his room bill, if it's no bother."

"Certainly, Officer," the clerk said, returning her attention to the computer.

The printer cranked out the bill. Eric Langsford had rented a suite for two hundred dollars a night—pricey for El Paso, where wages were low, unemployment high, and not too many high rollers had any reason to stay. On top of that, he'd booked the room before arriving.

Supposedly Langsford had been too drunk to remember what he'd done after leaving the band in Marfa, Texas. The room bill proved otherwise. Plus, it was solid evidence that put Langsford within easy striking distance of the crime scenes just prior to the murders.

"Where is the El Paso Police Department located?" Robert asked.

The registration clerk spread out a tourist map on the counter and circled the location.

According to the phone book advertisement, California Coeds offered a discreet dating service and accepted all major credit cards. Robert ran down his investigation to Oscar Olivares, the El Paso PD vice detective on desk duty, and learned that California Coeds provided in-room lap dancing, erotic massages, lingerie modeling, and whatever else the client privately negotiated with his date.

"For El Paso, it's a high-class operation," Olivares said. "The girls are mostly Anglo babes—fair-skinned blondes. They cater to businessmen up from Chihuahua and Mexico City who stay at the hotel. It's owned by a Mexican consortium."

"The hotel or the call service?" Robert asked.

"The hotel."

"Any prostitution or racketeering busts on the call service?" Robert asked, eyeing the vice cop, who looked like a kid trying to pass for a grown-up. His dark curly hair covered his shirt collar, and a pencil-thin mustache adorned his upper lip.

"Not yet."

"How do I make contact with the owner or whoever runs the operation?"

"I'll take you to him."

"It's your turf, detective," Robert said with a smile.

Mario Lopez Humberto operated the California Coeds Escort Service out of an expensive foothills residence with excellent views of the El Paso city lights. A white stretch limousine and several luxury cars were parked in the well-lit semicircular driveway.

Humberto opened the front door talking Spanish into a cordless phone, promising that Bambi would be somewhere at ten o'clock. He nodded nonchalantly when Olivares flashed his shield and kept talking.

Humberto looked like retired Mexican mafia muscle. Stocky, with a body slightly gone to seed, he wore three gold chains around his neck, fully revealed by his mostly unbuttoned white linen shirt.

He punched the phone button and smiled at Olivares. "Are you looking for a date?" he asked in Spanish.

"We need to talk to the girl you sent out to Eric Langsford's hotel room last Wednesday night," Robert said, speaking in English.

"What about?"

"Langsford is a murder suspect," Robert said.

"Here?" Humberto asked.

"In New Mexico."

"This has nothing to do with me?"

"Nothing."

"Brandy was his escort. She's in the green room," Humberto said, motioning the men inside.

"What's that?" Robert asked.

"It's a room where my girls check in before going out on a date. I gotta make sure they look good."

"And you call it the green room," Robert said, following Humberto through the house.

"Yeah, and it's not even green. I heard that actors stay in green rooms before a performance. I don't know why. Since my girls are like actors, I call it the same thing."

In a den filled with comfortable easy chairs and a big-screen television, Humberto took them through a side door to where Brandy stood in front of a full-length mirror adjusting the straps on a skimpy mini dress that barely covered her butt. In her early twenties, Brandy had long blond hair, baby-blue eyes, and a drop-dead body that would fulfill any man's fantasy of a California coed.

"Cops need to talk to you, babe," Humberto said.

"About?" Brandy said, turning around. Whatever she wore under the dress pushed her breasts up like round melons.

"Eric Langsford," Robert said.

"What a flake," Brandy said.

"He was your date last Wednesday night."

"Yeah."

"Did you go anywhere?"

"No, it was a room date. Lingerie modeling and lotion massage only."

"Did he do any talking about himself?"

"Not really."

"Or his immediate plans?"

"No."

"Why do you say he was a flake?"

"He liked the fact that I looked like his sister. Called me Linda. Wanted me to call him 'Daddy.' That's all. It wasn't scary or anything like that. Just flaky."

"Did he get physical with you?" Robert asked.

"No."

"Did you see him again, after Wednesday night?"

"No."

"How did he pay?"

"Cash," Brandy replied.

"Did he give you any gifts?"

Brandy hesitated and cast a furtive glance at Humberto before answering. "Why are you asking me about him?"

"He's a possible murder suspect," Robert replied, reading her uneasiness. "Six people were killed and robbed. What did he give you, Brandy?"

Her voice lowered to a whisper as Humberto scowled at her. "Nothing."

"Let's go down to the police station."

"You can't do that," Humberto said. "She's working."

"Why do I have to go with you?" Brandy asked, keeping her gaze on Humberto.

"Because I think you're lying, and we need to get this straightened out."

Brandy's pretty face lost color. "He didn't give me anything the night I was with him. But he sent me something in the mail. It came two days ago."

She got her purse from the makeup table and handed Robert a ruby ring surrounded by a cluster of diamonds in a gold setting.

Humberto's scowl turned mean.

"I have to take this into evidence," Robert said. "If it was stolen, you won't get it back."

"Give her a receipt," Humberto said, eyeing the treasure.

"Sure thing. Did a note come with the ring?"

"Yeah," Brandy said.

"Do you have it?"

"No."

"What did it say?"

Brandy thought about her answer before replying. "Something like thanks for a nice time."

Doubting Langsford's note had been so prosaic, Robert scribbled a receipt for the ring. The two cops left Humberto and Brandy in the green room—which was really soft peach in color—and walked outside.

"Brandy's in some deep shit with Humberto," Olivares said.

"It's not smart to hold goodies back from your boss," Robert said.

"No sympathy?"

"I doubt Humberto is going to damage his merchandise."

"Not so it shows, anyway," Olivares said. "You think the ring is real?"

"It sure looks it to me. Can I use your office phone?"

"You bet," Olivares said.

* * *

When Robert Duran reached him by phone in his Alamogordo motel room, Lee Sedillo immediately started taking notes.

"Get up here as soon as you can with that ring," Lee said. "I need to get it photographed and faxed to all the victims' families for an ID. You may have busted this case wide open."

"We can drive a tank through the holes in Langsford's alibi," Robert noted. "Tell Chief Kerney he's got probable cause to book him on multiple murder-one counts."

"I'm sure the chief will do that, as soon as we find Eric Langsford," Lee replied.

"Langsford's not in jail?"

"He got bailed out by his sister and ran off," Lee explained.

"That sucks," Robert said.

"Did Langsford use a credit card to book his hotel room?" Sedillo asked.

"Nope."

"Too bad. We would have a tighter case if he'd used one of the victims' charge cards."

"I'll see you in a little while, LT," Robert said.

"Good job, Bobby."

Lee walked down the corridor and knocked on Kerney's door. "We've got some good news, Chief," he said, when Kerney opened up.

Kerney heard Sedillo out and shook his head. "I'm losing my touch, Lee. I didn't think Eric Langsford had the chutzpah to pull off the murders, let alone the capacity to do it."

"It's looking more likely all the time," Lee said.

"Did Duran tell you everything he learned?"

"Just the highlights. I told him to get back here fast."

"Do you have a good description of the ruby ring?"

"Yep. It's an oval ruby lady's ring, about a carat in size, surrounded by diamonds, with a gold band."

"That will do. Let's call the victims' families. You take three, and I'll do the others."

Lee went back to his room to make his calls while Kerney pulled out a list of phone numbers and started dialing. He struck out on the first two and punched in Linda Langsford's number.

"Did you find Eric?" she asked, after he identified himself.

"No, but we may have recovered a piece of jewelry taken during the crime spree."

He described the ring and listened to Linda's sudden intake of breath.

"My father gave my mother a ring just like that on their twentieth wedding anniversary."

"Do you have a fax machine at home?"

"I do." She gave Kerney the number.

"I'll fax a photo of the ring to you for confirmation."

On the way to Lee Sedillo's room, Kerney thought about Eric's rip-off of his father four years ago. He wondered if Kay Murray would be able to ID the ring as one of the items Vernon had turned over to Eric. If not, a reasonable assumption would be that Eric had taken the ring from the motor coach after the murder.

That would simplify Kerney's life, let him pull the pin on his shield, and finally get out of the cop game for good.

He stopped at Lee's door. He was good at his job and he liked the work. Did he really want to quit just because he was about to become rich enough to buy a ranch? Or was the Shockley shooting making him feel like he had to bail out?

8

Kerney checked by phone with Linda Langsford after faxing a picture of the ring to her. She positively identified it as once belonging to her mother, said it had been promised to her, and wanted it returned as soon as possible. She hung up without waiting for a response.

The agent who'd showed a photograph of the ring to Kay Murray reported back that Eric had taken the item from his father during his staged robbery. That cooled Kerney's hopes for conclusive evidence needed to link Eric to the murders.

Eric still remained the only viable suspect in the case, so Kerney decided an early morning trip to El Paso was in order to meet with Brandy Wine and see what more he could learn about Langsford.

Agent Duran's report had included a fact sheet on Ronda Shields, aka Brandy Wine. She was twenty-four years old, a native of Nebraska, and had been runner-up in a statewide beauty pageant during her senior year in high school. She had two solicitation convictions out of southern California and a drug possession bust in Phoenix. No arrests had been made since her arrival in El Paso six months ago.

Before leaving, Kerney made sure Lee Sedillo had the team looking for Eric Langsford, working background investigations on the Langsfords, Murray and Gibben, and canvassing all businesses along the murder route one more time.

Ronda lived in an apartment on the west side of El Paso within striking distance of a major shopping mall and the Interstate. Her limp blond hair was pinned carelessly behind her ears, and her red-rimmed eyes looked wide and vulnerable.

Agent Duran's report noted that Eric had commented on Ronda's resemblance his sister. Kerney saw the similarities: she was the same height and weight as Linda, and her blond hair was a perfect match.

Ronda led Kerney into a cove kitchen where two large birdcages on the floor held a noisy cockatoo and a squawking parakeet. Birdseed crunched under Kerney's feet as he joined her at a counter that separated the kitchen from a dining area. She sat stiffly on a stool and winced, and while there were no visible signs Ronda had been beaten, Kerney guessed she'd been punished in some unpleasant way by her pimp for withholding the ring.

"You called Eric Langsford kinky," Kerney said. "What did you mean by that?"

Ronda lit a cigarette and blew smoke in Kerney's face. "I said he was flaky. Kinky has a whole different meaning. I don't do kinky. If a client wants that, I walk."

"Okay, flaky. How so?"

"Guys get off on different things. He wanted me to pretend like I was, like, a Lolita. All innocent and seductive, if you know what I mean. So, I baby-talked him and acted all coy."

"And he wanted you to call him Daddy."

"Yeah."

"Any spanking?"

Ronda shook her head. "That's not what I do."

"Did he ask?"

"No."

"Any sex?"

"No. He was into watching. I'm a pretty good actress. He just sat on the bed drinking whiskey from a bottle. I'd say something to him like did he want to see my panties, then I'd do it, and he'd call me a bitch or a slut."

"It went no further than that?"

"He asked me to take a bath, and he watched through a crack in the door."

"Just watched?"

"Well, no. When I got out of the tub, he dried me off with a towel."

"Was he aroused at any time?"

"Yeah, in the bathroom. He jacked off, and then I got dressed and left."

"Did you lend him a hand?"

Ronda made a face at Kerney's word play. "That's real cute. No, he just wanted me to watch, and believe me, it didn't take long."

"Was he free with his money?"

"He gave me a nice tip."

"How much?"

"A hundred dollars."

Eric had given Kerney the impression he'd been short on cash during his drinking binge. Yet he'd not only paid for an expensive hotel room, but also an expensive woman, whom he'd tipped heavily. "What denomination were the bills?"

"Five twenties."

"Did he flash a bankroll?"

"No, he kinda snuck the bills out of his wallet."

"You told the other officer Eric wanted you to act the part of his sister."

"That's what I meant about the Lolita thing. He was real excited about that."

"Excited?"

"Like animated, if you know what I mean—ready to get started right away."

"Did he talk to you about it in any detail?"

"No, he just told me what he wanted me to do."

"What did you do to get him to send you the ring?"

"Nothing, I swear. I thought he was just acting like a big shot and trying to impress me."

"Did he tell you what he was going to give you as a present?"

"No, he said it would be a surprise, something pretty, and I'd like it."

"Had Langsford ever been your client before?"

"No, but Crystal saw him once."

"Who is Crystal?"

"Betty Cook is her real name. She works with me. I can give you her phone number."

Kerney left and used a public phone to speak to Crystal, who reported that Eric had asked her to undress and masturbate while he watched from the bathroom door.

"Did he make any other requests?" Kerney asked.

"When he called for the date he asked for a blonde. But there wasn't one available. So Mario had me wear a wig. He wasn't too happy when he found out I was a redhead."

"What did he say?"

"Nothing. But he didn't tip me, and I put on a really good show."

He stopped at the hotel and asked the reservation clerk to check if Langsford had any prior stays at the hotel. She came up with four overnight registrations and calls to three additional dating services in the last year, all occurring around the time Eric received his quarterly checks for serving as a corporate board member for one of his father's companies.

Working a lobby phone, Kerney tracked down the women who'd been sent to Langsford's room, and got basically the same story: Eric liked to play Peeping Tom, wanted to be called "Daddy," avoided any actual sexual contact, and always asked for blondes.

Other than Ronda, none had received any surprise gifts in the mail. Or if they had, weren't admitting to it.

Eric's disappearance from Roswell, the inconsistencies in his alibi, his hatred of his father, and his proximity to the crime scenes added up to strong circumstantial evidence against him. But Kerney wanted some tangible proof of Eric's guilt, either in the form of physical evidence or a voluntary confession. He preferred both if possible.

Through the hotel lobby window he watched a parking attendant wheel a new Jaguar to the curb, where a slightly pudgy man in an expensive suit stood waiting. The car had Mexican license plates. That was the third luxury car in a row the attendant had parked, all with Mexican tags, all for men in expensive suits.

Business in the border city was obviously profitable, and Kerney didn't think for a second that all of it was legitimate.

As the most junior agent on the team, Mary Margaret Lovato got the drudge work assignments. Ordered back to Carrizozo, she'd spent the morning on a door-to-door canvas of every business and government office in town, showing photographs, asking questions, and trying to find one witness who could put any of the possible suspects in the area before the first homicide at the Valley of Fires campground.

No one Mary Margaret spoke to was able to ID Kay Murray, Penelope Gibben, or Linda and Eric Langsford.

Situated at the north end of the Tularosa Basin, Carrizozo was bracketed by mountain ranges, some near and some distant. While the landscape was lovely to look at, the winds were constant, swirling out of the mountains from all directions.

After a few minutes of small talk with the county sheriff outside the county administration building, Mary Margaret went to her unit, ran a comb through her hair, and wrote up her field notes. Her next scheduled stop was the village of Tularosa, fifty miles south.

She doubled-checked her list against the local phone book to make sure every possible contact had been made, crossed out the names of businesses no longer in existence, and noted down for later follow-up the few places where she'd been unable to speak to anyone.

The phone book included listings for the village of Capitan, a short twenty-mile drive southeast into the mountains. Famous as the birthplace of Smokey Bear, Capitan had not been canvassed. Mary Margaret cranked the engine. It was worth a shot.

She arrived in the village and made a quick tour. Nestled in a valley with mountains to the south and rolling hills to the north rising to a high range that extended in an easterly direction, it took its name from the peak that dominated the skyline. Businesses were concentrated along the highway and on several short blocks of side streets.

In the town center was the Smokey Bear Historical State Park, which celebrated the rescue fifty years ago of the famous Forest Service icon from a nearby wildfire.

Behind the somewhat quaint main drag, residential streets crisscrossed a narrow flat area for a few blocks before giving way to open grassland. Mary Margaret swung back on the main drag, stopped at a mom-and-pop motel, placed photographs on the office counter, and showed them to a slow-moving overweight woman who had emerged from the apartment behind the office.

The woman jabbed a finger at Eric Langsford's photo. "He stays here."

"When was the last time?" Mary Margaret asked.

The woman paged through her register. "Last month."

"Was he alone?"

"He checked in as a single." She picked up Kay Murray's picture. "But this woman meets him here," she said, waving the photo at Mary Margaret.

"You're sure?" Mary Margaret asked.

"Uh-huh. I've seen them both before. They just stay in his room for a while and then go to the restaurant next door."

"How often do they meet here?"

"Three, four times a year. It's been going on for a while."

"How long is a while?"

"At least four years."

"Does the room get used?"

"You mean for sex? Not unless they do it in the shower. The bed is never mussy."

"They arrived in separate cars?"

"Yes."

"How long do they stay?"

"No more than an hour or two," the woman said, nodding at the office window. "I can see all the vehicles in the parking lot from here."

"What name does he use when he checks in?"

The woman put the photo down and studied the register. "Eric Langsford. He pays in cash."

Mary Margaret tapped Kay Murray's photo. "Has he ever met with anyone else besides this woman?"

"Not so far as I know."

Mary Margaret passed her hand over Penelope Gibben's and Linda Langsford's photographs. "What about these two?"

"I've never seen either of them."

"I need the dates of all his previous stays," Mary Margaret said.

"For this year, that's easy. Anything before that, I'll have to dig out the guest books. It will take some time."

"I'll wait."

The woman huffed in frustration about the inconvenience and retreated into her apartment. A smile lit up Mary Margaret's face and she clapped her hands together in delight.

*   *   *

The uniformed officer sent to Ruidoso to find Kay Murray and bring her to Alamogordo called in a five-minute ETA. Kerney complimented Mary Margaret for a job well done, left the command trailer, and waited for Murray in the district captain's office.

His decision to have Murray picked up and escorted to him was calculated to make her feel vulnerable and at risk.

Murray knocked at the open door, and Kerney studied the papers on the desk for a minute before looking up. She glared at him when he motioned for her to enter, and stalked in with her back straight, her chin set, and a cutting look in her eyes.

"What is this all about?" she demanded.

"Sit down," Kerney said.

"I will not."

"You refuse to cooperate?"

"Why did you drag me down here?"

"Are you willing to cooperate?" Kerney said.

"I've done that already."

Kerney pushed the phone across the desk. "Call a lawyer, Ms. Murray."

"What for?"

"I may be filing conspiracy charges against you."

"Conspiracy to do what?"

"Colluding with Eric Langsford to kill his father and five other innocent people."

"That's ludicrous."

Kerney nodded curtly at the empty chair. "Sit down and cooperate."

Murray sat in cold silence, her expression frozen in restrained anger. He decided to change tactics.

He moved his chair to the side of the desk, closer to Murray, and smiled. "This doesn't have to be that difficult."

"What, exactly, do you want me to confess to?"

"Let's back up a bit. You were seen with Eric Langsford at a motel in Capitan less than a month before the murders. What was that all about?"

"I'd rather not say."

"You've met with him eleven times over the past four years in the same motel."

"Is that a crime?"

"Not necessarily."

Murray's laugh was brittle. "You think I'm a slut, don't you?"

"I'm not assuming your meetings with Eric had anything to do with sex."

"How generous of you."

"But I do believe the killings were planned and executed to conceal the fact that Vernon Langsford was the principal target. Your rendezvous with Eric, so close to the time of the murders, brings the possibility of your participation into question."

"I did not meet with Eric to help him plan a murder."

Kerney's skepticism rose. People who denied accusations quickly always made him more leery. "I'd like to believe that."

"Then by all means do."

"Why are you protecting Eric?"

"I'm not. Eric can take care of himself. I'm protecting my right to privacy."

"I know that's important to you."

"Very."

"Is it also important to those you care about?"

"Of course."

"Including Dr. Joel Cushman?"

"Since you know about my relationship with Joel, why do you bother to ask?"

"He's been your therapist, lover, and friend."

"Yes, all of those things."

"And you care about him."

"That doesn't deserve an answer. I know you threatened him with exposure to the Board of Psychological Examiners. But I would have to file a complaint against him, and I have no intention to do so."

"That doesn't necessarily protect him from an arrest."

"Of course it does."

"I've researched the law, Ms. Murray. Under the statutes, psycho-therapists who have sex with current or past patients, even if the consent is mutual, can be charged with criminal sexual penetration through the use of force or coercion. It's a third-degree felony."

"That's a stupid, intrusive law."

"I have your statement and Cushman's admission. That's all I need to ask the DA to press charges."

Murray's voice wavered when she spoke. "And of course you'll do it if I don't cooperate. You really are a son of a bitch."

"You can keep Cushman out of jail. What was the reason for your meeting with Eric?"

"I brought him money."

"How much?"

"I don't know."

"It wasn't your money?"

"No."

"Whose money was it?"

"His sister's. All of my meetings with Eric were to take him money. Linda would send me a sealed envelope with a note asking me to pass it along to Eric. I'd call Eric and arrange to meet him in Capitan."

"Why Capitan?"

"Because Linda didn't want her father to know that she was helping Eric financially."

"How did you know it was money you delivered?"

"Eric told me. He gets a kick out of the fact that the sister he despises gives him money."

"And what did you get for your trouble?"

"Nothing."

Kerney waited a beat. "Are you sure?"

"That's what I said."

"Why would Eric rent a motel room if all he had to do was wait for you to show up with an envelope?"

"You can't stay away from the sex thing, can you?" Kay said.

"I can't see you spending an hour or two in a motel room with Eric on eleven different occasions without a good reason."

"We would talk for a time, that's all."

"Do you always tell the truth, Ms. Murray?"

"The one thing I can't stand is a liar."

Kerney tapped a finger against his lips. "I wonder what a search of your car and house would turn up."

"You have no cause to do that," Kay said. She brushed an imaginary hair away from her forehead and broke eye contact. "I want to speak to a lawyer."

Kerney leaned forward. "I think I know what's happening here. There is always at least one thing a person would rather not have the police know about. It doesn't have to be a big thing. What is it for you, Ms. Murray? Do you smoke a little pot?"

Kay Murray raised her eyes to the ceiling and sighed.

"What is it you'd rather not have the police know?"

"Nothing."

"What would I find in your house, Ms. Murray? In your purse? In your car? If you're arrested, we'll take a very close look. You'll be strip-searched as well."

Murray's hand tightened on her purse, and her eyes snapped back to Kerney's face. "You'd find grass, okay? I smoke grass, and I buy it from Eric."

"He deals?"

"Only to friends and people he knows well. He's a doper, not a dealer."

"How much money does his sister give him?"

"It depends; between five and ten thousand dollars each time."

"For what?"

"I don't know."

"I believe you," Kerney said, getting to his feet. "Do you know where Eric is right now?"

Murray shook her head and stood. "I haven't seen him since we met in Capitan."

"When you meet with Eric in Capitan, do you wear a blond wig?"

Murray looked bewildered. "I've never worn a wig in my life."

"You can go, Ms. Murray, but we may need to talk again."

"Are you going to arrest Joel?"

"That will depend on how truthful you've been with me."

Kay protectively tucked her purse under an arm, her eyes narrow and hostile. "You really enjoy shattering people's lives, don't you?"

"That usually happens long before I ever get involved," Kerney said.

"I don't like you at all, Mr. Kerney, and I doubt there are many people who do."

Her cutting condemnation said, she hurried out the door, avoiding Kerney's hard-eyed scrutiny of her purse. She'd revealed her use of marijuana too easily, Kerney thought, and he wondered what still-undisclosed secret went with her.

Unnoticed, Andy Baca stood in the open office doorway watching Kerney as he scribbled notes on a pad. Kerney looked up, and the troubled expression on his face smoothed out.

"What are you doing here?" Kerney asked, forcing a smile as he dropped the pen on the desk.

"I see you haven't lost your touch with women, Kerney," Andy replied. "That was one pissed-off lady who flew by me in the hall. Who was she?"

"I'm not sure. A suspect, a witness, a victim of some sort. Maybe all of the above. Her name is Kay Murray."

Andy eased himself into a chair. "I haven't heard much from you in the last couple of days."

"There hasn't been much to tell. You could have called from Santa Fe if you wanted a progress report."

"I'm not here to check up on you. I came down to put Captain Catanach and Lieutenant Vanhorn back on the job."

"You're not going to terminate them?"

Andy shook his head. "It wouldn't be fair. Nate's Internal Affairs people tell me Catanach and Vanhorn aren't the only district supervisors who were lax about evidence protection. Seems my predecessor didn't pay it much attention, so things got sloppy. That's changing fast."

"I bet it is. How is Nate doing on the job?"

Andy grinned. "I should have made him my deputy chief a long time ago. He doesn't give me half the grief you do."

"How about I turn in my shield now so you can make Nate's appointment permanent?"

Andy cocked his head and studied his old friend. "Feeling a bit grumpy?"

"Stymied is more like it."

"Bring me up to speed."

Kerney took Andy through the high points of the investigation, the subsequent dead ends, and the circumstantial evidence that implicated Eric Langsford.

"Motive and opportunity sound like sufficient probable cause to me," Andy said, when Kerney finished up. "Find Eric Langsford and arrest him. Let the district attorney decide if he's got enough to file murder-one charges."

"Are we trying to make ourselves look good here?" Kerney asked.

"Making an arrest in a multiple-murder case always looks good," Andy replied.

"You sound like a careerist protecting the department's reputation, Andy."

Andy absorbed Kerney's words like a slap. "This has nothing to do with maintaining the self-interest of the department. You've got a viable suspect and enough cause to arrest him, so do it."

"Is that an order?"

"If you want it to be," Andy replied evenly.

Kerney's deep-set eyes became almost invisible, and anger darkened his face. "Fine," he said without emotion.

"What in the hell is the matter with you?"

Kerney swallowed his anger. "I want this case wrapped up right."

"That's not what's eating at you," Andy said.

"Maybe not."

"Want to talk about it?"

Killing Shockley and discovering Clayton to be his son had unsettled Kerney in ways he'd never imagined possible. For the past two days he'd been questioning everything. He could talk to Andy about any one of his worries, but not all of them at once. It would sound like babble.

"No," he said, breaking into a rueful smile as he stood. "Let me get out of here and do my job. I guess I do give you grief, Andy. Sorry."

Andy got to his feet and smiled back. "No sweat."

As Kerney came out from behind the desk, Andy gave him a reassuring pat on the shoulder. Kerney squeezed Andy's arm in response and continued out the door.

Kerney's shot-up gut didn't handle coffee very well, and he rarely drank it. He sipped water while Lee Sedillo waved his empty coffee cup at the waitress. She stepped over to the table, poured a refill, and moved on, looking for more customers wanting top-offs.

The restaurant catered to the German military personnel and families stationed at Holloman Air Force Base a few miles outside of Alamogordo. Most of the menu items Kerney had never encountered before, nor did he want to. Every plate the waitress carried past the table was loaded with dumplings and overcooked meat covered with a sludgelike gravy. He wondered if stomach pumps were offered as a courtesy after the final course.

"I'll get everybody looking for Eric Langsford," Lee said.

"Let's hope he hasn't left the state," Kerney said. "Put out a national APB, just in case. What have we missed, Lee?"

"I don't know, Chief. We haven't found any handgun sales made to the suspects, or any record of firearms training. Our interviews with people who knew the Langsfords turned up squat. On the surface, they look like the all-American family."

"We know better," Kerney said. "Go over every agent's field notes, investigation reports, and activity log. Look for undeveloped leads, incomplete witness statements, or possible hard evidence that might have been missed."

Lee nodded. "The owners of the bed and breakfast in Creede confirmed that Linda Langsford was a guest the night her father was killed. That leaves only Eric as a primary suspect."

Kerney put a few dollar bills on the table to cover the coffee and the tip. "I'm going to Roswell for a couple of days. You run things here."

"What's up with that, Chief?"

Kerney shrugged. "A fishing expedition."

"You're not convinced Eric is our boy, are you?"

"I won't be until we get either a voluntary confession or hard evidence that confirms his guilt."

Sedillo bit his lip.

"What's on your mind, Lee?" Kerney asked.

"Remember that rape case we worked together in Santa Fe when you were with the PD? Those three punks who got the victim loaded and raped her in a hot tub? The DA wouldn't prosecute because the girl voluntarily got into the tub wearing her bra and panties."

"I remember. He didn't want to risk losing the case in court; it would make his yearly conviction rate look bad. What's your point, Lee?"

"Maybe you're expecting too much."

"Meaning?"

"I know you'd like to nail down an ironclad conviction. But cases don't always break the way you want them to, especially after prose-cutors and judges get their hands on them."

"You think my ego is too wrapped up in this?"

"Mine would be, if I was in your shoes."

"Did Andy Baca ask you to have a little chat with me?" Kerney asked.

A pained look crossed Lee's face. "You know me better than that."

Kerney got up from the table. "I take it back, Lee. Forget I said anything. You're right; we can only take it as far as it goes. But I'm still heading out to Roswell."

"I wasn't trying to change your mind, Chief."

A knock at the motel room door came just as Kerney finished pack-ing. He opened it to find Isabel Istee looking up at him with sober eyes, her hands clasped together primly at her waist. A dark skirt, de-mure white blouse, and sensible shoes accented the reserved look on her face.

"Do you have some time to talk?" she asked.

"Come in," Kerney replied.

Isabel hesitated before cautiously stepping into the room. "Please leave the door open," she asked.

Kerney grabbed a travel bag from the bed and used it as a door-stop. He turned to find Isabel standing stiffly in the center of the room.

"What would you like to talk about?" he asked.

"Although he appreciates the fact that you are his father, Clayton sees no purpose in establishing a relationship with you," Isabel said.

Her words sounded rehearsed. Kerney took a crack at breaking through the formality. "In other words, he thinks I'm a racist."

"That isn't the issue."

"That's the impression I get from him," Kerney countered.

Isabel shrugged a shoulder slightly in concession. "I know he tested you. He's cautious when it comes to prejudicial attitudes. All of us are."

"I've tried not to be intrusive. Has that been misunderstood as a lack of interest on my part?"

"No."

"Then what is it?"

Isabel measured Kerney with unsmiling eyes that seemed to be asking an unspoken question.

He waited for a long minute and said, "Tell me why you're here, Isabel."

"Clayton will become a tribal leader someday, Kevin. He will be our next chief of police, and when his career in law enforcement ends he'll serve on the tribal council. He has much to offer, and he is highly regarded by the elders."

"I can see that potential in him," Kerney said. "But it still doesn't answer my question."

"We have a strong tradition of tolerance when it comes to relationships outside the tribe," Isabel said, coloring slightly. "Having you as a father is not a barrier to him."

"So, it's politics," Kerney said, thinking that Clayton's tribal ambitions would be a good reason to keep his distance from a gringo parent.

"You could say that."

"Whose politics are we talking about?" Kerney asked.

"Partially mine, partially his, partially the tribal elders."

"I see." Kerney said. "Was Clayton's assistance in my murder investigation politically motivated?"

"The tribal administrator and police chief asked him to informally give you the information. Otherwise, you never would have been allowed to question any tribal members. We wanted you to understand that no Mescalero had a part in either the murder of Judge Langsford or his wife."

"We?"

"I played a role in that decision. I serve on the tribal council."

"Have I been given all the facts, Isabel?"

"Nothing was withheld from you."

"So why all the game playing?"

"Allowing the state police to conduct an official investigation was unacceptable. Your department has no authority on our land, and we have no desire to set a dangerous precedent. Another way had to be found to give you the information you wanted. That's where I played a role. I've always believed you to be fair-minded, and I argued that you would not act in a way that would be detrimental to the tribe."

"That's nice to hear." Kerney flashed back on the laughing, spontaneous, lusty, spirited Isabel of his youth. "The world has certainly changed us since we were in college together."

"Not really, Kevin. I never had a desire to make you a part of my world, or be part of yours."

"Obviously."

"Do we have an understanding?"

"It was good of you to come and see me. I know this wasn't an easy thing to do. I won't be a bother."

"Thank you." Isabel smiled, her eyes searching Kerney's face with a hint of warmth. "I never meant to hurt you."

"I know that," Kerney said with a smile.

"When Clayton was a child, I often wondered what you would do if you'd learned of his existence."

"I would have exercised my rights as a parent."

"I thought so," Isabel said. "Even against my wishes?"

"Probably."

"It would have meant that much to you?"

"Yes."

"And now?" Isabel asked.

"I have an empty feeling that I've missed out on something important."

"Yes, I can see that. It speaks well of you. Are you angry with me?"

"No, just disappointed by the circumstances. What would you have done if I'd showed up, way back when?"

"I'm not sure. I never was sure. It was always a question." For a split second Isabel's dark eyes turned playful. "Maybe I would have changed my mind about letting you into my life."

"We'll never know," Kerney said. "But if that were the case, I would have had a hard time walking away from such an opportunity."

She flushed, her eyes brightened, and a small smile crossed her lips. She extended her hand and Kerney shook it, said good-bye, and walked her to the door.

He waited a few minutes before grabbing his bags and heading to the parking lot. Isabel's life was far different from his own, and he respected her decisions, her traditions, and her heritage. He had unwittingly become a father, and feeling bad about the situation wouldn't change anything. Maybe it was time to get out of his Clayton funk.

Kerney smiled as he thought about Isabel, Sara, Erma Fergurson, his mother, and one or two other women who'd been important to him throughout the years. Each was fiercely independent, smart as a whip, and an extraordinarily interesting person in her own unique way.

The smile vanished when he reached his unit. Someone had scrawled COP KILLER in paint on the windshield, in broad daylight.

The lot was almost empty of cars, and there were no people around. Careful not to touch anything outside the vehicle except the door latch, he unlocked it and made radio contact with Agent Duran.

"Come take a look at my unit," he said. "I'm at the motel."

"I'll be there in a few, Chief. Is the damage bad?"

"No damage, just the words 'Cop Killer' painted on the windshield."

It took the better part of an hour for Duran to dust for prints, lift some paint samples, and take photographs. As he worked, Kerney questioned him about his investigation and learned there were no suspects and no leads.

"But I'm thinking now that maybe it's somebody close by," Duran said. "Or a motel employee. This happened in broad daylight, which means that whoever did it saw you drive up."

"Nobody followed me," Kerney said.

"I'm gonna canvas the neighborhood as soon as I finish here," Robert said.

After scraping off the paint and cleaning the windshield, Kerney fired up the unit and rolled onto the street, thinking that whoever was sending him a message needed to be taken very seriously.

9

Traffic along the highway from Ruidoso to Roswell was light. Kerney parked near the mile-marker post where Arthur Langsford had been killed by a hit-and-run driver and studied the accident investigation report. The incident had occurred just inside the Chaves County line in low foothills that once defined the edge of a shallow inland sea. The long flowing mountains beyond looked serene and inviting. But in the high country away from the villages, towns, and settlements there were narrow zigzag canyons, deep unbroken cliff walls, and sharp elbow passages that could disorient the unsuspecting and the unprepared.

Kerney walked on the shoulder of the road thinking he needed to find out from the highway department if any changes or alterations to the right of way had occurred since the accident. He checked the photographs in the accident report and eyed the bend in the road where Arthur Langsford had been hit head-on. It wasn't a blind curve by any means. Supposedly a road hazard had caused the driver to swerve into Langsford's lane, and a setting sun had impaired the driver's vision. He wondered how, without any witnesses, the now-retired sheriff's deputy had ascertained his facts.

Motor vehicle collision analysis wasn't one of Kerney's special interests or skills, and it had been years since he'd handled a traffic accident. He consulted the deputy's field sketch and located the approximate spot in the road where skid marks showed the driver had braked and swerved into the opposite lane. Why had the driver veered across the center line in a no-passing zone when the most typical reaction would've been to steer away from any oncoming traffic?

The report noted that three empty cardboard boxes, each twenty by eighteen inches, had been found on the shoulder of the road approximately twenty feet beyond the point where the skid marks began. The deputy had assumed the boxes had been in the road prior to impact, but there was no substantiation of that finding. Further, he'd concluded that inattention had caused the driver to swerve quickly to avoid the apparent hazard.

Looking down the highway from the impact point, Kerney wondered how inattentive the driver had been. Even with a low, setting sun, the obstacles should have been visible in time for the driver to slow and approach with caution.

The report of conditions on the day of the accident indicated that the road was dry, traffic was light, and the weather was clear. No debris or paint particles from the vehicle had been found at the scene, either on the road or—according to the forensic analysis—embedded in Arthur Langsford's flesh, bicycle, or clothing.

Kerney decided he needed to find and talk to the retired deputy who handled the call, and locate an expert to reconstruct the accident.

In a traditional sense, Midway couldn't be called a village or a settlement. Just south of Roswell, close to a newly expanded four-lane highway built to carry radioactive shipments to the underground Waste Isolation Pilot Project eighty miles down the road, Midway consisted of a sprinkling of aging mobile homes and houses on flat, dirt-packed acre-size lots. The absence of lawns and trees, the presence of half-finished or abandoned attempts by residents to build sheds, decks, and carports, and the rundown condition of the neighborhood generally gave it a feeling of depleted energy.

Delvin Waxman, the retired deputy, lived in a trailer that looked no better or worse than any others. He was bent over the engine compartment of an old black-and-white state police cruiser that had been stripped of all decals and equipment and sold at auction. He raised his head when Kerney drove up, wiped his hands on a rag, and approached the unit. He had a small head, a narrow face, and a slightly off-center nose. From the lines and wear on his face, he looked to be pushing sixty.

Kerney showed his shield and introduced himself.

"What can I do for you?" Waxman asked.

"Tell me about Arthur Langsford's death."

"I remember that case. It would be hard to forget, seeing that the victim was a judge's son and all." Waxman stuffed the rag in a back pocket and glanced at the file in Kerney's hand. "You've read my report?"

"I have."

"Then there's not much to tell. It's all there."

"How long did it take you to get to the accident?"

"About twenty minutes. State police were tied up at another collision and I was the only unit available."

"Was it dark when you arrived?" Kerney asked.

"Just about."

"Then how did you know the sky was clear and the sun was setting at the time of the incident?"

"Witness report. A driver traveling east out of the mountains was first on the scene. He stopped and directed traffic until I got there. Another driver drove to a gas station outside of town and called it in."

"Did you inspect the cardboard boxes?"

"I gave them a look. They weren't crushed or run over, if that's what you're asking."

"You assumed the boxes were originally in the road."

Waxman nodded. "Probably dropped out of the back of a pickup truck hauling trash."

"Any garbage, newspaper or packing material in the boxes?"

"They were empty."

"Any lettering on them?"

"Just the manufacturer's name. They were plain brown boxes, like the kind used by moving companies."

"Did you preserve the boxes as evidence?"

"I saw no reason to."

"How long was it from the time Langsford got hit to the time the first driver stopped?"

"I'd say no more than five minutes. The driver told me Langsford was bleeding freely from the head when he got there."

"Was Langsford alive when the driver arrived?"

"The guy didn't know," Waxman said. "All he told me was the bicyclist looked dead and he didn't want to touch him. Langsford sure wasn't alive when I got there. His helmet had been split open and his brains were seeping out of a deep wound in his left temple."

"Did your witness pass any cars traveling in the opposite direction before he arrived at the scene?"

"He didn't think so, but he couldn't remember for sure. He was pretty shook up. You know how most civilians get when they see a fresh corpse for the first time. Especially one all torn to hell."

"Did you get a name and address of the guy who found Langsford?"

"I didn't have time. I had to block both lanes with flares and cones, handle traffic, and preserve the scene until backup and the first responders arrived. There were cars pulled off to the side for a hundred yards in either direction, and about twenty people trying to see what happened. It took volunteer firefighters and EMTs a good ten minutes to reach my location."

"You got nothing on the witness?" Kerney asked.

"He was a local. Said he worked at a furniture store in Roswell."

"Give me a description."

Waxman rubbed his chin and thought about it for a minute. "Late sixties, gray hair, above average height, mustache. That's all I can remember."

Kerney glanced over Waxman's shoulder at the single wide mobile home. It didn't look like much to live in for anyone, especially a retired cop pushing sixty.

Waxman read the look on Kerney's face and waved a hand in the direction of the mobile home. "Not much, is it? I spent twenty years in the Air Force and twenty more with the county sheriff's department. The ex-wife got half of both my pensions. Is this a great country or what?"

"That's too bad," Kerney said. "Did you ID Arthur Langsford at the scene?"

"Nope. He wasn't carrying any identification, just a small fanny pack with some change, bills, a few bike tools, and a first-aid pouch. His family reported him overdue from his cycling trip about three hours after he got turned into roadkill. We made the ID based on the information they provided."

"In your follow-up, you reported forensics came up empty on any physical evidence."

"That's right. I think the vehicle that hit him had one of those vinyl front end covers and a composition grill and bumper to absorb impacts. I never could determine the make or the model."

"Did you put the word out to auto dealers and repair shops?" Kerney asked.

"You bet. I did phone calls, bulletins, drop-bys, and got zilch." Waxman watched Kerney thumb through the paperwork. "Any more questions?" he asked, when Kerney looked up.

"That's it."

"This is about the judge's murder, isn't it?"

"Three deaths in one family raise interesting questions," Kerney replied.

"That accident was a clear-cut hit and run."

"You're probably right," Kerney said. "But I'd love to know who was behind the wheel of the car."

*   *   *

Kerney toured the Roswell furniture stores looking for an elderly salesman with gray hair and a mustache. At a downtown family-owned establishment he met up with Harry Bodecker, a part-time employee who matched Waxman's description. Bodecker nodded his head vigorously when Kerney asked about the hit-and-run accident.

"How could I forget that," Bodecker said. "It was just awful. Seeing that young man with his brains splattered on the pavement."

"Not a pretty sight," Kerney said. "You told the deputy you didn't recall a vehicle passing in the opposite direction just before you came upon the accident."

Clearly nervous for some reason, Bodecker cast a glance at the back office, looked around the empty showroom, and fiddled with the cuff of his shirt. "Let me ask the boss if I can take a break. He wouldn't want me talking to you on company time, and I don't want to lose my job. It's hard to get by on Social Security."

"No problem," Kerney said. "I'll wait."

Bodecker made a short trip to talk to someone in the office and then beckoned Kerney to follow him through double swinging doors into a storage room.

Outside on the loading dock, Bodecker smiled and lit a cigarette. "Too addicted to stop and too old to care," he said, as he sucked in the smoke. "I didn't see a car pass me."

"Are you positive?" Kerney asked.

"Almost certain. There wasn't a lot of traffic on the road. I think the snowstorm in the mountains may have had something to do with it. It was coming down really heavy when I left Ruidoso."

"Didn't you tell the deputy the sun was setting when you got to the accident?"

"It was. You know how it goes out here. Snowing in one place and clear twenty miles away."

"No clouds?"

"Sure, but the sun broke through for a little while right around dusk."

"For how long?"

"About the time I found the bicyclist on the road."

"Did you give this information to the deputy?"

"The only thing he asked me is what time I got there and what the weather was like when I arrived. Then he got busy setting up things so people wouldn't pile into each other."

"You directed traffic until the deputy arrived."

"On the eastbound lane. Another driver stopped and did the same in the opposite lane."

"Did you let cars go through before the deputy arrived?" Kerney asked, wondering if any evidence could have been scattered or destroyed by vehicles passing by.

Bodecker nodded and took another drag. "On the shoulders. It wasn't my place to stop them."

"About how many cars went by?"

"Maybe ten or twelve."

"Did you see anything in the road? A hazard, any litter?"

"Not in the road. There were some cardboard boxes off to one side. I moved them so the cars could get by."

"Where were the cardboard boxes before you moved them?"

"When I first got there? Near the dead man. Then the wind picked up and blew them across the highway."

"Into the eastbound lane?"

"Yes."

"Did you tell that to the deputy?"

"No," Bodecker replied. "Like I said, he was real busy. As soon as the first firefighters showed up I left."

"What about the other driver who stopped?"

"He drove away the same time I did." Bodecker brushed ashes off his jacket, ground out his smoke with the toe of his shoe, and kicked it off the loading dock. "I've gotta get back. I work only the slowest sales days of the week, so I don't earn much in commissions. And the salary isn't all that great, either."

"That doesn't sound fair."

Bodecker smiled ruefully and shrugged his slightly stooped shoulders. "Old geezers like me don't get the gravy jobs. But it beats eating canned pork and beans for a week before my Social Security check arrives."

Kerney sat in the newsroom with the meteorologist of a local television station and asked him to confirm weather conditions on the day of Arthur Langsford's death. Round-faced, with a toothy smile and a swept-back stylish haircut, the man swung his attention to his computer, punched up data from the National Weather Service, pointed a stubby finger at the monitor, and traced a series of contour lines.

"A fast-moving low pressure front from the Gulf of Mexico entered the state that morning, crossed the southwest quadrant, stalled over the Sacramento Mountains, dumped eight inches of snow on Ruidoso, and then petered out," he said.

"Did it move east toward Roswell at all?" Kerney asked.

The man shook his head. "It was dry as a bone on the plains. Compared to Ruidoso we had a twenty-degree difference in our high temperature that day. Warm and sunny."

"What about the cloud cover around sunset in the foothills?"

"By the ten o'clock news that night, Roswell was mostly cloudy with a sharp drop in temperature. I'd say we probably had the same conditions in the foothills at sunset. The front slowed as it broke up."

"So with the winter sun low in the sky, it's likely there wouldn't have been a problem with glare or blinding sunshine in late afternoon."

"That would be my bet," the meteorologist said, as he swung the task chair to face Kerney, his television-camera smile firmly in place. "This is a first for me. I've never been asked by the police to verify weather conditions. It must be important. What kind of case is it?"

The man's interest put Kerney's guard up. He didn't need a TV weatherman passing along a hot tip to the newsroom staff. "It's an internal matter."

Recognition showed on the man's face. "Wait a minute, aren't you the officer who shot the state police sergeant in Alamogordo? Yeah, you are. Deputy Chief Kerney. Now I've got it."

"I'll let you get back to work," Kerney said, as he crossed to the door. "Thanks for your help."

Behind him, Kerney heard footsteps. At the door, he glanced back and saw the man whispering to a young female reporter at a nearby desk. She looked at Kerney with blatant curiosity, reached for a notebook, and dogged him out of the building, calling his name and firing questions.

He made it to his unit without comment, waved, cranked the engine, and drove off. She trotted alongside the unit shouting questions as he picked up speed. In the rearview mirror he watched her slap the notebook against a leg in frustration and hurry back inside. He doubted that her interest in pursuing the story had cooled.

Senior Patrol Officer Tim Dwyer had a brisk, intelligent look, a self-confident manner, and a straightforward style. Had he been wearing a business suit instead of his state police uniform, Kerney would have pegged him as an up-and-coming corporate executive. One of a handful of accident reconstruction experts in the department, Dwyer was frequently used to handle complex vehicular investigations.

In a small office at the Roswell district headquarters, where Dwyer was assigned, Kerney laid out the facts and his suspicions surrounding Arthur Langsford's death.

Dwyer had greeted him with guarded detachment, which Kerney figured to be directly related to the Shockley incident and the back channel gossip about it circulating within the department. When he finished telling Dwyer want he wanted, the officer nodded curtly, asked for the accident report, and read it without comment. Kerney watched in silence as Dwyer spread Waxman's photographs, field sketch, and his field reconstruction drawing on the desk, and gave them a close look.

When he was done he stacked the paperwork in a neat pile and looked up. "Ninety percent of all vehicle accidents are caused by driver error," he said. "This one fits the profile, but what made the driver swerve is anybody's guess. If those cardboard boxes were empty, the wind could have been blowing them back and forth across the road between the fence lines like Ping-Pong balls. Or maybe the driver was daydreaming or changing stations on the car radio."

"Waxman was wrong about glare blinding the driver," Kerney said.

Dwyer shrugged. "That takes away a contributing factor, but you can add a dozen more guesses. Like the driver's state of mind, for instance. Was the driver drunk, angry with a spouse, or pissed off at a boss? Since the driver left the scene and Waxman had no witnesses, his hypothesis was as good as any others."

"Am I spinning my wheels?" Kerney asked.

"The typical reason for leaving an accident scene is to avoid arrest. Beyond that, trying to determine driver intent gets real iffy, especially when there's a lack of physical evidence."

"Is it worth your time to take another look?"

Dwyer nodded. "I'll visit the site and rework Waxman's figures, just to make sure he did them the right way. Distance, speed, skid resistance, the radius of the curve, the coordinates—that sort of stuff."

"According to the highway department, the roadway hasn't been changed since the accident," Kerney said.

"That's good to know. I'm going to need to use the same reference points."

Kerney's bum knee had locked up. He stretched his leg and rubbed the aching tendon. "There's nothing in the report that piques your interest?"

"One thing," Dwyer replied. "Waxman should've gone back to the accident scene the next day to re-photograph the skid marks in full light, and he didn't do it. These prints you brought along don't show me anything. For example, I can't tell where the skid marks changed. Without that, determining point of impact is almost impossible."

"Waxman's report says the driver braked ten feet prior to impact," Kerney said.

"I'd like to see the proof, and the pictures don't show it. Since it's still an open case, the sheriff's department should have the negatives in evidence. I'll get them, scan them into the computer, and do enhancements. It might tell us something."

"Good enough. Thanks for your help."

"Anytime, Chief."

Tim Dwyer watched Kerney limp out. He had wanted to ask why the chief deputy was working a homicide instead of running his division. And why was Major Hutchinson sitting in Kerney's office up in Santa Fe? Was Kerney on his way out, as many officers hoped? Or was the speculation true that Chief Baca was protecting his old friend's ass and retirement pension?

Dwyer decided he didn't want to know. He picked up the phone and dialed the sheriff's office.

Once a residence, the funeral home near downtown Roswell looked like a southern plantation manor house. A two-story portico was supported by large Georgian columns, and the building was painted a pristine white. It sat in the middle of a carefully manicured lawn enclosed by an ornate wrought-iron fence.

Kerney introduced himself to the funeral director and asked to see the guest book for Vernon Langsford, who was on display in the main viewing parlor.

"We've had literally hundreds of guests," Barry Bishop said as he handed Kerney the guest book. "I expect a great many more will come to visit before tomorrow's service."

Close to Kerney in age, Bishop had a puffy face, wore a suit jacket that hung loosely on his skinny frame, and spoke in hushed tones.

Kerney scanned the book. It would be impossible to attempt contact with everyone who'd been by to pay their respects. "When is the service?" he asked.

"Tomorrow morning at nine, with interment to follow," Bishop said, noting the name of the church.

"Has Ms. Langsford given you a preferred seating list for family and friends?"

"Yes."

"I'd like a copy."

Bishop's eyes stopped smiling. "Surely, you're joking."

"I can get a court order, if need be," Kerney said.

"That's not necessary. I'll get it for you." Bishop stalked into a office, returned with a typed piece of paper, and handed it over.

Twenty names were on the list. Kerney didn't recognize any of them. "Do you know any of these people?" he asked.

"Those who are local, I do," Bishop replied.

"Run them down for me," Kerney said.

"People are grieving," Bishop said stiffly. "I don't think this is an appropriate time to be conducting police interviews."

"Would you rather have me stop them for questioning outside the church?" Kerney asked.

Bishop blanched at the thought, and Kerney left with the low-down on twelve of Linda Langsford's preferred guests.

Rather than wait for the evidence officer at the sheriff's department to find the film negatives and call him back, Tim Dwyer decided to use his time at the accident scene. The state highway was a major east-west artery and big trucks and motorists roared by in both directions, only marginally slowing down when they caught sight of the warning lights flashing on Dwyer's unit.

He parked at the bottom of the hill and walked up the asphalt shoulder. At the top of the incline he looked down the road in the direction Arthur Langsford had been traveling. Even at top speed on a bicycle, coming out of the curve, the rider should have been able to stay on the shoulder, see the oncoming car, and make an adjustment. Waxman had made no mention of bike skid marks in his report, which Dwyer founding interesting. The most common panic reaction to avoid a crash is to hit the brakes.

At the bottom of the curve, Tim located the culvert and the

county line sign Waxman has used as his reference points. As traffic allowed, he ran measurements to verify Waxman's distances and found the spot Waxman had identified as the point of impact. He sprayed the location with orange paint, and photographed it from various angles.

Back at his unit, he punched in numbers on a pocket calculator, entered the formulas, and checked Waxman's math. Waxman had been right on, if he'd found the true point of impact.

Tim looked back up the hill. What was the first point where the driver could spot a hazard in the road? He popped the trunk of his unit, grabbed his metal file case, carried it up to the impact point, and placed it on the shoulder. At the bottom of the hill, he could see the case clearly, and it was less than half the size of one of the three cardboard boxes.

Figuring driver distraction, Tim cut the distance in half, and found himself thinking there was still time to slow and veer to avoid hitting the boxes or Langsford.

He returned his file case to his unit just as his call sign came over the radio. The sheriff's office had found the negatives and still had the pieces of the bicycle in evidence.

"Good deal," Tim said to the dispatcher. "I'm on my way."

In the sheriff's department evidence room, Tim sifted through the box containing the mangled parts of Arthur Langsford's mountain bike. The struts, front wheel, and handlebars were crumpled, and the control levers connected to the brake and gear shift cables dangled from the handlebars. Deep scratches in the metal showed that the bike had skidded across the pavement for a considerable distance before coming to a stop.

Tim opened the manila envelope attached to the lid and read through Waxman's forensic analysis request and the lab's results. Waxman had asked only for the identification of any foreign paint, and none had been found.

The back wheel, tire, and the support piece that anchored the rear brakes to the frame were intact. Tim took a closer look. The brake pads were frozen in a closed position against the sidewall of the tire, which was pretty good proof that Langsford saw the car coming and reacted. That, coupled with the fact that most of the road damage to the handlebars was concentrated on one side, made it very likely that Langsford had both braked and turned to avoid the collision.

Coming down that hill at thirty-five or forty miles a hour, Langsford must have put skid marks on the pavement. Waxman had flat-out missed them.

Tim's interest in the negatives jumped several notches. He dumped the bike parts in the box, resealed the lid, signed the evidence slip, and got back to district headquarters in a hurry. At the computer terminal, he scanned in the negatives and punched them up on the screen one at a time. He played with background colors until he had the right mix that highlighted the vehicle skid marks.

He looked, and looked again. The tread marks were thick and conspicuous on the outer side of the left front tire, and on the inner side of the right front tire, but otherwise barely discernible. What Waxman had taken to be skid marks was clearly a hard turn of the front wheels. But at what speed?

He punched up another image and the slender lines of the bicycle skid marks jumped out at him. He put the two photographs side-by-side on the screen, leaned back in his chair, and studied them intently before thumbing through the autopsy report. Then he factored in the new information and reworked Waxman's original calculations.

The new figures didn't work. He checked his wristwatch, printed hard copies of the negatives, and headed for the door. He needed to take new measurements at the site and visit with Marcos Narvaiz, the first volunteer firefighter on the scene, to see if he could fill in any of the remaining blanks.

Working the list of locals for preferred seating at the funeral services didn't yield anything of value. Death had cleansed Vernon Langsford of all human frailties, and Kerney found himself listening to clichéd eulogies that gave no true sense of the man, the most notable ones coming from a sitting district court judge, a former district attorney, and a retired city police chief.

He called around to motels and bed and breakfast inns and located six of the eight out-of-town guests who were on Linda Langsford's list. He got to the Bitter Lake Bed and Breakfast just as Leonora Wister was leaving her Santa Fe–style cottage accommodations.

"Vernon was my first cousin," Leonora said, as she stood next to a late-model white Cadillac with Texas plates. "We grew up together."

"Were you close as children?" Kerney asked, trying not to stare at Leonora's blue gray curly hair. She clutched a large purse against her stomach in an attempt to hide her thick waist from view.

"Yes, until high school, when my family moved to San Antonio. After that, I would see him during occasional visits to Roswell."

"What kind of kid was he?"

"Wild," Leonora replied.

"In what way?"

"He became interested in girls at a very early age."

"Can you give me specifics?"

"Not really. Maybe Danny Hobeck can. He was Vernon's best friend all through school."

Kerney scanned his list. Hobeck was one of the out-of-town guests he'd been unable to locate. "Do you know where he's staying?"

"With his sister," Leonora replied.

Kerney asked for and got a name and address.

"How can prying into Vernon's childhood possibly help you catch his killer?" Leonora asked.

"I'm not sure it will," Kerney said.

Danny Hobeck was out renewing old acquaintanceships, but his sister, Margie, was home. A thin, nervous woman in her late sixties with rounded shoulders and apprehensive eyes, she reluctantly let Kerney in. He sat with her in a living room entirely given over to her three cats. There were scratching poles in each corner for the tabbies to use. Rubber mice, tennis balls, and pet toys were scattered across the oak floor. Next to the pet door that offered access to and from the front porch, three food bowls were lined up, each inscribed with a name—Frisky, Mellow, and Violet. Framed photographs of the cats were prominently displayed on top of a television set.

The tabbies padded back and forth across the room, tails upright, giving Kerney a wide berth.

"I understand Vernon and Danny were best friends," Kerney said.

"I wouldn't call it a friendship."

"What would you call it?"

"Vernon led Danny around by the nose," she said after some hesitation.

"You don't sound well-disposed toward Vernon."

"He wasn't a very nice boy."

"Care to tell me why you feel that way?" Kerney asked.

Margie leaned forward in her easy chair and snapped her fingers. One of the cats turned and jumped into her lap. She stroked it and said nothing.

"How much younger are you than Danny?" Kerney asked.

"Five years."

"Does he have a family?"

"Two grown children. His wife died last year."

"And your family?"

Margie recoiled slightly and wet her lips. "I never married."

"Will you be attending the funeral services?"

Margie scratched the cat's chin while the ignored felines converged at her feet. "No."

"Care to tell me why?"

She patted the arm of the chair and the animals jumped into her lap. "I don't want to go." She ran a hand over the yellow cat's back, and it arched and purred.

"Would Danny be able to tell me why you don't like Vernon?"

"He would never do that." Her tone was biting.

"When will he be back?"

"I don't know."

"I'll call for him this evening."

"He won't talk to you."

Kerney let himself out wondering why so many people in Langsford's life, past and present, needed to keep secrets.

"I remember that call," Marcos Narvaiz said. He poured Tim Dwyer a cup of coffee at his kitchen table, returned the pot to the stove, and ran a hand over his shaggy, curly gray hair.

"Tell me about it," Tim said.

"I was the first responder on the scene. The whole thing was a mess. Waxman did the best he could under the circumstances."

Narvaiz's house was in the high foothills on the highway to Ruidoso. It sat between the village post office and the volunteer fire department. Marcos served as fire chief, a position he'd held for ten years, and his wife ran the post office. Tim had worked many accidents with Marcos and knew him well.

"I know the victim was separated from the bicycle, but Waxman didn't get a photograph of where it came to rest," Tim said.

Marcos laughed. "He ran out of film after he did the three-sixty shots of the victim and the skid marks. You should have heard him cursing about it."

Tim pulled out Waxman's field drawing. "So where did the bicycle wind up?"

Marcos pointed to a spot. "About here."

"You're sure?"

"Yeah. I helped him inventory and bag the bike parts for evidence. He wanted the debris cleaned up fast so he could reopen the highway."

"How long was the debris trail?"

"The bike shattered on impact," Marcos said. "From the rear wheel to the handlebars, I'd say it was a good thirty feet."

Tim marked the spot on the field drawing Marcos had pointed to and nodded. "About the same distance Langsford was catapulted over the vehicle."

"What are you looking for?" Marcos asked. "It was a clear-cut hit-and-run."

"The driver's intent," Tim replied.

"What kind of magic do you use to figure that one out?"

"It's guesswork, and I can't prove it, but I think the driver deliberately ran into that bicycle."

"What if the driver was drunk?" Marcos countered.

"Even drunks hit the brakes and take evasive action before impact. Their reactions are way too late and slow, but they do it."

"You got the skid marks from the car," Marcos said.

"They're front-end yaw marks from a hard turn of the wheels into the cyclist," Tim said. "I calculated distance, speed, and zero skid resistance at the scene. The vehicle was traveling at sixty miles an hour. Langsford went flying, landed on his head, and bounced like a deflated rubber ball, according to the autopsy. His internal injuries were equivalent to falling from a three-story building."

"Jesus," Marcos said. "You're saying this was murder, not vehicular manslaughter."

Tim nodded. "I'd never be able to prove criminal intent in a court of law, but Waxman blew the investigation, big time."

After talking with the on-duty motel employees, all of them women except for the manager and the cook in the restaurant, Robert Duran left fairly well satisfied that none had a vendetta against Chief Kerney. Most of them recognized Kerney only as part of the state police contingent staying at the motel, and the few who knew the chief had been responsible for shooting Randy Shockley didn't act distressed about it. On top of that, no one admitted to personally knowing Randy Shockley.

He started working the businesses along the strip across the street from the motel, concentrating on those within easy walking distance. He stopped in at a fast-food joint, a service station, a package goods store, and a run-down motel that catered to low-budget travelers, and then took a break at a mom-and-pop restaurant. He sat at the counter and ordered a cup of coffee. When it came he asked the woman if she'd heard any talk about the shooting of Sergeant Shockley.

"Everybody talks about it, but a little less each day," the woman said.

Maybe pushing fifty, the woman had a pudgy nose and very tiny ears. She swatted at a fly with a counter rag and missed.

"Are people still upset about it?" Robert asked.

"I wouldn't say that. Most of them just think cops are plain stupid. They steal and then shoot each other. It doesn't make folks feel real safe and protected, if you know what I mean. Why do you ask?"

Robert took a sip of his coffee before answering. "I'm a cop."

"Hey, I'm not one of those people who badmouths the police."

"I can see that. Have you heard anybody express outrage about the shooting? Somebody who felt sympathetic toward Sergeant Shockley?"

"Henry Waters come to mind. But nobody pays any attention to him."

"Why is that?"

"He's obsessed about police work. He's in his forties and has always wanted to be a cop. He's a sweet guy but not too bright. He once had a job as a security guard some years ago but got canned. He usually stops in before and after work for a cup."

"Has he been here today?"

"Yeah, this afternoon. He usually sits at the counter, but today he drank his coffee at a window booth and then left in a hurry."

Robert looked out the window. It had a clear view of the motel parking lot. He asked the woman if Henry had been in for coffee on the mornings Kerney's unit had been vandalized.

"He's been here every morning this week and last," the woman answered.

"What did he say about the Shockley shooting?" Robert asked.

"Something like no police officer deserved to die just because he did a little stealing, and that a cop killer, no matter who he is, was the worst kind of animal."

"Know where Henry lives?" Robert asked.

"I sure don't, but it's in the neighborhood."

"Where does he work?"

"He's a bagger and stock boy at Shop n' Save Hardware."

"Mind if I look in your outside trash bin?"

"Sure. What for?"

Robert put a five-dollar bill on the counter. "You make a good cup of coffee."

Outside in the trash he found a partially used quart of white latex paint and a cheap fifty-nine-cent brush, the bristles stiff with dried paint. Shop n' Save price stickers were still attached.

He bagged them, tagged them, and went looking for Henry Waters.

10

After meeting again with Tim Dwyer, Kerney stood outside the Roswell district headquarters, his thoughts fixed on the officer's assessment of Arthur Langsford's death. Knowing that three members of one family had been murdered in a nine-year span still didn't answer the fundamental questions of who and why. Were the murders linked or unrelated? If they were linked, one killer might well have murdered eight people, and was targeting Linda Langsford as his next victim. If not, three killers were at large, all with different motives.

Each crime had a unique signature, which made the likelihood of distinct killers a strong possibility. Add in the nine years separating Arthur's death from Vernon's murder, and the argument for different perpetrators gained even more credibility.

Kerney wasn't willing to lay aside the equally plausible notion of a vendetta against the Langsfords. What could have caused it remained obscure. In whatever direction he chose to look, no clear-cut motives emerged. All he had was a very rich, highly respected judge with a not-so-secret love life, a dead wife who may have been murdered by mistake, and a son killed for reasons unknown.

As for suspects, there was only Eric Langsford, who still hadn't been found, according to the latest update from Lee Sedillo.

Commuter traffic rumbled along the highway and a faint sunset put an anemic yellow glow on the western horizon. Kerney stepped toward his unit just as Clayton Istee drove up and cut him off.

Kerney nodded a greeting.

"My mother doesn't speak for me," Clayton said bluntly through the open car window. He got out and slammed the door.

"I never assumed that she did."

"How would you know what my mother does or doesn't do?"

"I don't," Kerney replied.

"Then don't try to bullshit me about something you know nothing about."

"That wasn't my intent," Kerney said.

Clayton stared hard at Kerney and took a deep breath. "Forget it," he said, turning on his heel.

"Wait a minute," Kerney said.

"What for?" Clayton said, as he swung back around. "You're too damn hard to talk to. I keep thinking I should try to get to know you better. But every time I see you, you just shut me down."

"I'm not very good at opening up to people."

Clayton paused. "I hear the same thing from my wife." The harshness in his voice eased a bit.

"There you go," Kerney said with a smile. "Maybe it's both of us."

Clayton's shoulders tightened. "I'm not like you."

"Would that be so terrible?" Kerney asked.

Clayton didn't answer.

"Let's find a better place to talk," Kerney said. "I'll buy you a drink or a cup of coffee."

"Coffee will do," Clayton said. "I don't drink."

At a strip-mall diner, where most of the stores sold antiques, used books, old furniture, and knickknacks put on consignment by the sons and daughters of parents who had retired to Roswell before passing on, Kerney tried to break the ice by telling Clayton the story of how, as a boy, he'd helped his father deliver cattle to the Mescalero village where the resort and casino now stood.

"My mother grew up in that village," Clayton said.

Kerney nodded. "My father sold those cattle to her father. We used to joke about it in college."

"Joke about what?"

"About how we might have met a lot sooner."

"Why did you walk out on her?"

"Excuse me?"

"She was carrying your baby."

"Isabel never told me about you."

"I don't believe that."

"Is that what's been troubling you about me?" Kerney asked.

"You couldn't see that she was pregnant?"

"She broke off the relationship six weeks before our graduation. I went into the army and she went home to Mescalero. Count back from your birthday and do the math. She wasn't showing."

"And she never said anything to you about being pregnant?"

"That's right. You haven't heard this before?"

"No," Clayton replied, dropping his gaze from Kerney's face.

"So, as far as you were concerned, I was just some jerk who took advantage of your mother."

"What else was I supposed to think?"

"You never questioned Isabel about me?"

"You don't question my mother." Clayton paused and raised his eyes to Kerney's face. "Are you being straight with me on this?"

"I'd be a fool to bullshit you. Maybe you need to have a talk with Isabel."

"Maybe I do. Were you serious about feeling bad about missing out on being my father?"

"It would have meant a lot to me."

"Having a lot of uncles around is one thing," Clayton said, letting the thought fade away.

"But it's not the same as having a father," Kerney said.

All Clayton could do was nod. "Did you like my mother, Kerney? I mean, really care about her, back in college?"

"I more than liked her. I thought we had a good chance to make it as a couple. I tried to get back together with her."

Clayton's expression hardened. "Now I know you're fucking with me. My mother never heard from you again."

"I wrote her letters for the next six months, before I shipped out to Vietnam," Kerney said. "She never answered any of them."

Clayton stared at the wall. "She never told me about that."

"There's a lot neither of us know about your mother's decisions."

"Maybe so." Clayton stood and dropped some bills on the table. "I've got to go."

"Clayton."

"What?"

Kerney got to his feet. "Have you told your children about me?"

Clayton blushed slightly before answering. "Not yet."

"Do what you think is best."

"This whole thing is a mess," Clayton grumbled.

"Give it some time."

"I'm a grown man. I don't need a father."

"Maybe we could be friends," Kerney said.

"I don't make friends easily."

"You could give it a try."

"Yeah, maybe," Clayton said, as he turned and left.

From his motel room, Kerney tried several times to reach Danny Hobeck at his sister's house. All he got was Margie's answering machine. He left his number, asked Hobeck to call, and started unpacking. He was down to one set of clean clothes and needed to find a Laundromat. The phone rang as he was about to leave with a bag full of dirty laundry, and the Roswell dispatcher patched through a call from Clark Beck, the trucker who'd broken down at the Three Rivers turnoff.

"My wife said you needed to talk to me," Beck said. "What can I do for you?"

"You lost your water pump at Three Rivers and had to get towed to Alamogordo."

"That's right. Cost me eight hours of down time," Beck said.

"Did you see any cars coming or going on the Three Rivers road?"

"Yeah, I saw one come out and make the turn heading for Tularosa."

"What time was that?"

"Maybe fifteen minutes after I broke down."

"Did you get a look at the vehicle?"

"Just the back end," Beck replied. "It was one of those Japanese import sport-utility vehicles. A Honda."

"You're sure of that?" Kerney asked.

"Mister, I'm sure. I look at the ass-end of cars six days a week, all day long. Honda SUVs have vertical taillights that run along the sides of the rear window. It's real distinctive."

"It wasn't a minivan?"

"Minivans have a rounded roofline; not boxy like the Honda SUV."

"You just saw the Honda?" Kerney asked.

"A few cars passed me on the highway. But the Honda was the only one I saw on the Three Rivers road."

"Thanks."

"No sweat, officer. Hope it helps."

Kerney grabbed his dirty laundry and headed out. As far as he knew, no one on the suspect list drove or owned a Honda SUV. He called Lee Sedillo from his unit, gave him the vehicle information, and asked for a canvas of car-rental companies in the state.

"Will do, Chief," Lee said.

"Give Tim Dwyer a call at the Roswell district office."

"What's he got?"

"Evidence that says Vernon's oldest son, Arthur, was murdered."

"So somebody is systematically wiping out the family," Lee said.

"Possibly," Kerney replied. "Or we've got three different killers who need to be caught. Is anything happening with Eric's sister?"

"Nada. She's home. Family and friends have been dropping by."

"Keep a close watch on her."

"Ten-four."

The fast-food hamburger Kerney bought after leaving the Laundromat didn't sit well in his gut. He sat in the unit across from Margie Hobeck's house with binoculars and watched her walk back and forth in front of her living room window. He dialed her number on his cell phone and Margie froze in front of the telephone but didn't pick up. The answering machine clicked on and he left another message for Danny Hobeck. Margie punched a button on the machine, and Kerney figured she'd deleted it.

She bent down out of view for a moment and came up holding one of the cats. She cradled it like a baby in her arms and started pacing back and forth in front of the window. She finally left the living room and Kerney settled in to wait.

After two hours, a car made a wide turn onto the street and came to a messy stop in front of Margie's house. A man pulled himself out and wobbled slowly up the front walk.

Kerney intercepted him at the porch step. "Danny Hobeck?"

The man lurched to a stop. "Who are you?"

Kerney flipped open his badge case. "State police. I have a few questions."

Hobeck pulled his shoulders back, straightened up, and squinted at the shield. His breath smelled of alcohol. "If this is about Vernon, I've got nothing to say to you."

"Have you been drinking, Mr. Hobeck?"

"I've had a few."

"More than a few, I'd guess."

Hobeck adjusted his tie and said nothing.

"Would you like to spend the night in jail?" Kerney asked.

"For what?"

"Driving drunk," Kerney answered.

Hobeck snorted and gestured at his parked car. "I'm not driving. I'm standing in my sister's front yard, on private property, minding my own business."

The porch light came on, revealing Hobeck's tanned face, thinning gray hair, and watery brown eyes. Margie Hobeck stared fearfully at Kerney through the front window, stroking the cat she held in her arms. The animal twisted its torso and clawed Margie's arm. She released it and remained motionless.

"Let's do a field sobriety test," Kerney said, turning his attention back to Danny.

"Don't be ridiculous," Hobeck said, as he tried to push his way past Kerney.

Kerney held him up. "Do you know what a lawful order is, Mr. Hobeck?"

Hobeck nodded his head in disgust. "Yeah, it's something a cop tells you that you have to do. Ask your damn questions."

"You were Vernon's boyhood chum."

"That's right. I've been his friend all my life."

"What was Vernon like?"

"As a kid? Starting out, he was just like all the rest of us, until his father started making big money in the oil and gas fields."

"That changed him?"

"He got spoiled."

"How so?"

"By the money, what else? His father gave him everything, and Vernon got used to it real fast."

"Did he make any enemies?"

"I wouldn't say he made enemies; mostly kids were envious of him."

"What about later in life?"

"Vernon won folks' respect as a lawyer and a judge. He had a good marriage and a good family life. He never acted high and mighty because he had money. Hell, he took what his daddy left him and built on it. People admired that."

"Your sister doesn't seem to think much of Vernon."

Danny chuckled sourly. "My old maid sister? She doesn't like anybody much."

"Why doesn't she like Vernon?"

"Because she's strange in the head," Hobeck replied. "Hates men. Hell, she barely tolerates me. She's not gay or anything like that. She's just a dried-up old maid."

"Has she always been that way?"

"Forever."

"Is she under any kind of special care?"

"You mean like a shrink? No, since she retired she just lives in her own dreamworld. Collects these ugly salt and pepper shakers, dotes on her cats, gardens, refuses to go out except to run errands or shop."

Kerney glanced at the living room window. Margie was gone. "She has no particular grievance against Vernon?"

"Like I said, Margie is strange. What is all this bullshit?" Hobeck asked, suddenly suspicious. "You can't be thinking she had anything to do with Vernon's death."

"Has she said anything to you about his death?"

"Not a word."

"Why would she tell me Vernon wasn't a nice boy?"

"Who knows what gets into her head? I don't see her much, and we rarely talk. Mostly I just send her money now and then. She's my kid sister, so I feel a sense of responsibility. But if you do anything she doesn't like, she shuts you down and won't talk about it. That's just the way she is."

Hobeck forced a friendly smile and continued, "Look, I'd really appreciate it if you'd just leave her alone. There's no sense upsetting her. The way it is, she'll probably spend the night walking up and down the stairs. She does that when she gets agitated."

"Talking to you has been sufficient, Mr. Hobeck."

Relief flooded across Hobeck's face. "Thanks. Sorry I sounded so abrupt." He smiled sheepishly. "I guess I did raise a few too many glasses in Vernon's memory."

"That happens. Don't drive anymore tonight."

Hobeck reached for the porch rail, steadied himself, and planted a foot on the step. "I don't plan to. Can't hold my liquor like in the old days. I'm going to bed."

"Good idea."

Margie was back at the window again. She smiled as Kerney stepped off the porch and waved bye-bye, folding her fingers over the palm of her hand.

In the morning, before the funeral services for Vernon, Kerney stationed three agents inconspicuously outside the church: two with video cameras to record everyone in attendance, and one to keep watch in case Eric made an appearance. A fourth agent stayed on Linda Langsford.

He left after the mourners arrived and drove to Margie Hobeck's house. Danny's car was gone, the front curtains were drawn, and his knock went unanswered. An older sedan was parked in the detached garage, so Kerney went to the backyard to see if Margie was in her garden. Only Margie's cats greeted him.

When he came around the side of the house he found Agent Duran waiting for him.

"What brings you to Roswell?" Kerney asked.

"Last night I arrested the guy who trashed your unit, Chief. Lieutenant Sedillo sent me over to fill you in."

"Was it a cop who did it?"

"Nope. He's a civilian by the name of Henry Waters. He's forty-three and has a steel plate in his head from an automobile accident that happened when he was in high school. He's got an IQ that puts him in the mildly retarded range, and a fixation about law enforcement. He made a voluntary confession, and I've got some solid physical evidence to go with it. He's locked up."

"Did he act alone?"

"Yeah. You should've seen his apartment, Chief. The walls are plastered with photos and newspaper articles about cops, he has a collection of patches and caps from about a hundred different law enforcement agencies, and he keeps a police scanner going full time when he's home. He has study guides for police officer examinations, dozens of law enforcement equipment catalogs, and an outdated set of criminal statutes the local library discarded. He met me at the door wearing a city PD shirt with a security guard badge pinned on it. He filched the shirt from an unlocked cruiser a couple of years ago."

"Did he give you a reason for his actions?"

"He said you shouldn't have shot Sergeant Shockley."

"He's right about that. Is he crazy, dangerous, or both?"

Robert didn't agree with Kerney's self-criticism, but knew better than to comment. "According to his doctor, because of the head wound he's got organic brain syndrome, which screws up his thinking. But he's stable and not dangerous."

"Any priors?" Kerney asked.

"He's got a clean sheet, and everybody I talked to said he never caused any trouble. It's kinda sad, Chief. He was a normal kid until the accident. After that, his mental functioning went downhill. His sister told me that he's always wanted to be a cop."

"Did he give you any problems?"

"Just the opposite. He talked freely about what he'd done. After I finished taking his statement, I told him a few things about Shockley. He got real apologetic. Said he was sorry. Wanted me to be sure and tell you. Then he asked if I could help him join the department as a recruit."

"That is sad," Kerney said.

"His public defender wants him to cop a plea. She's asked for a psychiatric evaluation. I don't see Henry getting anything more than some county jail time out of this."

"Thanks, Robert," Kerney said.

"Anytime, Chief. Lieutenant Sedillo asked me to tell you there's no record of any of the suspects renting a Honda SUV around the time of the murders."

"I'm not surprised," Kerney said.

One family had been out of town during the door-to-door canvas of Penelope Gibben's neighbors. Kerney stood on a lovely wraparound porch of a Queen Anne Victorian one street over from Penelope's house, and rang the bell. The woman who answered stood six feet tall and looked to be in her mid-thirties. Dressed in workout sweats, she was breathing hard and had a sheen of perspiration on her face.

"Mrs. Peters," Kerney asked, holding up his shield.

"I'm Dr. Peters."

"Are you a medical doctor?"

Peters ran a hand towel across her face and nodded. "I work in the ER at the hospital. So does my husband. What can I do for you?"

"Do you know Penelope Gibben?"

"Of course. I've known her almost all my life."

"How long have you lived in the neighborhood?"

"I grew up in this house. Has something happened to Penelope?"

"No, she's fine. I'm investigating Judge Langsford's murder. Did you know the judge at all?"

"I knew he was a frequent visitor at Penelope's. His car was parked there quite often when I was a child."

"What did you think of Judge Langsford?"

"As a kid? To me he was just another adult."

"Did you know Penelope and Langsford were lovers?"

"That was the common assumption among some of the neighbors."

"Was it yours?"

Peters laughed. "Not at the time. I was too young to pay any attention to that kind of thing. I used to play occasionally with Linda and Penelope's niece. It was all very ordinary and innocent."

"Kay Murray?"

"Yes. Kay stayed with Penelope during summer vacations for three or four years. Judge Langsford often brought Linda with him when he came to visit. Except he wasn't a judge then."

"Did Mrs. Langsford ever bring Linda over to play with Kay?"

"I never saw or met Mrs. Langsford. It was always Linda's father who brought her to Penelope's."

"How old were you at the time?"

"Eight."

"Were you good friends with Linda and Kay?"

"I wouldn't say that. I was much more interested in sports than either of them, and we traveled in different circles. We played together once in a while. We'd ride our bikes to the park or I would visit with them if they were out in Penelope's front yard."

"Would you say that Linda and Kay were good friends?"

"They got along well."

"But they weren't close?"

"I got the feeling they tolerated each other."

"What gave you that feeling?"

"They would argue a lot."

"About?" Kerney asked.

"They liked to play with dolls, and I wasn't really into that. They'd bicker about which doll would be the bride, or the mother, or the daughter. They liked to play dress-up and pretend they were adults. Then they'd argue about who would be the wife or the child."

"Did you get to know Kay better later on, when she moved in with Penelope?" Kerney asked.

"No, I was away at college, and I didn't see her much. We'd wave to each other when I was home. That was about it."

"Thanks. I won't keep you any longer," Kerney said.

Kerney walked to his unit wondering why Gibben had failed to mention that Kay spent several summer vacations with her as a child. Did it matter?

He wasn't sure, but decided to follow up anyway. He checked the time. It was too soon to expect Penelope to be home from the funeral services. He would swing by later.

Deedee Hall lived in an upscale Roswell neighborhood near the country club, where the streets were named for trees, and the houses were mostly two-story affairs with garish touches such as towering entryways supported by faux Greek revival columns.

Kerney sat with Mrs. Hall in her spotless country kitchen and asked her about Linda Langsford.

Deedee gave him an immaculate smile. Her blond hair was perfect, her face was perky and cute, and her figure looked trimmed and toned. Except for the first touch of age lines at the corners of her mouth, she didn't look much different from the picture taken of her as a member of the high school cheerleading squad almost twenty years ago. She even sounded like a cheerleader.

Just back from the services for Langsford, she was wearing a conservative dark gray dress.

"Linda and I were *best* friends," she said, "from kindergarten on."

"Tell me about her as a child," Kerney asked.

"She was always at my house. *Always.*"

"She didn't like it at home?"

"Her mother was usually sick with allergies, headaches, and such. It just wasn't any fun to play there. We had to be so quiet. Mrs. Langsford wasn't a well person."

"Did Linda get along with her brothers?"

"Not with Eric. He's always been weird. She was much closer to Arthur and her father."

"What about her mother?"

"Linda never minded her."

"Never?"

"Well, hardly ever. Sometimes they would argue."

"About what?"

"Where Linda could go, what she could do, who she could play with. Normal stuff. If Linda *really* wanted her own way, she'd just go to her father."

"And Judge Langsford would cave in?"

"Almost always. He couldn't deny Linda anything. It invariably threw her mother into a tizzy."

"Were there parental arguments about the children?"

Deedee shook her head. "Mrs. Langsford would just stop talking. She would barely speak to anybody. When that happened, the judge would take Linda and Arthur camping, or on a trip to Albuquerque, or some other outing."

"But not Eric?"

"He was included until he was about six years old."

"What changed?"

"He started to act like his mother, really sullen and angry all the time in a shut-down sort of way. It was like the two of them were the family outcasts."

"Did Linda and Arthur remain close?"

"Until Linda started high school and Arthur went to college. After that, they didn't see much of each other."

"What did you think of Arthur?"

"He was okay. Big man on campus type. Real popular."

Her cautious reply caught Kerney's attention. "You had reservations about him?"

Deedee nodded. "He was real randy, if you know what I mean. He thought he could have any girl he wanted."

"Did that include you?"

Deedee laughed. "He tried."

"How did Linda get along with boys?"

"She was a real Miss Goody Two-shoes."

"She dated?"

"Sure, and had boyfriends. But none of them got anywhere, if you know what I mean. I don't think she's met the right man. Either that, or she's just not interested in getting married again."

"Tell me about Linda's ex-husband."

"Bill? He's a sweet guy. He dated Linda in high school and then started seeing her again after she came home from law school. It was a whirlwind romance: they got married within a few months. Bill's father is the pastor of the biggest Baptist church in town."

"What happened to the marriage?"

"I guess they just weren't compatible. It didn't last a year. Bill left his job with the bank and moved up to Albuquerque before the divorce was final. Linda wouldn't talk about what happened, although I heard rumors that she was having an affair."

"Did Bill talk to you about it?" Kerney asked.

"Not really. I saw him in Albuquerque about a year after he'd moved. All he said was it had been a big mistake and that Linda wasn't the person she appeared to be. I thought that was *really* strange."

"Why?"

"Because they seemed like such lovebirds before the wedding."

"Have you kept in touch with Bill?"

"Sometimes I see him when he brings his family down for a visit. He remarried, has a nice wife and a cute son."

"I take it Linda doesn't like to talk about family or personal problems."

"Not ever."

"Was that true when she was younger?"

"Oh, yes. Whatever went on in the family stayed in the family. About all anybody knew was that Mrs. Langsford was sick most of the time and Eric was a problem child. That, they couldn't hide."

"Thanks."

"How can any of this possibly be helpful to you?" Deedee asked.

"It may not be."

On his way out of the neighborhood, Kerney noticed golfers in their carts puttering along on the paved pathways adjacent to the street, cruising toward the links. He noted the absence of parked cars, the clean gutters and curbs, the groomed lawns that showed no sign of the first kiss of autumn leaves, the uniform placement of mailboxes in front of each house.

Such a tidy little neighborhood, he thought, with nothing out of place. Just right for all those people who find comfort and safety in a world of uncluttered sameness.

Parked a block down from Penelope Gibben's house, Kerney watched Kay Murray's Explorer coast to a stop in the driveway. The women talked for a considerable time before Gibben got out of the car and Murray drove away. He gave it a good five minutes before approaching the house.

Penelope greeted Kerney with a haughty look, ushered him into the living room, and immediately made her feelings known.

"This is hardly the time to be bothering people with your pointless investigation," she said.

She wore a simple black mourning dress with a single strand of pearls. No grief showed on her face, only displeasure.

"I understand Kay Murray spent several childhood summer vacations with you."

"What a perplexing man you are, Chief Kerney. You come up with all these little tidbits and wave them around like important facts. Yes, she did. My sister and her husband had very little money, and it was my idea to have Kay stay with me. I wanted to expose Kay to a better way of life. Was I remiss in not telling you?"

"Vernon would bring Linda over to play with Kay."

"Yes, he would, upon occasion. Looking back on it now, surely, it must have been a capital offense."

"Were you sexually involved with Vernon at the time?"

Penelope smiled with tight lips. "Looking for more little tidbits, Chief Kerney? I was not."

"Have you heard from Eric since he left Linda's house?"

"I have not. Good day, Chief Kerney."

Frustrated by meaningless tidbits, Kerney left, thinking that Gibben's sarcasm might well be right on the mark.

It was lunch hour and the executives had not yet returned from the funeral services when Kerney arrived at the corporate offices of Ranchers' Exploration and Development. The only employee on duty, a young secretary seated at the reception desk, greeted him as though his arrival was a relief from absolute boredom.

Kerney explained that he needed to compile a list of all past and present employees as part of the investigation into the judge's murder.

The young woman nodded gravely, escorted him to the personnel director's office, showed him how to access files on the computer, and returned to the reception area to answer phones. While the printer reeled off names, addresses, and phone numbers, Kerney read through Penelope Gibben's personnel file.

She'd begun her rise up the corporate ladder long before she'd become Vernon's lover. After that, the promotions came more quickly and the salary increases were more substantial. Presently, Gibben was drawing a hefty six-figure income and held a nice chuck of corporate stock options.

For Roswell, Gibben was doing very well indeed.

Kerney shut down the computer, thanked the secretary on his way out, and went looking for Eleanor Beyer, a retired employee who'd joined Ranchers' about the same time as Gibben.

She lived in an older two-story apartment complex that had been converted into an assisted living center for senior citizens. Four rectangular buildings were sited around a central courtyard. One had been transformed into a community center consisting of a visitor's lobby, recreation area, dining room, infirmary, and offices for the administrator and medical staff.

Kerney got directions to Beyer's living unit and walked down the pathway. Mature shade trees and freshly painted park benches graced the landscaped commons, but the effort to soften the stark facades of the concrete block buildings failed. It looked like a way station for low-income seniors slated to eventually move on to equally depressing nursing homes.

It made the prospect of growing old—an idea Kerney had never found particularly appealing—even less inviting.

Eleanor Beyer opened the door to her first-floor apartment and looked at Kerney's shield.

"Ms. Beyer?" Kerney asked.

Considerably older than Penelope Gibben, she was small in stature and suffered from osteoporosis that bent her almost in half. She looked up at Kerney through thick, heavily scratched glasses that were taped together at the nose piece.

"Why are the police here?" she asked in a frail voice. "Has someone died?"

"Nothing like that. I'd like you to tell me about Penelope Gibben and Vernon Langsford."

"I haven't seen either of them for several years."

"You worked at Ranchers' Exploration and Development."

"I was the senior billing clerk until my eyesight got bad and I had to retire," Eleanor said.

"You do know Judge Langsford was murdered."

"I heard it on the evening news."

"Did you know of Penelope Gibben's relationship with the judge?"

"Everyone in the office knew about it. But if you wanted to keep your job, you never mentioned it."

"When did the affair start?"

"Some years after Penelope joined the company. I can't say exactly when. I never understood why Vernon took up with her."

"Why do you say that?"

"She was so standoffish and cold. But I suppose every man has a type of woman he's attracted to."

"Did you know Vernon's wife?"

"Oh, yes. I saw her quite often until the children were born. She was a local girl, so I knew her even before she married Vernon. He really shocked everybody when he proposed to Marsha."

"Why is that?"

"She wasn't his type at all. Vernon had a reputation as a man who only dated the best-looking women in town. Marsha wasn't particularly popular or exceptionally pretty. She was more the homemaker type. Few people expected the marriage to last. I don't think it was a happy marriage, especially after Linda and Eric were born. The children held them together."

"Did Penelope ever talk about her affair with Vernon?"

"Not that I know of. Certainly not with me. But you can't hide that sort of thing in a small town."

"Marsha never learned about it?"

"I don't think she cared to know."

"Did the judge have any enemies?"

"I really couldn't say."

"Who would know?"

"Talk to Bud and Jean McNew. He had some business dealings with Vernon that went sour, and she was about Marsha's only friend for a time."

Kerney spent an interesting hour with Bud and Jean McNew at their small ranch east of Roswell. The adobe home McNew had built on his two sections of land looked out over a sweep of sand hills that changed color from warm yellow to dull brown as passing clouds cut the sunlight.

Bud McNew, who once owned an oil drilling supply company, had been screwed by Langsford on a couple of equipment contracts back when crude prices made drilling new wells unprofitable. McNew had sued, and Langsford settled with him before the civil case went to trial.

Bud didn't think Langsford had any serious enemies, just a number of jobbers and suppliers who got rubbed the wrong way by his habit of not paying the corporate bills on time. All that changed when Langsford became a judge and corporate management was assumed by a blind trust set up to ensure that he would have no conflict of interest in any legal matters involving his companies. During Langsford's tenure on the bench, the companies had cut back on gas and oil drilling and expanded into land development, which increased his wealth several times over.

Kerney got Bud talking about Langsford and his associates and learned that Vernon had used Danny Hobeck as a contract geologist to assess state trust lands and bid on gas and oil leases for his company.

Jean McNew talked about the early days of Marsha's marriage, and how happy Marsha had seemed at the time. She never knew what soured the relationship, but always suspected it was Vernon's womanizing. According to Mrs. McNew, Vernon had a string of extramarital affairs before he "settled down" into a relationship with Penelope Gibben.

When Kerney asked her to describe Marsha Langsford's personality, Jean said that she was a submissive person who never asserted herself. She characterized most of Marsha's illness as psychosomatic. Although she couldn't say for sure, Jean felt that Marsha knew about Vernon's philandering and had simply retreated in the face of it. Arthur's tragic death had pushed her over the brink into an almost total self-imposed isolation.

After leaving Bud and Jean McNew, Kerney tried a second visit to Margie Hobeck. His knock at the door was answered by the three cats and a woman Kerney didn't know.

"Margie has gone away with her brother," the woman said. "I'm watching the cats for her." She nodded at the adjacent house. "I live next door."

"Where did she go with Danny?"

"Albuquerque. That's where he lives."

"How long will she be gone?" Kerney asked.

"Three or four days."

"Has she ever asked you to watch her cats before?"

"No, but I'm delighted to do it," the woman said with a smile. "It's about time she did something more than just stay at home."

"Did you see her or speak to her before she left?"

"No, her brother called and then brought the house key over before they left."

Kerney decided it was time to talk to Leonora Wister, Vernon's first cousin, again.

The afternoon sky had clouded over when Kerney arrived at the Bitter Lake Bed and Breakfast where Leonora Wister was staying. Her Cadillac was parked outside and a light was on in the cottage. She answered the door dressed in traveling clothes.

"Danny wasn't very happy with me for telling you where to find him," she said.

"I don't see why," Kerney said, again trying hard not to stare at Leonora's blue gray hair. "We had a pleasant conversation."

"You threatened to arrest him on the night before his best friend's funeral."

"But I didn't."

"That's true."

"I came here to ask you for your help. I know you must want Vernon's killer found."

"Of course I do, but everyone is saying that Eric killed his father."

"We don't know that for sure," Kerney said.

"How can I be of any help?"

"The more I know about Judge Langsford, his family, friends, and associates, the more I can narrow down my investigation. I know it's an uncomfortable time for me to be interviewing people, but I have no alternative."

Leonora's expression softened. "You do have a job to do, don't you? What would you like to know?"

"Tell me about Danny."

"Danny couldn't kill Vernon. Vernon meant everything to him.

Vernon's father gave Danny's father a job—the best job he ever had—and paid Danny's way through college. He was Vernon's roommate. He's had a contract with Vernon's company ever since he became a registered geologist. Without the support he got from Vernon and his father starting out, Danny would have probably been a roughneck oil worker, living in a trailer park, drawing unemployment six months out of the year."

"Did Vernon's father help any of Danny's other friends with their schooling?"

"Not that I know of. It was a special situation. Danny and Vernon were inseparable—almost like brothers. Vernon told his dad that he wouldn't go to college unless Danny went with him. And when Vernon took over the companies, he made sure that Danny had a chance to build his reputation as a petroleum geologist. He's considered one of the best in the Southwest."

"That makes a lot of things clearer. Did you know he took Margie with him to Albuquerque?"

Leonora's eyes widened. "That's amazing. I've never known Margie to budge from her house for anything other than work and necessary errands. Good for her. It's about time Margie did something besides stay at home."

"She doesn't speak highly of Vernon."

"She never got over feeling that Vernon stole her brother away from her. She used to adore Danny; followed him everywhere until Vernon took over Danny's life."

"Took over, how?"

Leonora shrugged a shoulder. It made her thick upper arm jiggle. "You know how boys are, one always has to be the leader. Vernon led and Danny followed."

On his way back to town, Kerney called Lee Sedillo and asked if any correspondence from Danny Hobeck had been found during the search of Judge Langsford's house.

"Nothing, Chief," Lee said, after checking the inventory of reviewed documents. "And no long-distance telephone calls, either."

From the parking lot of a family-owned grocery store near his motel, he called Penelope Gibben.

"Does Ranchers' have a current consulting contract with Danny Hobeck?" he asked.

"Yes."

"How much do you pay him?"

"It's in the hundred-thousand range."

"Annually?"

"Yes."

"How long has he been under contract?"

"For many years."

"What does he do to earn the money?" Kerney asked.

"I'd have to pull the contract for the specifics."

"I'd like a copy of every contract."

"I can't do that without our lawyer's permission."

"I'll have an officer at your house within an hour with a court order," Kerney said. He disconnected and dialed up the district office.

In the grocery store Kerney picked through the fresh produce section and got what he needed to make a good salad.

His motel, close to the New Mexico Military Institute, was an improvement over his room in Alamogordo. He had a suite that came with a kitchenette, a sitting room, and a separate sleeping area.

At the checkout counter he stood behind a woman who had also shopped for an evening meal. Only she would be cooking for two and serving a nice bottle of red wine with dinner.

Kerney looked down at the few items in his hands and started missing Sara. He watched the woman swing her way out the automatic doors and bit back on the feeling of loneliness that nipped at him.

He walked into the motel lobby carrying his groceries and saw

Clayton sitting at a couch with a woman and two small children. They stood in unison when Kerney approached.

"You wanted to meet my family," Clayton said, rubbing the head of the little boy at his side. "This is Wendell." He pointed to the child in the woman's arms. "That's Hannah. And this is my wife, Grace."

Wendell stepped forward and with a serious look extended his hand.

Kerney bent down and shook it.

"Hello, Grandfather," Wendell said.

"Hello, Wendell. It's nice to meet you."

Wendell nodded and, well coached for the occasion, stepped back to his father's side.

"Mrs. Istee," Kerney said, as he stood upright. She was a small-boned pretty woman with a narrow face and even features that gave her a classy look.

"Chief Kerney," Grace replied, nodding her head as she scooped up Hannah, who had started to toddle away.

Kerney looked from face to face. Clayton and his family had dressed for the occasion: father and son wore pressed jeans and fresh shirts, and mother and daughter each wore white blouses and dark skirts.

His eyes settled on Clayton. "Please be my guests for dinner," he said.

Clayton shook his head. "We can't, but thank you anyway. We just stopped by a few minutes ago so you could meet my family. We have a lot of errands to run before we go home."

"Some other time then," Kerney said, smiling at Grace.

"I'd like that," Grace said, giving Kerney a small smile in return.

"So would I," Kerney replied, switching his gaze back to Clayton. "Thank you for doing this."

"My mother kept your letters," Clayton said. "But she wouldn't let me read them."

"Thank her for saving me from the embarrassment," Kerney said.

"Were they that mushy?"

"Yeah, I guess they were."

Clayton nodded a good-bye and led his family through the lobby doors. Looking at Kerney over her mother's shoulder, Hannah waved.

Kerney waited a beat until they were out of sight, then approached the registration clerk and asked how long Clayton and his family had been waiting.

"Way over an hour," the woman said, glancing at the wall clock.

11

In the morning, Kerney lathered his face in the bathroom mirror at the motel and forced himself to stop grinning. But the image of Penelope Gibben stalking into the corporate offices late yesterday afternoon, forced by a court order to release the Hobeck contracts, brought the smile back. She'd said nothing during the time it took to find the records and left giving Kerney a spiteful look. Making Penelope Gibben angry and uncomfortable served no purpose, but it felt good nonetheless.

The Hobeck contracts spanned a period of almost fifty years, and the money Danny had received in total exceeded four million dollars. On an annualized basis it was a healthy chunk of cash.

After reading through the contracts last night, Kerney had called a local petroleum geologist to get a reading on the compensation Hobeck had received for services rendered. According to the geologist, Hobeck had been more than fairly reimbursed for the scope of his work.

He toweled off the remaining lather and at the small writing desk wrote out some questions before dialing up Hobeck's company in

Albuquerque. When a woman answered, Kerney gave her a fictitious name, sounding as officious as possible.

"I'm with Rubin and Thayer," he continued. "We're conducting the annual corporate audit for Ranchers' Exploration and Development.

"How I can help you?" the woman said.

"I need to speak with your chief finance officer."

"That would be me, I suppose," the woman said with a laugh. "I handle all of Mr. Hobeck's office work. Now that he's semiretired, there's just the two of us, and he's out of town."

"I see," Kerney said. "Part of our audit process includes reviewing a sampling of the consultant contracts issued by Ranchers'. We show that Mr. Hobeck is contracted to provide professional services, and that year-to-date payments in the amount of ninety thousand dollars have been made to him through the month of September. Is that correct?"

"Yes, it is. I make the deposits. The checks come after the first of each month."

"Would you please access your billing statements to Ranchers' for this year?"

The woman paused. "I can't do that."

"We really need to verify the services that have been provided to the corporation," Kerney said.

Worry crept into the woman's voice. "Mr. Hobeck doesn't bill Ranchers'. He says it isn't necessary. As far as I know, he's never billed them."

"I wouldn't be concerned about it. I'm sure the information I need is available through Ranchers'. You say he's never billed the company?"

"Not in all the years I've been with him."

"That's not a problem," Kerney said smoothly. "But I will need to speak with Mr. Hobeck for verification purposes. Is there a way I can reach him?"

"He called yesterday from Roswell saying he was taking a four- or five-day holiday before returning home."

"He's not in Albuquerque?"

"No. He always calls first thing in the morning if he's in town."

"Is he traveling alone?"

"I believe so. He's a widower."

"Will he be checking in with you?"

"I wouldn't think so. He has no pending projects."

"Is Ranchers' his only contract?"

"Yes, it has been for the last few years."

"I'd really like to close out this part of the audit as soon as possible. Does Mr. Hobeck have another residence where he might be staying?"

"He has a cabin outside of Ruidoso. But he always tells me when he's planning to go there."

"Do you have a phone number for it?"

"Yes, of course."

Kerney got the number, thanked the woman, and hung up. Why would Danny Hobeck tell Margie's neighbor he was taking his sister back to Albuquerque and tell his office manager a completely different story? It didn't make any sense unless Hobeck had something or someone—like Margie—to hide.

He tried the Ruidoso phone number, hung up after a dozen unanswered rings, got on the horn to Lee Sedillo, and gave him a summary on Hobeck's connection to Vernon Langsford.

"I'll nail down the location of the cabin," Lee said.

"Put full-time surveillance on it as soon as you do," Kerney said. "And I want the same coverage at his Albuquerque house and office."

"That means pulling in some additional help from the districts," Lee said. "Do you want him picked up?"

"Don't pick him up."

"Roger that."

"Any news from your end?" Kerney asked.

Lee sighed heavily. "I wish there was, Chief."

* * *

Assigned to look for Eric Langsford in Cloudcroft, Mary Margaret
Lovato had been to every bar, business, and government office in the
village trying to get a lead on him.

Eric was known throughout the community as a screwup who
couldn't hold a job, who moved around a lot, and who would disappear for months at a time. He didn't date, had no close male friends,
and the people he hung with were hard-core barflies and dopers.

No one she talked to admitted knowing where he might be. She
did learn that when Eric was in town, he liked to drink with Willie
Natter, an ex-felon and drug user who had done time for forgery.

Natter had moved from the address supplied by his parole officer,
and Mary Margaret was deep into the morning, still trying to find him.

High on the western slopes of the Sacramento Mountains, twenty
miles away from Alamogordo, Cloudcroft was a resort community
surrounded by National Forest. It wasn't at all like the isolated, pas-
toral northern New Mexico high-country village where Mary Margaret had been raised. Here, it seemed as if every bit of privately held
land had been turned into subdivisions for vacation cabins, year-
round homes, golf courses, hunting lodges, sportsmen's ranches,
campgrounds, and mountain retreats on five- and ten-acre parcels.

Mixed in with the vacation chalets, condominiums, and high-end
homes on heavily timbered lots were scuzzy rental cabins, old camping trailers on permanent foundations tucked into hillsides, and
economy tourist parks that looked right out of the 1950s.

With the information supplied by people who knew Natter, Mary
Margaret tracked him from job to job, slowed down by traffic pouring
into the area for a bluegrass music jamboree, a chamber of commerce–
sponsored art gallery extravaganza, and a mountain-bike rally that
had drawn over two hundred enthusiasts grinding their way up and
down narrow mountain roads.

In a small settlement east of Cloudcroft marked with a plaque
commemorating a site where Apaches had seriously kicked some
U.S. Army butt during the Indian Wars, she found Natter washing

dishes in a restaurant. She cuffed and marched him out the back door, where last night's raccoon raid on the garbage cans had not yet been cleaned up.

A hair net covered Natter's greasy ringlets, and old needle tracks ran up his arms.

"What are you busting me for?" Natter whined through a mouth full of chipped and stained teeth.

"Parole violation," Mary Margaret said. "You moved without reporting it to your PO. But maybe we can work something out."

"Like what?"

"Where is Eric Langsford?"

"I haven't seen him."

"That's not good enough," Mary Margaret said, yanking Natter along by the cuffs in the direction of her unit.

"Wait a minute," Natter said.

"Give me something."

"He's got a place in Cloudcroft. An old trailer he turned into a recording studio. He doesn't like people to know about it. Sometimes he stays there when he wants to hide out or when he's working on his music."

"Where is it?"

Natter gave Mary Margaret directions. She took off the cuffs, marched him back inside the diner, and had him call and report to his parole officer.

Natter hung up the phone, relief showing on his face. "He won't violate me if I go see him after work today."

"Be a good boy," Mary Margaret said, "and do as you're told."

The road to Langsford's secret recording studio wound past a nineteenth-century resort hotel with a lush nine-hole golf course into a wooded area away from the center of the town. The trailer was stepped down on the hillside so that only the roofline and stairs leading to a wooden deck showed from the road.

Mary Margaret approached cautiously, hand on her holstered

9 mm. From the stairs to the deck, electric lanterns strung on overhead wire glowed dimly in the bright afternoon light. She heard music coming from inside as she moved quietly across the deck, ducking under the trailer's windows. It was combination of flamenco and jazz chords played flawlessly on an acoustic guitar.

She eased up to the side of the door and saw a note taped on it that read COME IN. She took out her weapon, turned the knob with her free hand, and pushed the door open. The music grew louder. Crouching low, she called out Eric's name and got no answer. But the guitar playing continued. Raising her voice, she identified herself and ordered Langsford to step outside. Nothing happened.

She took a quick look and pulled her head back. Inside against the far wall was a built-in soundboard on a long table, with green dials glowing on the control panel. She looked once more and saw two monitor speakers mounted on a side wall. White light coming from an interior window made the silver-colored soundproofing on the walls and ceiling glisten. She called out again, and the music continued uninterrupted without response.

She sank down on her knees and considered her options—go in alone or call for backup. As she reached for her handheld the music stopped and a hushed hissing sound began, followed by a repeat of the same melody playing again.

Staying low, she ducked inside, plastered herself against a wall, and scanned for movement. After visually clearing the room she looked through the interior glass window of the sound studio. What might have been Eric Langsford was sitting in a straight-back chair.

It was impossible to tell for sure. There was a shotgun on the floor, and the lower half of the man's face had been blown off. Above the closed door glowed a red warning light. She opened the door and almost stepped in a pool of sticky blood. On the ceiling were wads of flesh, clumps of hair, and what looked like fragments of bone and teeth.

Mary Margaret took a deep breath, finished a sweep of the trailer,

keyed her handheld, and reported the death of an unknown subject—
possibly Eric Langsford—to Lieutenant Sedillo.

"Is it Langsford?" Kerney asked, as he signed the crime scene log.

"Positively," Mary Margaret replied. "Major Hutchinson is flying
in from Santa Fe. Lieutenant Sedillo is picking him up at the airport.
ETA fifteen minutes."

Kerney figured Nate was probably coming down to pull the plug
on the investigation. An onsite briefing was unnecessary, and no
other reason for his visit made sense. He'd have to convince Hutch
to give him more time.

"Was it a suicide?" he asked, as he entered the trailer.

"Without a doubt," Mary Margaret said, following along. "He's
been dead for less than six hours. Langsford videotaped it, Chief, and
left the time and date stamp running on the camcorder."

Crime scene technicians were photographing, vacuuming, and
sketching inside the recording room. Kerney watched through the
plate glass window. "Did he confess before he killed himself?"

"Just the opposite, Chief. He denied murdering anybody. That
doesn't mean he wasn't lying."

"You did a good job finding him, Agent Lovato."

"Too little, too late, Chief."

"Take the compliment, Agent," Kerney said.

"Thank you, sir," Mary Margaret said, slightly jarred by Kerney's
uncharacteristic gruff tone. "He recorded his statement for you,
Chief. I have the tape ready to view in the small bedroom."

"Thanks. Let me know when Major Hutchinson arrives."

In the bedroom behind the closed door, Kerney played the video-
tape. It began with handheld shots of the soundboard and the
recording room, then Eric Langsford's slurred speech broke the
silence.

"I lied to you about why I ripped off my father, Kerney. This is what I
spent the money on. Pretty neat, isn't it? After I bought the trailer, I

soundproofed it, ordered the components from catalogs, and put every-thing together myself. Wait a minute."

The scene jiggled a bit and then froze. Eric came into view, sat at the soundboard, and swiveled to face the camera. He looked drugged, drunk, and exhausted. His two-day beard, the dark circles under his eyes, and the strands of hair plastered against his forehead gave him a demented appearance.

"I'm gonna play you some of my music and leave it on so you can lis-ten to it when you get here. It's kinda like a funeral dirge, except it isn't very mournful. Wait a minute. I need to get something."

He rose on unsteady legs, came back with a whiskey bottle, took a long swallow, and plopped back down.

"Good stuff. Daddy's favorite single mash. I used to steal bottles of it from his liquor cabinet when I was a kid."

He giggled and put the bottle on the soundboard.

"I don't know when you'll get here, Kerney, so I'm gonna leave the music on for you. Hope you like it; it's from my Latin Suite. I call it 'The Day of the Dead.' The Mexicans make a big deal about death—they cele-brate it every year with a special day. Isn't that nice?"

He turned to the soundboard and with a shaky hand punched a few buttons and fiddled with the controls. The bass tones swelled. Eric nodded his head in time with the music and took another long pull from the bottle.

"There. I did the rhythm, bass, and two lead guitars on this track back when I was trying to get straight. Took me a month to get the licks down the way I wanted them. It could've been my best work, but then I started getting stoned again and never finished it."

He took another swig from the bottle, threw it against a wall, and pulled himself out of the chair.

"Time to go, Grasshopper."

He stepped out of view and then the camera moved jerkily as it was carried into the recording room and positioned to face a straight-back chair. Eric walked into camera range cradling an old shotgun.

"There are some really good riffs on this tape, but nobody listens to acoustic music anymore. It's all that techno and hip-hop crap."

He broke open the single-barrel shotgun, inserted a shell with a shaky hand, and snapped it shut.

"Like my new toy? I traded some pot for it. The guy threw in a box of shells for free. Who's that doctor that helps people die and films it? Maybe I should have gotten him to assist me, 'cause I'm starting to get a little scared."

He composed himself, sat in the chair, and patted the stock of the weapon.

"Okay, time to get serious. I know you want my confession, so here it is: I didn't kill my father or any of those other people. I never killed anybody. Does that piss you off? I bet it does. But the Judas Judge's murder got me thinking. Now just Linda and me are left, and the world would be a better place if the whole family was dead. So I'm gonna make my contribution to the cause."

He placed the shotgun between his legs, locked it in place with his knees, and rested his chin on the barrel. His unblinking eyes stared into the camera.

"I saw this once on one of those dumb television movies about a bad cop. Why do they always show cops killing themselves with guns? Can't you guys do it any other way? Would you use a gun to kill yourself, Kerney?"

Eric smiled as his finger found the trigger.

"This is gonna be real messy."

He hesitated and took his chin off the barrel.

"Make sure my sister sees it—it should make her happy."

He nestled his chin on the barrel, and the smile exploded into a bloody ruin of shattered bone and mangled flesh that splattered against the camera lens.

Kerney played the videotape for Nate Hutchinson, who'd arrived looking serious and slightly uneasy. During the viewing, Hutch didn't speak. Outside on the trailer's wooden deck, birds chirped and fluttered in the tall pines, and a breeze jingled some wind chimes that hung from a branch arching over the deck.

"I've never seen anything like that before," Nate finally said, his eyes fixed on a hummingbird darting by. "Do you believe him?"

"Yeah, I do," Kerney said.

Hutch leaned against the deck railing, furrowed his brow, and fell silent.

"You want to pull the plug on the investigation," Kerney said.

"I can't see any reason to keep it going. Not at the current level, anyway."

"I may have another target: a lifelong friend of Langsford's named Danny Hobeck, who's been feeding at Vernon's corporate trough big time for almost fifty years. He got his sister, Margie, out of town in a hurry after I talked to her. Aside from Eric, Margie was the only other person who seemed downright happy that Vernon was dead."

"Do you have anything substantial on Hobeck?" Hutch asked.

"Not really. Hobeck told Margie's neighbor he was taking her to Albuquerque to stay with him for a few days and gave his office manager a completely different story. I've put surveillance on his house, cabin, and office."

"Is there anything that points to Hobeck as the murderer?"

"I think he's hiding something," Kerney replied, "along with everybody else closely connected to the judge."

Nate bit his lip. "You can't keep running a full-scale investigation indefinitely based on hunches, Kevin."

"We've got three murders and a suicide in one family, Hutch. It isn't just a hunch."

"Okay, work the Hobeck angle. But from now on it's just you, Lee Sedillo, and the core team. Don't pull in any more district personnel for assistance. The field commanders are griping to Andy about it."

"How much time have I got?"

"Not much. If Hobeck doesn't pan out, or you can't get a handle on a motive, the case goes to open status, and I assign it to one agent."

"I'll work it solo, if I have to," Kerney said.

"Even if that means deferring your retirement?"

"I'll step down from my position and take a reduction in rank to do it."

The worry lines on Nate's forehead cleared. "You'd be the best man for the job, no doubt about it."

"Then it's a deal?"

"Yeah."

"How's the new job treating you?" Kerney asked.

"There's a lot to learn. But I like it so far."

"Have you given Andy any grief yet?"

Nate grinned. "That starts when I tell him what you plan to do. I was supposed to shut you down immediately."

"Andy slicked me into staying on for this case in the first place," Kerney said, "and he gave me thirty days. Remind him of that."

Nate nodded. "Eric Langsford could have been lying. The video-tape doesn't prove anything."

"I know it."

He left Hutch and spent a few minutes working out team reassignments with Lee Sedillo. Sedillo had found Hobeck's Ruidoso cabin and put an agent on-site.

"Keep him there and have our agents relieve the field officers covering Hobeck's residence and office in Albuquerque," Kerney said. "Have them pull double shifts."

"That spreads me thin, Chief."

Kerney nodded in the direction of the trailer. "When the techs finish, do a full search, and let's take another look at Eric's cabin in Pinon."

"I'll give it to Agent Lovato; she's the primary on the suicide."

"I want a full background check on Danny and Margie Hobeck, plus information of their whereabouts at the time of the murders."

"Senior citizens usually don't commit spree murders, Chief. Especially premeditated ones." Lee shook his head. "Jesus, is that a contradiction in terms, or what?"

"Nothing about this case is ordinary, Lee. Nothing fits or makes any sense."

"Man, I'm glad to hear you say that. I've been starting to think I was the only one totally bewildered by it. Are you going to tell Linda Langsford about her brother?"

"I'm leaving now."

"Do you have a few minutes?" Kerney asked.

Linda Langsford gave him a weary, exasperated once-over. Her port-red tunic-length shirt magnified a careworn expression and ashen complexion. Without a word, she turned and walked from the screened porch into the living room.

"What is it?" she asked, as she arranged herself on the couch and pushed her hair away from her face.

"I've come to tell you about Eric."

Interest flickered in her eyes. "Have you found him?"

"Yes."

"Have you arrested him?"

"No."

"Then what do you have to say?"

"Eric is dead," Kerney said. "He shot himself. We found him several hours ago."

Linda's eyes lost focus. She covered her face with her hands and sucked in a deep breath. When she looked at Kerney her eyes snapped with anger.

"Eric wouldn't have killed himself if you'd left him alone."

"He videotaped his suicide. On it, he said something I thought you should know."

"What did he say?"

"He thought the whole family was better off dead. What did he mean by that?"

Linda's mouth barely moved. "I don't know."

"He wanted you to watch the tape."

"Did you bring it with you?"

"No. Why would he want you to see his death?"

Linda forced herself to her feet, her body taut. "I don't know."

"It might help if you talked to me about your family, Ms. Langsford."

"Don't play therapist with me. It's insulting."

"Eric said his death would make you happy. Does it?"

"He was sick in the head. Can't you see that?"

"You gave him money: large sums delivered to him by Kay Murray."

"I had it to give, and Eric needed help financially."

"You had no other reason?"

"He was my brother, Mr. Kerney. Family."

"Why did you use Kay Murray as an intermediary?"

"Eric wanted it that way. Besides, he didn't like me. Surely, you noticed."

"There's one more point that concerns me, Ms. Langsford. I believe Arthur's death was a homicide, not an accident."

Linda recoiled, visibly shaken. "Impossible."

"Four violent deaths in one family worries me. I can't help wondering what could have caused it."

"What kind of fiction are you concocting?"

"I'm sorry to raise the issue right now, but I'm concerned for your safety. Can you think of any reason why Arthur may have been murdered? His death was the first in the family, and it could be an important link to what has happened since."

Linda's face hardened. "I can't take any more of these ridiculous speculations. Please go."

"I know it's difficult, but when you're able, think about it, Ms. Langsford."

"I'll try. Now, please, leave me alone."

Kerney had seen many people deny reality when given the devastating news of the unexpected, violent death of a loved one. It was an instinctive human response. Kerney hadn't seen that reaction in Linda Langsford until he'd raised the possibility that Arthur had been murdered. He wondered why it had surfaced for Arthur only.

* * *

Kerney caught Dr. Joyce, Eric's former shrink, between sessions and told her about the suicide.

Joyce let out a resigned sigh. "How tragic."

"I need to know more about Eric and his family relationships," Kerney said.

"You know I can't disclose that."

"Your former patient is dead, Dr. Joyce. What harm can it do?"

"But his sister is very much alive," Dr. Joyce replied.

"Is Linda Langsford in treatment with you?"

"I have a patient to see, Chief Kerney."

"When did you start seeing her?"

"You need to be going."

Joyce's deflection convinced Kerney that Linda had recently started treatment. He leaned forward in his chair. "Help me out with some analytic theory, Doctor. I've been focused on family dynamics ever since we last talked, but I'm not a psychiatrist."

Lillian Joyce adjusted the hem of her skirt and shifted her weight in the chair. "I can do that. Generally speaking, most serious emotional problems are rooted in late infancy and early childhood, Chief Kerney. The bond between parent and child is of particular importance in psychosocial development. If the healthy growth of a child is corrupted, most likely the individual becomes a maladjusted adult, unable to achieve close personal relationships."

"Corrupted?"

Dr. Joyce stood and ushered Kerney to the door. "My secretary has an office dictionary. Feel free to look the word up. Pay particular attention to the first entry."

Dr. Joyce had flagged the dictionary page with a yellow tab. The first entry read, "Marked by immorality and perversion; depraved."

Kerney smiled. Not only had Joyce expected him back, but she'd found a clever way to give him another hint.

Motorcycles dominated the traffic traveling to Ruidoso. Vintage hogs, expensive touring cycles, bikes with sidecars, and customized racing machines flowed around Kerney's unit, tailpipes rumbling. Riders traveled solo, in pairs, or as part of a convoy, many of them carrying female passengers wearing club leathers.

Kerney dialed up the Ruidoso PD frequency and learned that the annual weekend motorcycle rally was under way. On the main drag in town, choppers snarled traffic, hundreds of them moving slowly in both directions. All the parking spaces along the street were filled with gleaming, polished motorcycles, carefully arranged in neat rows. People wandered the sidewalks checking out the impromptu exhibition and talking to the bikers.

Stalled in traffic, Kerney consulted a street map and found an alternative route to Kay Murray's town house. After crawling slowly to the next intersection he peeled away from the snarl of motorcycles and down a narrow side canyon road that crossed the river.

Houses, cabins, and vacation retreats filled the hillside under a canopy of tall pines, and the warm afternoon had brought people out onto their decks and porches and into their yards. Small groups ambled along the roadside on their way to the event on the main street.

It all looked very pleasant and festive, and Kerney yearned for a quiet weekend with Sara, far removed from anything to do with murder.

Kay Murray opened her front door and shook her head as though the act would make Kerney disappear.

"No," she said flatly.

"We have more to talk about, Ms. Murray."

"If I give you a blow job, will you leave me alone?"

The offer stopped Kerney cold. "What?"

"I'm serious."

"No, thank you," Kerney said. "Do you know that Eric Langsford committed suicide?"

"Really?"

"Linda didn't call to tell you?"

Murray looked away.

"Did she call?"

"Yes."

"Was Eric blackmailing Linda?"

"That's the way he liked to put it, but I always considered it another one of his sick jokes."

"Did he ever tell you why Linda gave him money?"

"No."

"Why would you stay with Eric in a motel room for two hours, when all you needed to do was deliver Linda's money and score some grass?"

"He liked to talk to me."

"He never asked you to shower in the motel bathroom while he watched?"

Murray laughed harshly. "Does that sort of thing interest you?"

"Answer the question."

"No."

"You helped Eric rob his father, didn't you?"

"Excuse me?"

"How else could he have known exactly what Vernon had in the house?"

"I don't know how he knew."

Kerney took a step toward Murray, breaking into her personal space. She pulled her chin back as if she expected to be hit, and a vein throbbed rapidly in her neck.

"I know you want to stop playing this game with me," he said softly. "It's wearing you down. I can see it. You don't have to protect anybody."

"I haven't lied to you."

"I'm not talking about that. Help me get this settled and you can walk away from it."

"You don't need my help and I don't want yours," Murray said, as she pushed against the front door, forcing Kerney back.

It closed in his face with a thud.

*   *   *

Cushman's house sat on a crest-line road with a view of Sierra Blanca Mountain, where the Mescalero Apache Tribe operated ski lifts and ran a lodge as part of their resort amenities.

Contemporary in style, the residence had a tile roof, stucco exterior, and a privacy wall that hid the entryway from view. Both cars in the driveway wore bumper stickers that read JESUS LOVES YOU.

Kerney rang the front doorbell.

The door opened, and the smile on Joel Cushman's face collapsed into a distressed grimace. "Why have you come here?" he asked in an anxious whisper.

"You weren't at your office," Kerney replied. A pathetic fear showed in Cushman's eyes.

Cushman stepped outside and closed the door. "I'm home with my family. Can't this wait?"

"Why were you treating Kay Murray? Your answer could allow you to remain in practice, Doctor."

Cushman kept walking, his breath coming fast in his chest. He stopped next to the privacy wall and looked at Kerney with frightened eyes. "She had a relationship problem with Vernon."

"What kind of problem?"

"A sexual one. Vernon began wanting Kay to do things she wasn't comfortable with. Some of it was sadistic, some masochistic, but mostly it was a simulated bondage fantasy associated with bizarre imagery."

"What kind of imagery?" Kerney asked.

"He wanted Kay to dress and act like a prepubescent girl."

"Did she comply?"

"No. She stopped him from even touching her until he gave up trying."

"And after he quit making his demands?"

"According to Kay, she never slept with him again, nor did he ask her to. He was a paraphiliac: without the proper imagery or paraphernalia, he simply wasn't aroused."

"Isn't that pathological?" Kerney asked.

"It can be," Cushman answered. "If he had forced Kay to be a nonconsenting partner in the fantasy, it would have been. But he didn't. They settled into a nonsexual relationship after that, primarily because Kay began setting strict limits."

"Why would she tell me that she was still his lover up until the time of this death?"

"I don't know."

"She never explained her reasoning to you?"

"No," Cushman said, stepping into the driveway.

"Speculate about it," Kerney prodded.

Cushman cast a worried glance over Kerney's shoulder at the front of his house. "She was protective about Vernon, in her own way. She started therapy to learn how to manage his peccadilloes without alienating him. She wasn't bothered by Vernon's sexual needs; some of them simply didn't suit her tastes. For Kay, everything is basically a control issue."

"If you knew Kay had ended the sexual part of her relationship with Vernon, why did you tell me she was still his lover?"

"Because she asked me to."

Kerney studied the hangdog look on Cushman's face. "Didn't you find that odd? Usually people want to hide love affairs, not have them revealed."

"All I can think is that she did it for Vernon's sake."

"To preserve his reputation as a womanizer?"

"It would seem so."

"Isn't that somewhat off the wall, Doctor?"

"The dynamics are unusual."

"What is your clinical impression of Ms. Murray?"

Cushman's face turned red. "She's a highly sexual, intelligent, extremely dominant woman who knows how to meet her needs."

"Did she talk about her childhood in therapy?"

"No, she kept the issue focused on managing Vernon. I'm not proud of what happened between Kay and me, Mr. Kerney, and I've asked God for forgiveness."

Kerney nodded, wondering if Cushman had asked his wife for the same degree of understanding. He didn't think so.

Cushman licked his lips and gave Kerney a pleading look. "What happens now?"

"I'll get back to you," Kerney said, unwilling to let Cushman completely off the hook.

He left Cushman standing in the driveway and checked with Lee Sedillo by radio, who reported everything was quiet at the stakeouts, nothing had turned up at the trailer search, and the ball was rolling on the Danny and Margie Hobeck background investigations.

"I've got a message from your wife here, Chief," Lee added.

"What is it?"

"It says pick her up at the Albuquerque airport tomorrow morning or she'll file for divorce. Have you got trouble on the home front, boss?"

Kerney laughed. "Not yet, Lee. Give me her flight number and ETA."

12

After driving the state highway bordering the northern edge of the White Sands Missile Range, Kerney picked up the interstate in the Rio Grande Valley and passed by the suburban communities that oozed along the interstate south of Albuquerque. On once-empty desert rangeland housing tracts now mushroomed, lining either side of the road. To Kerney's eye it was uncontrolled sprawl that lacked any sense of scale, sensibility, or harmony with the land.

He grumbled about it, thinking the world needed fewer roads, fewer cars, and most important, fewer people.

Early in the evening he arrived at Bill Kendell's adobe-style house in Corrales, a semirural community sandwiched between Albuquerque and the burgeoning city of Rio Rancho. Linda's ex-husband, an affable man who seemed settled and comfortable with himself, introduced Kerney to his wife and son, and then took him into a small rear bedroom that had been turned into a home office. A glass door opened onto a covered backyard patio that provided an unobstructed view of the Rio Grande bosque and the distant Sandia Mountains.

"I don't have much time," Kendell said, easing his lanky frame into an overstuffed reading chair. "I've got a city league basketball game in about an hour."

"Tell me about your ex-wife," Kerney said.

The congenial look on Kendell's face vanished. "Boy, that was a mistake."

"In what way?"

Kendell struggled a moment to find the right words. "We were just incompatible."

"I sense there was more to it than that."

"How is knowing about my marriage to Linda going to help you find Vernon's killer?"

"I think the killer knew the judge, and his murder is tied to something in his past, or to his family."

"I'm not real comfortable talking about my problems with Linda."

"What you tell me may help keep her safe. Both parents have been murdered, we have reason to believe the death of her older brother Arthur was a homicide, and Eric has committed suicide."

"Jesus, what a mess," Kendell said, shaking his head.

"I'll keep whatever you tell me confidential."

Kendell took a deep breath, let it out slowly, and nodded. "Nobody deserves that kind of grief, not even Linda."

"I take it your relationship with her is less than cordial."

Kendell adjusted his position. "You could say that. We parted on pretty harsh terms. I'm old-fashioned when it comes to marriage. My parents raised me that way."

"And Linda wasn't?" Kerney asked.

"I thought she was before we got married," Kendell replied. "We messed around a lot before the wedding, if you know what I mean, but we never actually had intercourse. She didn't want to before the wedding, and I respected her decision."

"What went wrong?" Kerney asked, when Kendell stopped talking.

Kendell blushed. "This isn't easy to talk about."

"I understand."

"No, I don't think you do."

"I really need your candor, Mr. Kendell."

"She said she wanted to make me happy—please me sexually—and she did." Kendell shook his head as though warding off an unpleasant memory. "But looking back on it, it wasn't right."

"How so?"

"Well, she would . . ." Kendell stopped and smiled uneasily. "Shit. Okay. She'd give me hand jobs or oral sex. But it wasn't reciprocal, if you know what I mean. I could touch her, but only above the waist. I thought things would change after the wedding. You know, the virgin thing. But she wouldn't let me make love to her. She kept wanting to please me without any intercourse. At first, I just thought she was scared about it—some women are that way. But it never changed."

"When did things start to go sour?" Kerney asked.

"When I told her I wanted children. She said we could adopt. I didn't want that. I wanted a wife and a family in the full sense of the words."

"Were you aware of Linda's feelings before the wedding?"

"We never talked about having children. But I assumed we would. Otherwise, why get married? Looking back on it, I think she did it to prove something to herself."

"Prove what?"

"That she was normal. But she wasn't. The sex stuff she did was like an obsession. I wasn't a person who mattered to her romantically. I don't think she had a clue about what love is."

"How long did the problem go on?"

"For months. When she realized she couldn't seduce me out of having children of our own, she just walked out one day when I was at work and left everything behind. No discussion, no 'I'm sorry'—nothing."

"I heard a rumor that the marriage ended because Linda was having an affair."

"That wasn't it at all. I think Linda started that rumor herself."

"Was there anything else in Linda's behavior that you found strange or unusual?"

"You know, I never saw her naked—not once. She'd even lock the bathroom door when she brushed her teeth. I teased her about it one time and she almost went ballistic."

"What did she say?"

"That she needed her privacy; didn't like people spying on her—weird stuff. In a way, she was like two different people. Publicly she'd act all loving and affectionate toward me. But at home she would shut down when it came to snuggling or kissing, or anything romantic. She'd ask me if I needed a blow job maybe three or four times a week. That was the way she treated sex. After a while it made me feel vulgar and cheap."

"Did she ever talk to you about her family?"

"That subject was pretty much off-limits, and when she did say anything, it always had a double edge to it."

"Can you give me an example?" Kerney asked.

"It was always a mixed message kind of thing. She'd call Eric a sick little sneak and then say something about how it wasn't really his fault. Or she would chastise her father for not loving her mother and then blame her mother for being frigid. Frankly, I think Linda was frigid herself."

Kendell checked his wristwatch and stood up. "I've really got to go."

"Do you take your family to your ball games?" Kerney asked as he got to his feet.

Kendell's expression warmed. "They never miss one. They're my biggest fans."

After repeating his promise not to reveal the particulars of Kendell's failed marriage, Kerney left and checked into a high-rise hotel near the Albuquerque airport.

He opened the window drapes in his room and watched the lights of the city wink on as the last bit of dusk vanished in the western sky.

Bill Kendell seemed like a good man, happy with his life and his family, and the thought made Kerney long for similar circumstances. Having Sara in his life was a delight, but maintaining a long-distance marriage wasn't getting any easier. And Sara's interest in starting a family while continuing to serve on active duty made Kerney wonder how they could pull it off. He had no desire to be a military dependent following Sara from post to post.

He turned away from the window thinking he had to keep his priorities straight. He was married to a woman he loved deeply, and he was about to come into a sizable chunk of money that would give them more options. He needed to start thinking more creatively, but he didn't know where to begin.

His thoughts turned to the Langsford case. He decided to spend the evening piecing together what he knew about the family, to see what kind of profile developed.

In the morning, Kerney waited for Sara's flight to arrive. When it did, she was the first one out the jetway, and he started grinning the moment she appeared. Each time he saw her again he couldn't contain a feeling of elation.

She dropped her overnight bag, pressed up against him, and planted a long wet kiss on his lips while the other passengers flowed around them.

She pulled back and gave him a lascivious smile. "Do you have a room?"

"Nearby, milady."

"You're one smart man, Kerney. I may not have to divorce you after all." She grabbed her bag and folded her arm in his. "Let's go."

An hour or so later, after very little talking, Sara found the spot on Kerney's shoulder where she liked to rest her head. She reached over and started gently scratching his chest.

"I haven't heard from you much this week, Grandpa," she said.

Kerney groaned in response.

"Not funny, huh?"

"Unsettling."

"Tell me about it."

Kerney brought her up to date on Clayton, including the surprise introduction to his family at the Roswell motel.

"It sounds like an overture to me," Sara said.

"A small one, perhaps. We'll see where it goes."

"And the case?"

Kerney put the week's events into a series of highlights, concentrating on Eric Langsford's suicide, the disappearance of Danny Hobeck and his sister, and his difficulties dealing with Kay Murray, Penelope Gibben, and Linda Langsford.

"Murder, suicide, drugs, missing persons, sexual deviants, harlots, pushy women, family secrets," Sara said, when he finished. "What have you gotten yourself into?"

"The sex angle intrigues me. Vernon's bizarre need to have Murray dress up and act like a provocative schoolgirl, Eric's twisted voyeurism, Linda's aversion to intercourse, statements that Vernon's wife was passive and frigid. I've even wondered if Penelope Gibben may have groomed her niece, Kay Murray, to become Vernon's mistress."

"At Vernon's urging?" Sara asked.

"Perhaps. And why did Kay Murray tell me a useless lie about continuing to be Vernon's lover up until the time of his death, if the sexual relationship had ended?"

"Sex and secrets," Sara said. "A potent combination."

"Murray offered to give me a blow job if I left her alone."

Sara raised an eyebrow. "Really? Did you take her up on it?"

"No, it wasn't the type of bribe I usually accept."

Sara punched him on the arm in response.

Kerney shook off the love tap and tickled Sara's tummy. "What do you make of it?"

Sara pushed his hand away. "Stop it. I think you're right to follow the sex angle. Something has been going on in the Langsford family for a long time that everyone wants kept secret, and it's connected to the judge."

"That much I know. But what is it?"

"You'll figure it out. But not this weekend, if I have anything to say about it. I hope you haven't made any plans."

Kerney cocked an eye. "What have you cooked up?"

Sara pushed herself into a sitting position. "We're weekend guests at Dale and Barbara's."

"Don't you have to be back at the post tomorrow night in time for Monday classes?"

"Classes don't resume until Tuesday morning. I've rented a car to drive down to the ranch."

"Are we in a hurry?"

Sara lifted the bedsheets, looked at Kerney's crotch, and smiled. "Not necessarily. What have we here?"

"Has all this sex talk turned you on?"

"No more so than you, it would appear," Sara said. "Did I mention that I'm fertile this weekend?"

"Thanks for the late warning."

Sara laughed as she swung a leg over Kerney's torso. "Matrimony usually brings with it the promise of children, Kerney. That's a given, unless negotiated otherwise."

"So I've heard," Kerney said, thinking back to his conversation with Bill Kendell.

The Rocking J, Dale and Barbara's ranch on the western slope of the San Andres Mountains, bordered White Sands Missile Range and spread down to the Jornada del Muerto—the journey of death—a waterless, desolate savanna of cactus, creosote, and mesquite. Once part of El Camino Real that ran from Mexico City to Santa Fe, the Jornada earned its name because of the scores of lives it claimed during the early days of Spanish settlement.

The remote ranch headquarters stood on a ridgeline overlooking a deep canyon, with views of the basin below and the red-tinged forested mountains inside the missile range. Only the soothing sound of the wind in the trees and the call of Mexican blue jays broke the silence.

On arriving at the ranch, Kerney became pensive and somewhat quiet, and although he hid it well, his moodiness remained just below the surface.

Sara didn't press him about it, thinking that perhaps staying in the old foreman's quarters, where Kerney and his parents had lived after losing their ranch to the army, brought back sad memories, including the harsh reminder of the tragic death of his parents, who had died in an auto accident on the day of Kerney's return from Vietnam.

Kerney had buried them in a small family cemetery under a grove of old pine trees on the Rocking J. After greeting Dale, Barbara, and the girls and chatting for a while, he paid a solo visit to the grave site for the better part of an hour.

When he came back, Dale got him to help with some chores, and the routine of ranch life seemed to lift his spirits somewhat. Sara watched the two men for a while and then worked on supper with Barbara and the girls, all of them talking up a storm as they prepared the evening meal.

The two girls, Candace and Meaghen, were lovely, wholesome, spirited teenagers who made Sara yearn for a daughter. As she flattened bread dough with the heels of her hands, she wondered if her lovemaking with Kerney had turned that longing into reality. The possibility brought a smile to her face that made Barbara raise an eyebrow as she passed by on her way to the kitchen sink with a bag of potatoes that needed peeling.

Working with Barbara and the girls reminded Sara of her own family's Montana sheep ranch and her mother, who had taught her to work as hard as a man and cook as lovingly as a woman. There was something to be said for the country life, Sara thought, as she molded the dough, covered it with a towel, and set it on the top of kitchen windowsill to rise. If nothing else, it was a welcome break from the spit-and-polish routine of the military.

She looked at her three busy companions, took in the delicious smells of the roast in the oven, the handmade welcome wreath hung over the kitchen door, and the neat row of hand-painted antique food canisters on the shelf next to the stove. Barbara was still peeling potatoes, Meaghen was putting final touches on an apple cobbler, and Candace was busy snapping string beans.

"Why the big grin?" Barbara asked.

"This is just a lot of fun," Sara replied, as she found a paring knife and joined Barbara at the sink.

The remainder of the weekend went wonderfully well, and after an early Sunday supper, Barbara left the dishes for Candace and Meaghen and invited Sara on a walk. They followed the ranch road into the canyon, the creaking sounds of the lovely old wooden windmill next to the corral wafting along behind them on a slight breeze, before Barbara led her off on a game trail that wandered down to a distant stock tank on the flats.

The breeze had pushed away a light haze and the Jornada sparkled under a harvest-yellow sun. Barbara pointed out the bleak Fra Cristobal Mountains, named for a friar who'd died on his return journey to Mexico four hundred years earlier. The peaks cut into the sky like sharp incisors, blunted only by the towering expanse of the Black Range that filled a hundred miles of the horizon to the west. Sunlight bounced off the metal roof of a distant wine-processing shed near the railroad tracks that cut through the Jornada, past the remnants of Engle, once a thriving railroad and ranching community.

Water for the acres of adjacent vineyards on the tableland was piped across the desert from Elephant Butte Lake, the largest water impoundment reservoir in the state, which ate up forty miles of land along the Rio Grande.

"Is Kerney's heart still set on ranching once he leaves the state police?" Barbara asked, as they stood looking at the view.

"He hasn't been talking about it quite as much as he used to."

"I would never say this to Dale, but I wish there was a way for him to slow down and not work so hard. Except for our trip to Montana for your wedding, we haven't been anywhere as a family for the last five years."

Sara nodded, her thoughts turning to her father and brother on the Montana sheep ranch. "The work takes its toll."

"And you can't tell these kind of men that they might not be twenty years old anymore," Barbara said, turning to look at Sara. "And what about you? Do you want this kind of life?"

"I grew up with it," Sara said.

"That doesn't answer my question."

"I want Kerney to be happy."

"He's going to have a lot of options open to him," Barbara said. "Maybe he hasn't considered all of them."

"Do you think he's holding on to an unrealistic dream?"

"You two fit together like a hand and glove, Sara. If both of you were going to build a ranch together, I'd say go for it. Ranching may be hard, but it's a wonderful way to live."

"I know it is," Sara said.

Barbara smiled. "Want some advice?"

"I thrive on it," Sara said playfully.

"Help Kerney learn how to enjoy all that money he stands to gain from the sale of Erma's land. I don't think it's sunk in that he's going to be a rich man."

"Convince him to give up the dream?"

Barbara shook her head. "Heavens, no. But he could ranch in a small way, for the fun of it, and enjoy life without worrying about the price of beef on the open market, or the next drought, or the cost of doing business."

Sara bit her lip and thought about it. "I don't think he could stand the idea of being anything but a dirty-shirt cowboy."

Barbara patted Sara's arm. "Encourage him to change his attitude. Believe me, I'd be on Dale in a flash if we had the financial where-withal to ease up a bit."

"That might take some doing."

Wind blew Barbara's hair into her face. She pushed it away and settled down on a large boulder. "Do you really want to see Kerney sink everything into something so risky? His dream could turn into a disaster real fast."

"I've thought about that," Sara said, joining her.

"Would you be willing to give up your career to help him make a go of it?"

The sky lost color as mare's tail clouds masked the sun. Sara twisted her West Point class ring with her thumb. "No."

"Neither would I, if I had a profession I'd worked hard to achieve and was good at," Barbara said.

"Kerney doesn't change his mind easily."

Barbara giggled

"What?"

"You have an advantage. He's desperately, completely in love with you."

Sara's sparkling eyes smiled. "He does seem to adore me."

"Enough said," Barbara replied. She stood and started back up the trail. "You get no more sisterly advice from this gal."

"That's it?" Sara asked jokingly.

"For now. Let's get back and serve up some of that chocolate cake you made, if it hasn't already been devoured."

Kerney gave Sara a kiss, watched her enter the jetway, and left the airport wondering if he'd married a mind reader. They had stayed up half the night in the hotel room talking about the future, with Sara raising questions that had been bouncing around in Kerney's mind, giving him a voice to talk about his apprehensions about starting a ranch and leaving law enforcement for good.

Nothing had been resolved, but Kerney felt a weight had been lifted. Sara had suggested a range of options to be considered, all of them centered around the notion of more time together, establishing a permanent home, sharing responsibility—if indeed she was pregnant—for raising a child, and allowing Kerney to pursue his aspirations. She'd driven the point home by noting that the army might be willing to send her to law school, which was something she'd planned to do anyway sometime in the future. That would mean three years of detached duty and the chance for them to be together over an extended period of time.

The idea excited Kerney, especially when Sara made it clear she would apply to the University of New Mexico, which had an excellent program, as her first choice.

He drove out of the airport parking garage toying with ideas he hadn't considered before. For years, in different ways and for different reasons, both of them had been nomads. Marriage hadn't changed that. But now there was a possibility it could change, at least for a very large chunk of time.

Caught up in a delightful daydream, he barely heard his call sign on the unit's radio. He keyed the microphone and responded.

"Hobeck just pulled up at his residence, Chief," the agent on stakeout said.

"Is his sister with him?"

"Negative, but a visitor has been waiting. I ran the plate on his car. It's registered to Pomeroy and Associates. I checked the phone book. It's a law firm. This guy's a suit, fifty-five years old or thereabouts, chunky, with thinning hair."

"Give me your location and stand by," Kerney said, wondering what prompted Hobeck to seek legal counsel, hoping it had something to do with Margie.

Hobeck's house was in an upscale neighborhood in the foothills overlooking Albuquerque. The subdivision had been started during the brief time Kerney had been married to his first wife and attending graduate school in the city. Back then, the original developer had scarred the foothills with roads, clear-cut the vegetation, and built houses overlooking the city that sat like exposed Monopoly pieces on a life-size game board. It was now a hidden residential oasis for the well-off. Mature trees sheltered the homes, neat rows of decorative shrubs were carefully pruned, emerald green grass bordered brick walkways, and trimmed vines climbed thick stone walls.

Hobeck's residence sat on two lots at the end of a cul-de-sac. Surrounded by carefully arranged groves of evergreen trees, it presented a vaulted cathedral-style glassed entry to the street.

Kerney walked up the semicircular driveway and rang the bell. Hobeck answered with a look of dismay. In the daylight, Kerney could see the signs of years of heavy drinking etched on his face.

"You have no business coming here," Hobeck said.

"Where's Margie, Mr. Hobeck?"

"My family matters aren't your concern."

"I would think you'd want your best friend's murder solved."

"I've done nothing wrong," Hobeck caught his blunder and tried to adjust. "Of course I want the killer caught."

Kerney pressed the issue. "But you have done something wrong, Mr. Hobeck. Failing to reveal the whereabouts of a material witness constitutes obstruction."

"Margie had nothing to do with Vernon's murder."

"That's not my point. Talk to your lawyer."

"Have you been watching my house?" Hobeck asked.

"I'll wait here while you speak to him," Kerney said.

Hobeck closed the door. When it opened again, a middle-aged portly man in an expensive suit greeted Kerney with a quick, hard look.

"May I see some credentials?" the man asked.

Kerney held up his badge case. "Who are you?"

"Ronald Pomeroy. Hobeck's attorney."

"Is your client willing to cooperate with me?"

"We'll see," Pomeroy said, swinging the door open so Kerney could enter. He led the way into the living room, where a wall of glass mirrored the front entrance to the house, providing a view of a flagstone patio and a bubbling stone fountain.

Hobeck paced nervously in front of a tan leather couch positioned in front of a built-in bookcase that held a treasure-trove of antique African folk art, mostly of male and female fertility symbols with enlarged sex organs.

"How is Margie Hobeck a material witness in your case?" Pomeroy asked.

"Do you represent Margie?" Kerney replied.

"At her brother's request, I represent her best interests."

"In what way?"

"Margie isn't well. She has emotional problems. Mr. Hobeck doesn't think now is a good time for you to bother her."

"You're playing word games, counselor," Kerney said. "Does your client have any legal authority over his sister's affairs?"

"Margie is in a very fragile state, and Mr. Hobeck wishes to protect her from any additional trauma."

"Are you planning to file for guardianship?"

"Mr. Hobeck's reasons for meeting with me are privileged."

"Of course," Kerney said. "But whatever civil action you may take doesn't shield Margie as a material witness in a criminal investigation. Let me ask you again: Do you represent Margie Hobeck?"

"I do not."

Kerney looked at Hobeck. "Where's Margie?"

Hobeck glanced from Kerney to Pomeroy. "Do I have to answer?"

Kerney held up a hand. "Before you respond, counselor, let me make it clear that Mr. Hobeck acted intentionally when he took his sister out of town to avoid any further contact with the police. He lied to his employee and to Margie's neighbor about what he was doing and where he was going."

"Is that true?" Pomeroy asked.

Hobeck hung his head. "Can't you do anything?" he pleaded to Pomeroy.

"After I arrest you for obstruction of justice, he can," Kerney said, turning back to Pomeroy. "What will it be?"

Pomeroy nodded curtly. "I suggest you tell Chief Kerney where Margie is, Daniel."

With haunted eyes, Hobeck gave Kerney the name of a chemical dependency treatment program outside of Tucson. "She's addicted to tranquilizers," he added. "Has been for most of her life. You can't count on her to tell the truth."

"Perhaps you'd like that to be so," Kerney countered. "What does Margie know about Vernon Langsford?"

"I can't talk about that."

"Nor do you have to at this point," Pomeroy advised.

"Don't let your client contact Margie until after I speak with her," Kerney said.

Hobeck switched his gaze to Kerney. "You can't keep me from doing that. This is America, not some dictatorship, for chrissake."

"I suggest we follow Chief Kerney's advice," Pomeroy replied.

Defeated, Hobeck dropped heavily to the couch as though his legs had been knocked out from under him.

Kerney handed Pomeroy his business card. "You may want to hold off on any court petition until after my visit."

"I'm way ahead of you on that one," Pomeroy replied, giving Hobeck an inquisitive look.

The cramped seat on the plane ride to Tucson made Kerney's bum knee lock up. He hobbled through the terminal like an old man, signed for his rental car, and, using the map supplied with the keys to the vehicle, found his way to the treatment center where Hobeck had stashed his sister.

A drying-out resort and spa for affluent addicts and drunks, the center had once been a dude ranch, and the Western theme was continued in newly built clusters of rustic-looking private guest cottages and low-slung buildings with wide verandas, where a range of treatment options, from aroma and massage therapy to group and individual counseling, was available to speed the recovery process.

If the patrons didn't leave cured of their addictions, they would at least check out feeling pampered.

On the green in front of the administration building, a group of matrons in mix-and-match sizes were exercising under the guidance of a tanned, fit-looking young man who wore a body-hugging tee shirt that accentuated his toned upper torso. The young woman inside at a reception desk was equally toned, tanned, and dressed in a tee shirt of her own that emphasized a pair of remarkably different features from those of her male counterpart on the lawn.

The receptionist was busy on the telephone, so Kerney stood in front of the desk and fanned through an advertising brochure for the center that listed the levels of services available, optional packages, and the weekly rates. Even if Hobeck had selected the least expensive course of treatment for his sister, the cost was exorbitant.

"May I help you?" the woman asked, as she hung up the phone and gave Kerney a well-practiced welcoming smile.

"Margie Hobeck, please," Kerney replied, showing his shield.

The smile vanished and Kerney got directions to the Paloverde Cottages, which, according to the brochure, were the low-end accommodations. Before he left, he verified that Margie had voluntarily signed herself in for treatment.

She answered his knock at her cabin door immediately. Agitation showed on her face; perhaps withdrawal symptoms, Kerney speculated.

Hobeck had paid for a makeover; Margie's hair had been tinted and set, her nails were perfectly done, and her eyebrows and lashes had been dyed.

"I remember you," Margie said. "You're that policeman. Why did you ask my brother all those questions about me?" The question came out as a whine.

"I'm sorry if it caused you trouble."

"He took me away from my home and brought me here. I don't like it here. I need to be home with my cats."

"Would you like me to take you home?"

"Danny wouldn't like that. He wants me to stay. He said if I talked to you, he would sell my house. He said a judge would give him control of my affairs because I'm not responsible."

"I won't let that happen," Kerney said.

"You can stop him?"

"Yes, if you help me."

A hopeful look broke through Margie's uneasiness. "My cats liked you. They don't usually like men."

"They're lovely animals, and I'm sure they miss you."

"Take me home."

"Will you talk to me about Vernon Langsford?" Kerney asked.

"Danny said he told you everything."

"I need to hear your side of the story," Kerney replied, "in order for it to be official."

Margie nodded.

"Tell me about Vernon."

"He was a bad boy."

"What did he do?"

Margie's eyes closed. "He made me play with his lollipop—that's what he called it. I had to let him put it everywhere."

"How old were you when this happened?"

"Very young. It went on for years." Margie's fingers touched her chest and she smiled ruefully. "Until I got breasts. They never did get very big."

"Did you tell anybody?"

"I told Danny what Vernon was doing to me the summer I turned ten and he turned fifteen. He said it was my fault."

"You told no one else?"

"I was scared to. But I think my daddy knew. He went to work for

Vernon's father that same summer and stayed with the company until he retired."

Kerney thought about Margie's years of pain and shame. "Vernon can't hurt you anymore."

Margie smiled bitterly. "I always thought Vernon's death would be a remedy. But it's not."

"Why don't you get packed," Kerney said gently, resisting the impulse to reach out and comfort Margie. Based on what he'd just heard, he doubted that a man's touch would soothe away any of her hurts.

13

The flight back to Albuquerque and the drive to Roswell took up the remainder of the day. Kerney got Margie home at nightfall, his mind reeling from her descriptions of Vernon's sexual assaults. In a tiny little voice, she'd recalled the events as though they were fresh and recent. The fact that Danny Hobeck had freely made his kid sister available to Vernon turned Kerney's stomach.

He stayed with her while she checked on her cats, fed them, called the neighbor to report her return, and then disappeared into the bathroom. Ten minutes later she emerged with a dreamy look on her face, all traces of agitation and worry gone.

He said nothing about her drugged condition and left thinking that if anybody had a legitimate reason to get loaded on tranquilizers, it was Margie.

Penelope Gibben's house was dark when he drove by. By phone he contacted a staff member at Ranchers' Exploration and Development and learned that Gibben was on a business trip to Dallas and wouldn't be back until midweek.

Linda Langsford's house was lit up, but the cars in the driveway, including her minister's Chevy and her law partner's top-of-the-line Volvo station wagon, canceled the possibility of a private conversation.

It was just as well, Kerney thought, as he drove away. He was drained from hearing Margie's gut-wrenching accounts and wasn't sure he could maintain the focus of another interview with either woman on the heels of what he'd recently learned.

Besides, the weakest link in the chain other than Margie was Kay Murray. As an admitted drug user, he could lean on her, if necessary. He'd see her in the morning when his mind was clear.

A bad dream forced Kerney into consciousness. He woke in his Ruidoso motel room with a jumble of ugly images in his mind. In it, Randy Shockley and Eric Langsford were stalking a prepubescent Kay Murray with shotguns, like hunters chasing a jackrabbit. Murray suddenly transmuted into Sara, and Kerney couldn't reach her in time to save her from the blasts that took her down.

He checked the time and stifled an urge to call Sara—she was long gone from her quarters to morning classes. In the shower he let the water beat on his head until the last remnant of the dream evaporated.

Kay Murray wasn't at her town house, but Kerney found a newly planted realtor's FOR SALE sign next to the walkway very interesting. He caught up with Murray at Vernon Langsford's, where she was loading personal belongings into the back of her Ford Explorer.

She wedged a box into the back of the vehicle and faced Kerney as he approached.

"You don't listen well," she said. "Let me be clearer: Fuck off."

"The more I think about it, the more I believe you never had a sexual relationship with Vernon," Kerney said. "At least, not as an adult."

"Excuse me?" Murray tried to step aside and Kerney crowded her back toward the Explorer.

"I talked to a woman yesterday who told me Langsford had been a pedophile since boyhood. I've been thinking that he used Penelope

Gibben as a cover for his pedophilia, and after his wife was killed and he moved here, he used you to fill the same role. Did you ever tell Linda her father was a child molester?"

"I don't have to listen to this."

"Yes, you do," Kerney snapped. "Answer the question."

She winced, fell silent, and lowered her head. "Linda always knew," she finally said in a harsh voice.

"I thought Linda hated her father because he was unfaithful to her mother. Wasn't that the party line you and Penelope gave me?"

Her head stayed down. "Linda always knew," she repeated.

"How long is always?"

Murray's head came up, and she averted her face. "From the time I was eight. Vernon didn't bring Linda to Penelope's house so I could play with her. He brought her there so that he could play with her." She snapped her cold eyes in Kerney's direction. "Now do you get it?"

"Who else knew?" Kerney asked, his stomach twisting.

"Eric, Arthur, their mother. All of them knew or at least guessed at what was going on."

"How many?" Kerney asked.

"What?"

Kerney couldn't contain his antagonism. "How many little girls did Vernon molest while you and your aunt were busy protecting his reputation?"

She looked over Kerney's shoulder with dead eyes. "He gave that up when I started working for him."

"In exchange for what?"

"My attention."

Kerney studied the woman, looking for anything that signaled regret. All he saw was misery. "Was it worth it? The money? The gifts?"

Her eyes strayed to Kerney's face, remote and narrow. "After Vernon tired of Linda, he grew fond of me, if you get my meaning."

Kerney's anger dissipated as though doused by a chilling rain. He waited for more.

"I've learned to cope with life in my own way," she added.

"Did Penelope know Vernon sexually assaulted you during the summers you stayed with her?"

"She more than knew, she helped it happen. But she also made sure I got opportunities I never would have had otherwise. She's done a great deal for me." There was no gratitude in her voice.

"Help me sort everything out," Kerney asked.

"What purpose would that serve?"

"You really don't have a choice."

"We'll see about that," Murray said.

"You helped Eric rip off his father."

"Inadvertently, Mr. Kerney. I didn't know Eric was planning a robbery. He told me he wanted to ask his father for a few family mementos and some of his personal belongings from his childhood, so I told him what Vernon kept in the house. I never expected him to show up waving a gun around."

"Weren't you angry with Vernon?"

"Whatever for?"

"His demands to have you act out his sexual fantasies about prepubescent girls?"

"His fixation became tiresome, that's all."

"More than tiresome, I'd say. You sought out Joel Cushman to find ways to deal with it. Did Vernon ask you to procure girls for him?"

"You don't know what you're talking about."

"Did he?"

"Never."

Kerney studied her. She was skittery, eager to get away. He wasn't sure if Murray had procured young girls for Langsford. But it wasn't outside the range of possibility. "Think about all the girls Vernon molested," he said. "Don't they deserve to know Langsford has been unmasked? Wouldn't it help them get beyond the trauma?"

"I have to go."

"I can't allow that." He reached out and took Murray by the arm. "I'm placing you under arrest."

She looked at his hand, surprised that he'd touched her. "You're arresting me? What for?"

"Armed robbery," Kerney said, feeling worn down by all the lies and perversion.

"You can't do that," she said, as though the force of her words could stop him.

"Watch me."

He cuffed her, did a quick pat-down search, put her in his unit, and got her purse from the front seat of her vehicle. It contained her passport, an airplane ticket to Amsterdam, and a sterling silver antique cigarette case filled with marijuana.

He drove away with Murray sitting woodenly in the backseat. Only the sound of her rapid breathing signaled any hint of panic. In the rearview mirror her face seemed carved in stone.

He keyed the microphone, reached Lee Sedillo, asked him to rendezvous at the jail, and made the remainder of the trip in silence. Lee was waiting when he arrived.

"Book her on armed robbery," he said, when Murray was out of earshot. "It's a stretch and she'll walk if we don't get something better." He filled out the charge sheet and gave it to Lee. "Search her car. See if you can find more grass we can use to bump a possession charge up to drug dealing. Another ounce will do it. Buy me as much time as you can."

"What does this get us, Chief?" Lee asked.

"I'm not sure yet."

He watched through the thick, shatterproof glass of the booking room as Lee entered the reception area and tried to steer Murray toward a wall phone so she could call an attorney.

She dug in her heels and looked at Kerney. "You motherfucker," she mouthed at him through the glass.

After reviewing the field report filed by the agent who'd checked Linda Langsford's alibi, Kerney called for a department plane, met it at the Ruidoso airport, and flew to Alamosa, Colorado. Not enough good questions had been asked during the agent's phone interviews, and Kerney wanted to fill in the blanks.

He drove seventy miles in a rental car to Creede, where Linda Langsford had started her fall vacation. He followed the grassland valleys along the Rio Grande into the high country, marveling at the remarkable change in the landscape that was so evident every time he crossed over into Colorado. The mountains were higher, the rangeland richer, the forests greener, and seemingly inexhaustible water rushed over rocky streambeds and through fast-moving channels where tall grasses grew thick along the banks.

Since Kerney's last visit many years ago, Creede had been gussied up and turned into a vacation spot. The town stood at the mouth of a narrow canyon that cut into the mountains. Two high peaks dominated the skyline and pressed against the village. At the south end of the village, the terrain fell away to a lush grassland valley.

The main street boasted Victorian buildings on a narrow paved road that petered down to a dirt track at a fire station housed in a converted mine shaft. Gift shops, restaurants, art galleries, and two small hotels, most of them closed for the season, fronted the main street. An old music hall had been renovated for use as a summer repertory theater, and the businesses that were still open catered primarily to local residences. Only a few cars were parked along the three-block strip that defined the town center, and the sidewalks were empty.

A smattering of hillside homes and vacation retreats overlooked the town, and a gushing watercourse roared out of the mountains behind the main drag where neatly tended former miner cabins and older homes on tiny lots fronted a narrow dirt lane.

Kerney found the bed and breakfast where Linda Langsford had stayed. Posted to the front door was a notice that it was closed for the season. A telephone number was listed if people were interested in booking advance reservations for next year.

At a nearby bar and restaurant done up in an old Western saloon motif with sawdust on the floor, two customers and a bartender were watching a sports channel on a wall-mounted television. He asked and got directions to the B & B operator's residence.

The middle-aged woman who opened the door of the hillside house looked at Kerney and shook her head. "I'm sorry, our bed and breakfast is closed," she said. "So are the hotels. You'll have to drive to South Fork if you want a room. I don't know why Eddie at the bar keeps sending people up here."

Kerney introduced himself, displayed his shield, and held up a photograph of Linda Langsford. "Do you know this person?"

"Of course. Linda Langsford. She stays with us for several days every fall."

"The notice on the door says that you close on the fifteenth of September. Ms. Langsford supposedly stayed at your bed and breakfast in early October."

The woman nodded. "We shut down the breakfast operation then, but we'll rent rooms into October, especially to returning guests. We get some overnighters who check in at the gift shop next door, but most who come when the season has ended make reservations through the mail or by phone."

"How do they get a room key?"

"I leave the place open with a key in each room."

"What day and time did Ms. Langsford check in?" Kerney asked.

"I think we mailed her a key at her request. Let me double-check."

She left and returned holding a open ledger. "Yes, she got a key and a reservation confirmation by mail." She read off the dates of Linda's stay.

"Did you see her on the day of her arrival?" he asked.

"I didn't see her at all, but her luggage was in her room."

"On the day she was due to arrive?"

"Yes. I stopped by to say hello. Her bags were there and she had started to unpack. I assumed she'd either gone out for a short walk to stretch her legs, or she was getting something to eat."

"What time was that?"

"Around two in the afternoon."

"Did you see her the next day?"

"No, I went to Alamosa for the day and didn't get back until long after check-out time."

"Did you give my agent this information when he called?"

"No, all he asked about was the dates Linda was registered as a guest."

"Was her room used? The bed? The bathroom?"

The woman nodded. "I cleaned it after she left. She was very sweet about not needing her room cleaned until then. She said there was no reason for us to bother since she was only staying two nights."

"When did she tell you this?"

"When she called to make her reservation. Why are you investigating her?"

"Did you have any other guests registered at the same time as Ms. Langsford?"

"Two couples. We only have six rooms."

"Would you give me their names, addresses, and phone numbers?"

"Certainly, but you didn't answer my question," the woman said in an eager tone. "And the detective who called wouldn't tell me anything, either."

Kerney shrugged and smiled. "We're not always free to do so, and this, unfortunately, is one of those situations."

The town hall and sheriff's department were just beyond the quaint string of Victorian buildings that defined the business and tourist area of town. A four-wheel-drive patrol unit was parked outside. Kerney entered the small office where he was greeted by a tanned, calm-looking uniformed officer who rose from behind a paper-cluttered desk.

The man matched Kerney's height and weight and looked to be in excellent condition. He had sandy hair about to turn gray and sharp eyes that took everything in and gave nothing away.

"I'd like to talk to the sheriff," Kerney said,

"I'm the sheriff," he said. "Ira Morley. What can I do for you?"

Kerney identified himself, told Morley why he was in town, and asked to use the phone to make two long-distance calls.

"Help yourself," Morley said, gesturing at the desk phone.

Of the two couples who'd stayed at the B & B the same time as Linda Langsford, he was able to make contact with only one, a retired southern California high school band director and his wife. Neither had seen Linda on the first day she was a guest at the establishment, but had visited with her the next day, before she'd left. All the man could remember was that they had made small talk for a few minutes.

"Was there anything unusual about the conversation?" Kerney asked.

"Not the conversation," the man said. "But she sure did look exhausted, and her clothes were all wrinkled like she'd slept in them."

He hung up to find Ira Morley paging through a small stack of printouts. "This is about that spree killer you're hunting, isn't it?" he said.

"That's right. Did anyone from my office contact you personally about this case?" Kerney asked.

Morley looked up. "Nope. My records show no car registered to a Linda Langsford in town on those dates."

"You run license plates?" Kerney asked.

"Especially during the tourist season," Morley said, "or when things get slow, which happens fairly often around here. It's just me and two deputies, and we don't have a lot of crime to speak of. Cabin break-ins, lost hikers, dead animals on the roadways, sick tourists—that's about the extent of it. We've had only one murder in the sixteen years I've been sheriff. Mexican fella from Alamosa killed by some drinking buddies and dumped in the forest. Occasionally we'll get a computer hit back on a stolen car."

Morley returned his attention to the papers in his hand. "The only New Mexico plate in town on the days you were asking about was registered to a Drew Randolph, out of Roswell."

"Make and model?" Kerney asked.

"A Volvo station wagon," Morley said. "One of those new fancy all-wheel-drive models."

If Kerney remembered correctly, Volvo station wagons had taillights that ran vertically along either side of the rear window, just like the vehicle Clark Beck, the trucker with the broken water pump, had described. Maybe Beck had been wrong about it being a Honda.

"What time was the license plate check run?"

"Eleven in the morning on the day of her arrival. But it was gone all night and most of the next day. We keep a pretty close eye on tourist vehicles."

Kerney did a quick mental calculation, figuring that if Linda had dropped off her bags and then turned around to make the long drive back to Carrizozo to start her killing spree, she had plenty of time to finish up, return to Creede, and establish her alibi. He smiled.

"You've got something?" Morley asked.

"Thanks to you, I may have," Kerney replied.

At the state police district office in Roswell, Kerney worked late into the night carefully preparing search warrant affidavits: one each for the residences of Murray, Gibben, and Linda Langsford, and one for the corporate offices of Ranchers' Exploration and Development.

Since the fruits of the investigation hinged solely on circumstantial evidence and the statements of Margie Hobeck and Kay Murray, Kerney knew he would need to mount a sufficient and convincing probable cause argument before a judge would agree to issue the warrants.

Using the information supplied by Margie and Kay, he summarized Vernon Langsford's known sex crimes and asked for permission to look for specific financial documents, notes, records, photographs, personal or business letters, personal or corporate checks, and any pertinent personal diaries, electronic mail, or computer data that could identify victims or could demonstrate payment of money to possible victims.

To strengthen his argument, Kerney listed the financial benefits Langsford had given Kay Murray and Penelope Gibben over the years to buy their silence, and specified the acts of collusion they had engaged in during the current investigation to protect Langsford's reputation from exposure. That should be enough to secure a warrant to search both women's houses and the corporate office.

Kerney tracked down Clark Beck, who answered on a cell phone. He was hauling culverts for a highway construction project, and Kerney could hear the sound of the engine and the truck radio in the background. He asked Beck to describe again the arrangement of the taillights on the vehicle he'd had seen exiting the road from Three Rivers.

"Like I told you," Beck said, "it had lights on either side of the rear window."

"Did the vehicle have a high-centered profile?" Kerney asked.

"Not a real high one. Those subcompacts aren't really built for off-road use."

"Did it have a spare tire on the tailgate?"

"I don't remember seeing one."

"Are you sure it was a Honda SUV?"

"It looked like one to me."

"Were the back up lights below the rear window?"

"Yeah, I think they were." Beck paused. "Now that you mention it, maybe it was one of those Swedish Volvos yuppies like to drive. That's the only other car I know that has a similar setup. It sure wasn't a minivan."

At midnight, he stopped working on the search warrant affidavit for Linda Langsford's house and set it aside until morning. He needed to nail down a few more pieces of information without telegraphing his renewed interest in her alibi.

He called Lee Sedillo, woke him up, asked him to have all the agents meet at the Roswell district office in the morning, and then went looking for a motel. In the parking lot of the first decent-looking one along the strip, he cut the engine, rubbed his bleary eyes, and stared at the flashing neon VACANCY sign above the door to the dark office.

He got out and rang the bell, wondering if he'd taken the investigation far enough, hoping the planned searches would yield something more tangible. Without it, the district attorney might balk at prosecuting a case based purely on circumstantial evidence. He'd feel a hell of a lot better about the chances for conviction with clear-cut proof of Linda's guilt in hand.

In the morning, Kerney held back the Langsford affidavit and got approval for the other search warrants. He sent an agent by plane to Dallas to pick up Penelope Gibben, where she was attending a business meeting, and bring her home. He detailed another agent to pick up Kay Murray, who was sitting in jail pending her preliminary hearing on drug dealing and armed robbery, and take her to her town house. Two more went to the corporate offices to start the financial records search.

Surveillance on Linda Langsford had been ongoing all night. When she left her residence to make funeral arrangements for Eric, he sent Mary Margaret Lovato off to gather up Drew Randolph, bring him in to the district office, and conduct a follow-up interview. She carried with her a list of questions Kerney wanted answered.

Kerney waited in the small conference room, watching as Lee Sedillo went through the draft affidavit line by line.

"Jesus, what a mess," Lee said, as he turned over the last page. "But we still can't physically put her at any of the crime scenes, Chief."

"The DA can make a reasonable assumption about it from the witness statements we have. That gives him enough to establish opportunity."

"What about the murders of her mother and brother?"

"I'll put the Cold Case Unit to work on it."

A knock came at the door and Mary Margaret stepped inside.

"Randolph confirms he lent Linda his Volvo for her vacation, Chief," she said. "He had the car serviced just before her trip and then took it back for an oil change after she returned. The garage owner who did the work reports a good thousand miles more on the vehicle than one would expect, given the trip itinerary Linda gave you."

Kerney smiled. "That tightens the noose."

"Randolph said Linda asked to borrow his car because her SUV needed an engine overhaul. I just got off the phone with the mechanic who works on her vehicle. He said it was in for a major tune-up, not an overhaul, and there wasn't anything wrong with the vehicle that would have kept it off the road. Linda asked him to store the SUV on his lot until she got back. The guy says she called him long distance on the day of her return and had him deliver the SUV to her house. She tipped him a hundred dollars to do it."

"When did she call him?" Kerney asked.

Mary Margaret smiled. "Right after she spoke to Lieutenant Sedillo to say she was in Taos and on her way to Roswell. She used a phone credit card, so I was able to verify the time."

"She had her moves carefully laid out," Kerney said, consulting his field notes. "There were only three cars at her house the night she returned home: Randolph's sports car, the minister's Chevy, and Linda's SUV. Where was the Volvo?"

"According to Randolph, Linda parked it in her garage so she could unload her camping and hiking gear."

"And hide it from view," Kerney said. "Knowing the cops were going to come knocking at her door soon after she got home."

"Too much planning can be a bad thing," Lee said.

Kerney thought about the five innocent people who had died in Linda's concocted killing spree. "A case of overkill, in this instance," he said, looking at Mary Margaret. "Keep Randolph entertained while I finish the paperwork and get it signed."

"Will do," Mary Margaret said, reaching for the doorknob. "Are you going for multiple murder counts, Chief?"

Kerney nodded. "Let's hope we can make them stick," he said, reaching for his pen and the unfinished affidavit.

After Mary Margaret left, Kerney twisted the pen in his fingers and gave Lee a long look.

"I want the agent who verified Linda Langsford's alibi sent back to Santa Fe," he said. "Tell him for me that until he learns to ask smarter questions, he can count rolls of toilet paper in central supply."

Lee swallowed hard and nodded.

Kerney hung back in his unit at the entrance to Linda Langsford's driveway watching Lee Sedillo and Agent Lovato serve the warrant. Even at a distance he could see Langsford freeze as she read the papers. She tried to bar the door, and Lee pushed past her while Mary Margaret took her by the arm and led her inside.

Kerney eyed the lines of the house that at first had looked contemporary yet out of place in its setting. Given what he now knew about the woman living inside, the structure presented a cold, barren feeling.

He'd staged the operation carefully. Lee Sedillo would spend thirty minutes creating as much disorder and noise as possible while he searched, while Mary Margaret kept Linda isolated and stonewalled any conversation. He wanted Linda to feel her safe haven had been breached and her crimes were about to unravel, in the hope that it would shake her up.

Kerney checked the time, adjusted his tie, and turned on the microtape recorder inside his coat pocket. He'd dressed in a suit to establish an air of authority. He walked into the kitchen and found Linda sitting calmly at the table, seemingly impervious to the noise Lee was making in the back of the house. Mary Margaret gave him a slight head shake to signal that nothing of consequence had transpired.

He looked around for kitchen implements that could be used as weapons. Nothing dangerous was in sight, and Linda sat too far from the drawers and cabinets to reach anything that could be used to mount an attack.

"Don't you look nice," Linda said with a derisive smile. "Did you dress up just for me?"

"We need to talk, Linda."

"There will be no talking."

Kerney didn't believe her. Killers, particularly successful ones who felt smug and superior, always wanted to talk or play a verbal game of hide and seek.

"Have you two had a good time?" Kerney asked Mary Margaret.

"Peachy, Chief. Ms. Langsford called a criminal defense attorney. She's on her way over."

"That's a very wise thing to do," Kerney said, as he turned to Linda. "You've read the warrant and the affidavit?"

"Every word," Linda said. "You're quite the fiction writer, Chief Kerney—a born storyteller."

"All a prosecutor needs for a conviction are compelling facts that lead to convincing proof. In your case, we have that plus the added benefit of a motive."

Linda waved a dismissive hand over the papers on the table. "So then arrest me."

"All in due course," Kerney said, inclining his head toward the door. Mary Margaret took the cue and left.

"Am I free to go until then?" Linda asked.

"You need to stay until the search is completed and the evidence is inventoried."

"Am I detained for questioning?"

"I'm sure you'll want a list of everything we take from your house. You must be very pleased, Linda. You've achieved a great deal of success over the years."

Linda's eyes smiled. "I'm very happy with my life."

"Eric did you a favor when he killed himself," Kerney said. "He saved you the trouble."

Linda pouted dramatically. "Don't be tedious, Chief Kerney. Why don't you sit down? Trying to intimidate me isn't going to work."

"I'll stand. At first, I thought Eric was the killer. He was single, never married, had no significant relationships, hated his father. He was a typical, asocial loner, always on the fringe, into drugs, an under-achiever, and more than a little weird."

Linda leaned toward Kerney and lifted her face. Her eyes turned serious, her tone conspiratorial. "You may be right. I've had a change of heart about Eric: I think he did kill my father and all those other people. I truly do. It's really too bad he couldn't own up to it. Then I wouldn't have to put up with this little staged production of yours."

"Eric didn't have the balls to act out his anger against his father. He couldn't even stand up to you."

Linda pulled back and gazed at Kerney. "You sound so sure of yourself."

"Vernon and the other victims were killed methodically without murderous rage."

"Which means nothing."

"It means a very well organized, intelligent person with a personal vendetta did the killing, and the only person with a reason to do it is you."

Linda laughed. "I have no reason to kill anybody, Chief Kerney. I overcame my childhood problems a long time ago, and I live a nor-mal life. And in spite of all his problems, Eric was brilliant. He could have pulled it off."

"I think Eric knew what was going on between you and your father."

"Unfortunately, we can only wonder what Eric knew," Linda said with a charming smile. "Now that he's dead, it's impossible to sort it out."

"I'm sure he was on your list."

A giggle fluttered on her lips. "How you do go on. I have no list."

"Perhaps he was a low priority because he never really victimized you, except to take your money in payment for his silence."

"Silence about what?"

"Things he saw, and what he knew."

Linda's eyebrows arched. "That's quite a stretch."

"I'm impressed with how you carried it out. You used a different MO and a different signature for every murder. You really did your homework. And making those anonymous phone calls to yourself was a brilliant strategy."

Linda tried to repress a smile but didn't quite succeed. "What are you talking about?"

"Killing off your family, one by one."

"You have an overactive imagination."

"You killed your father because he raped you, your mother because she stood by silently and let it happen, and Arthur because . . ." Kerney shrugged.

"Because?"

"Now it's only a theory, mind you."

Linda smiled like a child about to play a favorite game. "Let's speculate," she said, clapping her hands together.

"Daddy passed you on to Arthur."

Linda blinked and the playfulness disappeared. She forced it back on her face. "Oh, that's very good."

"And then there's Eric, who saw and knew things."

"Like what?"

"Your ex-husband helped me figure it out when he told me how you'd lock the bathroom door to brush your teeth, and wouldn't allow him to see you naked."

"Poor Bill. Such a conventional, narrow-minded man. I totally misjudged him."

"Voyeurism probably started for Eric at home when he saw you being raped and molested by Vernon or Arthur, or both."

"Or maybe he just kept bursting in on me while I was taking a bath, like kid brothers sometimes do. That would be enough to make a girl modest. Or maybe he was just sexually screwed up."

"Did you start seeing Dr. Joyce to keep her silent about Eric? That was very clever."

Linda smiled openly at the compliment. "She's teaching me ways to cope with my pain. It's been a very trying time."

"And is the pain gone?"

"Oh no," she answered mechanically. "Dr. Joyce says I have a lot of work to do in that regard."

"Talk to me about it, Linda."

"I can tell you one thing." She lowered her voice when Mary Margaret stepped into the room. "Daddy always used to say that giving a young girl an early start in life was a father's obligation. Don't you think he did a good job of getting me started?" She flipped her long hair and it covered her face.

"The lawyer is here," Mary Margaret said.

"Just a minute," Kerney said, keeping his attention fixed on Linda Langsford.

Mary Margaret slipped out the door and closed it.

Kerney had caught something in Linda's voice that made him think she wanted to keep talking. "What kind of start did he give you, Linda?" he asked lightly. "Was it a good one? One that you liked?"

Linda rose from the chair and pushed the hair back over her shoulders. "That's a very mean question. I really should talk to my attorney."

"I know you weren't bad, Linda. You were trying to be good and do what you were told. You haven't been arrested or read your rights so whatever you tell me can't be used against you. You know that; you're a lawyer."

"Are you truly that interested?"

"Very. I'd like to understand what happened."

Linda paused. "I'll tell you one story that will explain everything. When Daddy stopped playing with me and started playing with Kay, I had to play with Arthur. That's what Daddy called it, playing. I had my first abortion when I was twelve. Mother told people I had the stomach flu."

Kerney said nothing, hoping for more.

"I had the stomach flu again the next year, and the year after that. Daddy got really mad at Arthur about making me pregnant so many times."

"What about Eric? What did he do?"

"Do you think I'll be allowed to bury my brother?"

"I'm sure it can be arranged."

"Eric was so sad. He used to hide in my closet at home and play with himself while he watched me undress. He was too scared to do more, but he wanted to. I could tell. Funny, isn't it? All he had to do was ask. Daddy and Arthur had trained me well."

"But wouldn't you have hated Eric more if he had molested you?"

Her expression turned quizzical, as though the question was pointless. "Of course. As much as Daddy and Arthur. I've planned a very nice service for him. Nothing nearly as grand as Daddy's. I don't expect very many people will come. But Penelope and Kay might like to."

"Now if only Penelope and Kay were dead, that would tidy things up nicely," Kerney said, thinking all the tidbits had finally come together.

"What a lovely thought," Linda said, her sweet smile turning slightly crazy.

14

Among the items seized during the search, one of the most incriminating turned out to be a photo album with a series of neatly labeled and dated snapshots of Linda, Arthur, and Vernon Langsford taken during a camping trip made when the children were young. Their excursion had started at the Valley of Fires Park outside of Carrizozo and ended at Dog Canyon, now known as the Oliver Lee State Park. Overnight stops had included the Three Rivers Petroglyphs site and the nearby Three Rivers campground at the base of Sierra Blanca.

From the dates printed in a child's handwriting below each snapshot, Linda had been eleven years old at the time, and her brother fifteen.

There were pictures showing Linda cuddled in Vernon's arms, sitting in her brother's lap, her coltish legs spread wide, and striking a cheesecake pose with hands on her hips.

Kerney studied her face. Linda had been a naturally pretty girl with wide, innocent-looking, hopeful eyes. But a forced smile hid clenched teeth and a furrow creased her forehead like a tightly strung wire.

In one picture, Arthur stood behind her, his hands grasping Linda's hips as she bent forward toward the camera. In another staged shot, Linda sat facing her father, with her legs wrapped around his waist, her mouth open in a provocative pout.

In all the snapshots, Vernon and Arthur's eyes had been scratched out.

Kerney closed the album, convinced that the camping trip had been used to pass on the family tradition of incest from father to son. He now understood why Linda chose to kill her father at Oliver Lee State Park, and why spilling innocent blood along the way made a kind of cleansing, crazy sense to her.

He looked at the hardback books Lee had entered into evidence. Linda had amassed a small but sophisticated library on crime classification, homicide investigation, scientific evidence in criminal cases, and case studies of violent criminals. Lee had flagged a section in one of the books that outlined the typology and style of the spree killer, which had been heavily underlined.

From a dresser in Linda's bedroom, Lee had removed six individually framed photographs of Linda's parents, siblings, Kay Murray, and Penelope Gibben. On the back of each, with the exception of the Gibben and Murray photographs, were birth and death dates. For Penelope and Kay, birth dates were entered, but the spaces for the dates of death were blank, ready to be filled in.

It was all good incriminating evidence.

Kerney looked at the evidence boxes and stacks of papers taken from Linda's residence. They filled the district headquarters conference room table and spilled over to the floor. He would leave it to Lee and his team to do the tedious analysis and cataloging needed to strengthen the case.

Outside the closed door he could hear banging sounds as folding tables were being set up in the reception area to handle the large volume of evidence collected at the other search sites. He went to find Lee, who was directing the placement of evidence being carted in from the units.

"This is gonna keep us real busy for a while," Lee said.

"You can handle it."

"Are you bailing out on us?"

"As soon as I finish meeting with the district attorney, I'm heading back to Santa Fe."

"You did it, Chief."

Kerney smiled grimly. "We all did it, Lee."

Lee studied Kerney's solemn expression. "Are you okay, Chief?"

"I'm fine. Give the team my thanks for their good work."

He moved out the door and through the parking lot, past an agent who was unloading more evidence. Night had brought a light, cooling rain and the tangy scent of creosote filled the air. He shivered. Not against the chill, but in an attempt to shake off all he'd learned about the Langsford family and would rather never have known.

Slightly disoriented from a dreamless, heavy sleep, Kerney rolled out of bed. It took a minute for him to realize he was back in Santa Fe at his own place and the morning was half gone. He cleaned up, got dressed, drove to work, and tried to make an inconspicuous entrance through a side door. Before he could reach the second-floor landing, half a dozen officers and civilian employees had stopped him to offer congratulations on the Langsford case. A few others in the hallway, probably those unwilling to forget about the Shockley incident, greeted him with tight, curt nods.

He smiled at Andy Baca, who waited for him in the reception area outside his office. Kerney had worn his uniform to work and he watched Andy take in the unusual sight with a look of mock disbelief. In his office, they both sat on the couch that faced Andy's oak desk.

"Lee Sedillo says you've made a strong case," Andy said.

"The DA bought it after he heard the tape recording," Kerney replied. "He'll take Linda Langsford to trial. But he wasn't happy about prosecuting her without any hard physical evidence or not being able to use Linda's taped confession. He figures the defense will argue insanity."

"Is she?"

Kerney shrugged. "Insane or not, she's a cold-blooded killer. She murdered five people to conceal an act of revenge against her father, killed her mother and brother, and was planning to ice three more, if you include Eric, Kay Murray, and Penelope Gibben."

"Will you be able to arrest her for the murder of her mother and brother?" Andy asked.

"That's hard to say. I've asked the Cold Crimes Unit to reopen the investigations."

"What about Gibben and Murray?" Andy asked.

"I don't know how that will fall out. I'm hoping we can get enough information from the search warrants to at least track down some of Vernon Langsford's other victims. Then it depends on what they tell us."

"If Gibben and Murray didn't procure for Langsford, at the very least they colluded with him."

Kerney nodded in agreement. "There could be conspiracy charges filed."

"Will the DA follow up?"

"That's iffy right now. The perpetrator is dead, it's possible that the statute of limitations has expired, and only Margie Hobeck and Kay Murray have made statements. He's researching case law."

"Have any other victims come forward?"

"Not yet. The news about the case is just breaking, and the department shrink says it may take a while before any of them feel safe enough to want to talk."

"Langsford was a lifetime pedophile with multiple victims. That might win a jury's sympathy," Andy said.

"Sympathy won't wipe the slate clean for the five innocent people she left dead in her wake," Kerney replied. "It's gonna be some trial, that's for sure."

"You don't seem too happy about clearing the case."

"The really bad guy wasn't brought to justice."

"Getting shot to death by your daughter comes pretty close," Andy said.

"I rather he'd been caught and held accountable."

"We don't execute child molesters in New Mexico," Andy said.

"I wasn't thinking of legal action," Kerney said. "I had something more personal in mind."

Andy recognized the feeling. It had been a case to turn anyone's stomach, no matter how hardened. Kerney had been right in the middle of a dung heap of a family, and squashing Vernon Langsford would have made any cop feel better.

"This one got to you, didn't it?"

"Big time."

"What's with the uniform?" Andy asked. "You haven't worn it more than five times in the last year."

"I decided to put it on while I still had the chance," Kerney said, as he pulled at his shirt collar displaying the three stars.

"So, you really are leaving."

"Without fanfare."

"No party?"

"No party, no surprises."

Andy went to his desk, returned with a business card, and gave it to Kerney. "The Santa Fe city manager wants you to call him."

"About what?"

"I don't know. He was here for a joint criminal justice planning meeting and left his card with my secretary. You will let Connie and me take you and Sara to dinner before you leave, won't you?"

"As long as you don't get sloppy drunk and maudlin," Kerney said.

"Have I ever?"

"There's always a first time," Kerney said, smiling at Andy, "for both of us."

* * *

The thirty days Kerney had promised Andy stretched into two months. On the Friday before his last week at work, Kerney took the day off and drove to Las Cruces, where he met Milton Lynch, the executor of Erma Fergurson's estate, who was ready to close on the sale of Kerney's inherited land to the Nature Conservancy and file final papers with the probate court.

Lynch took Kerney through the paperwork, his back to the picture window in his office that gave a stunning view of the Organ Mountains, and finished up with an accounting of the net proceeds that Kerney would receive after the taxes were paid.

Even with the enormous tax bite and the sale of the land to the Nature Conservancy at below market value, Kerney was about to become a multimillionaire.

"How do you want the funds disbursed?" Lynch asked.

Kerney had consulted a tax attorney and CPA in Santa Fe earlier in the week. He gave Lynch a disbursement schedule for the joint accounts that he'd opened in his and Sara's names.

Lynch studied the schedule. "This is a good mix of conservative and growth investments," he said. "But you really need to buy some real estate fairly soon, and let your tax-free fund pay the monthly principal and interest."

"I plan to do that," Kerney said.

Lynch ran a stubby finger across the line that projected Kerney's annual after-tax income. He noted the amount and asked, "Will this amount adequately provide for you and your wife?"

Kerney laughed. Even after reinvesting most of the expected dividends and interest, his net disposable income was about to become more than double—almost triple—what he'd ever taken home in paychecks during the course of a year.

Lynch's bushy eyebrows flattened into a straight line as he looked up from the papers. "I take that to mean yes."

"Yes," Kerney replied.

"Now there's the matter of Erma's other bequest to you." Lynch rose, crossed to the office closet, and returned holding a wrapped package, which he placed in Kerney's hands.

Kerney tore away the protective paper to find an oil painting by Erma of his family's ranch on the Tularosa, as it had been before the army took the land to expand White Sands Missile Range.

He took the image in as memories of his childhood flooded back: setting new corral fence posts behind the house with his father, painting the eaves and the porch trim with his mother, climbing the nearby windmill in the early morning to watch the sun rise over the Sierra Blanca peaks as it cascaded down to Three Rivers.

"It's wonderful," he said, trying to keep his voice steady.

"Prices for Erma's work have escalated since her death," Lynch said. "Erma held this piece out of the retrospective of her work shown at the university the year before her death. I've been authorized to ask if you'd like to place it on permanent loan or give it to the university. They'd love to add it to their collection."

"Not a chance," Kerney replied.

"I didn't think so," Lynch said, holding out an envelope. "Here are the two accounts you asked me to set up. Each has the maximum tax-free gift amount you are allowed under the IRS code. You can add the same amount to the accounts annually, if you wish."

"I understand."

"Good luck, Chief Kerney," Lynch said. "I hope you enjoy being a rich man."

Kerney shook Lynch's outstretched hand. "I'll try to get used to it."

"I don't think you'll have any problems."

From a distance, it was a modest house at the end of a dirt lane, made even more unprepossessing by enormous pine trees that dwarfed the structure and allowed only the diffused, fading evening sunlight to filter in. Up close, the house was more substantial in appearance, rectangular and low to the ground with a bright red tin roof over a post-and-beam porch. New metal-clad wood windows had been recently installed, and the porch deck, made of long planks, had been carefully laid and thoroughly weatherproofed.

In a small clearing away from the house, a fenced vegetable garden held the drooping remains of tomato and squash plants killed by frost. A swing and slide set stood under a pine tree next to a sandbox.

Kerney knocked on the front door and Clayton answered, his expression changing quickly from surprise to impassivity.

"What brings you back to Mescalero?" he asked.

"I wanted to give you this," Kerney said, holding out the envelope.

Clayton read the certificates of deposit and with a stunned expression on his face shook his head. "I don't need your money."

"It's not for you; it's for your children's education. The enclosed letter explains everything. Consider it a scholarship fund."

"I don't know any cop who has twenty thousand dollars lying around to give away."

"I can afford it," Kerney said.

He waved the envelope at Kerney. "You really want to do this?"

"I do."

"Why?"

"Because it pleases me. If you decide not to keep it, send it back to the return address on the letterhead. I hope you won't do that." Kerney turned to leave.

"Wait."

"What?" Kerney said, swinging back around. Clayton's expression was uncertain.

"You want to give my children money, just like that?"

"Just like that."

"I don't know what to say."

"You don't have to say anything," Kerney replied, as he stepped off the porch.

Clayton waved the envelope again. "This is serious money."

"Relax, there aren't any strings attached to it."

Clayton inclined his head toward the open door. "You want to come inside?"

"I can't. I have to meet my wife at the Albuquerque airport."

"Well, maybe you can come down for dinner sometime, with your wife."

"I'd like that."

Clayton nodded. "Okay. I'll call you." The envelope flapped in his hand. "This is unreal."

A smile crossed Kerney's face as he thought about Erma's fairy-godmother bequest that had made his gift to Clayton's children possible. "It's part of a legacy from an old friend," he said, "and I'm just passing some of it along. I'm sure she would approve."

Sara asked for food and a drink when she got off the plane, preferably enchiladas with lots of green chile, and a margarita. Kerney took her to an Albuquerque Old Town restaurant where the drinks were generous and the chile was hot. They got there just before the kitchen closed and sat at a window booth in the nearly empty bar, which was decorated with Mexican masks, Day of the Dead folk art figures, and bullfighting posters.

As they waited for dinner, Sara nibbled chips dipped in salsa and worked on her drink while Kerney told her about his visit to Clayton.

"Do you think he'll ever be able to emotionally accept you as his father?" Sara asked.

"It's hard to say. With time, we may be able to become casual friends. I doubt it will go much deeper than that."

"You did a very nice thing for his children."

"Compliments of Erma," Kerney said, raising his wineglass.

Sara touched her glass to his. "I'm sure she's pleased. "Now that you're a rich man, what are you going to do with the rest of your money?"

"It's our money," Kerney said, "and I'm hoping you'll get the army to send you to law school, so we can actually live together for a while."

Sara made a face and shook her head. "Law school at the army's expense isn't going to happen. I should have looked into the opportunity years ago. Selection into the program is limited to captains and lieutenants."

"Can an exception be made?"

"The eligibility requirements can't be waived," Sara said. Disappointment showed on Kerney's face. She reached across the table and stroked his hand. "We'll figure something else out. Maybe I can get posted back to New Mexico after I finish up at Fort Leavenworth."

"What are the chances of that happening?"

"I can ask, and politick for it a bit, but I'll have to go where the army wants to send me."

"Would you mind if Santa Fe remains our home base for a while?" Kerney asked.

"I thought you wanted to get out of Santa Fe."

"The police chief is leaving at the end of the year and the city manager has offered me the position."

"Then Santa Fe it is," Sara said. "You are going to take the job, aren't you?"

Kerney nodded. "It's what I've always wanted."

"So, will we buy or build?"

"Build. On enough land to do something with, like keep a few horses or maybe run a few cows to keep the taxes down."

"Away from the sprawl, I hope."

"Definitely. I'm thinking a hundred acres or a quarter section in the Galisteo Basin would do. The land is pricey, but we can afford it."

"I don't want a trophy home, Kerney."

Kerney laughed. "Will a ranch house serve?"

"Perfect," Sara said, her eyes dancing. "We can work on the plans together. It has to have a nursery and be ready by next summer."

"Are you serious?"

"I am both serious and pregnant."

A waiter pushed through the swinging doors from the kitchen, dinner plates in hand, and paused halfway across the barroom until the couple at the window booth stopped kissing.